HER MOTHER'S PENDANT

HER MOTHER'S PENDANT

JOHN CHAMBERS™ BOOK ONE

MICHAEL ANDERLE

LMBPN Publishing
PMB 196, 2540 South Maryland Pkwy
Las Vegas, NV 89109

First US Edition, December 2020
ebook ISBN: 978-1-64971-384-1
Print ISBN: 978-1-64971-385-8

THE HER MOTHER'S PENDANT TEAM

Thanks to the Beta Team
Larry Omans, Jim Caplan, Mary Morris, Kelly O'Donnell, Rachel Beckford, John Ashmore

Thanks to the JIT Readers
Dave Hicks
Deb Mader
Diane L. Smith
Micky Cocker
Debi Sateren
Jeff Goode
Dorothy Lloyd
Paul Westman

If I've missed anyone, please let me know!

Editor
The Skyhunter Editing Team

*To Family, Friends and
Those Who Love
to Read.
May We All Enjoy Grace
to Live the Life We Are
Called.*

— Michael

John "Dick" Chambers studied the cards in his hand with the scrutiny of a pawnshop owner examining a diamond.

He was up considerably. Black, red, blue, green, and white chips littered his green felt corner of the table, and several towers threatened to topple. The surly expressions on his opponents' faces were the sweet little cherry on top of his cream cake.

Arnie Taft tapped the table with his knuckles to indicate a check on his turn. Dick expected nothing less. Taft had the shriveled balls of a cockroach, but his mammoth size made him demand a space at the table. He couldn't talk a hooker into a fuck with a handful of cash, but boy, could he knock her clear across the room in one clean punch.

Next, Connor would lay down a clean white chip to show that he was still in the game, but that was a ploy to hide his shitty hand. Tyrone and Jake would match the raise, Dick would up it another two levels, and soon they'd be sweating beneath their collars, each trying to save face as they went down swinging, hoping that Dick had a less than favorable hand for once.

Dick examined his cards again. A pair of twos. It was his first real stinker of the night, but he wouldn't let that stop him toying with the others.

It's right what they say about playing with meatheads. Bring a tenderizer, and you'll have them eating their putty from the palm of your hand.

Dick caressed the cool neck of his Blue Moon beer and brought it to his lips. All eyes were on him, and he could detect their impatience in the air. He swigged the foam around his mouth, then swallowed, and closed his eyes.

"Man, that hits the spot."

"Quit dawdling, Dick. We haven't got all night." Arnie's voice was deep and carried easily around the small tavern. A thin layer of smoke hazed the air and carved mystic patterns around the overhead fluorescents. At the bar, the owner scrubbed lazily with a cloth while a handful of patrons sat scattered in the dark corners, interested only in their business.

The way that everyone is in Atlantica. Out for themselves.

"Haven't got all night, huh?" Dick grinned. "In that case, I suppose I should wrap up and take my winnings with me. I thought you boys would want a chance to win back your dough, but if you're just going to hand it over to me, then…"

"You know that's not what he meant," Tyrone snapped. He stared at Dick through his one good eye, the other made of glass and fixed in one direction. He had a patchy layer of black curled stubble across his face and a bald head that reflected the light above and cast an ironic halo. "Get your ass in gear and let's play."

Arnie nodded. Connor grumbled his agreement. Dick scanned the table and noted the small bowls of salted peanuts, and his opponents' collection of beer bottles, which significantly outweighed his. Even if he had been as inebriated as the others, he knew he'd still have the upper hand. You didn't take drinking daily as a hobby for over a decade and not build up an impressive tolerance for the stuff.

"I see you. I raise you."

Dick threw a handful of chips at random and laughed internally, enjoying the fact he had made the others squirm. It was one of life's little pleasures, drawing in the lowlifes and exerting dominance. Every day it became harder and harder in the streets.

Arnie and Connor folded, while Tyrone and Jake matched. Arnie took the opportunity to head to the bar and order enough bottles of beer to last him the next few rounds, while Connor excused himself with a grunt to take a leak.

"You can't run on luck all night, sunshine," Tyrone crooned, which revealed gold teeth among his ivories. "Luck can only get you so far. You're bluffing out your ass."

Jake scrutinized his cards, the features of his thin face harsh in the limited light.

"That may be true," Dick replied. "But are you willing to take that risk?" He glanced at the decorated backs of Tyrone's cards on the table. "I know for a fact that you're playing with dirt. Bet you have little more than a pair in that deck. Maybe an ace-high at best, but you're not going to admit that, are you? Even though your tell is incredibly potent. I can smell bluffing on you like I smell dog shit on my shoes."

"Bullshit," Tyrone growled. Although he tried to keep his cool, his confidence faltered, if only slightly.

"Ironic how ex-cons make the worst liars."

Tyrone's fists clenched, which confirmed Dick's theory of his shitty hand. He grimaced, and it looked as though Dick was about to push him over the edge when a bell sounded at the door, indicating the arrival of a new patron.

Every head except Dick's turned to the door.

Jesus, the whole city has us trained like Pavlov's dogs. Hear a bell and look for the treat. Meanwhile, I'm the only one focused with my head in the game. Ain't no wonder I'm up on these fleabags.

Several patrons wolf-whistled across the bar. Dick ignored them. They were all testosterone-fueled pricks with eyes only for the pink bit between a woman's legs. Dick had his fair share of ladies, but when it came to a throwdown between women and cold, hard cash, he knew which he'd rather invite back to his place.

Dick took two greens from their pile, suspended them in the air, then threw them into the center. "Raise."

He waited patiently for Jake to make his move but soon noticed his eyes were far from the game.

Dick took a white chip and tossed it at Jake. His aim was true. The coin spun through the air and caught him in the middle of his forehead. Jake's brows knitted together.

"What d'ya do that for?"

"Your turn."

More voices rang across the bar.

"Whoa, foxy miss. I think you're in the wrong place, but I can help you find the right one."

"Here's a quarter, call your momma and tell her you ain't going home tonight."

"Mmhmm, day-*um*!"

Jake tried to focus on his cards, but his eyes kept dancing to his right. He absently ran a hand through his hair, which neatened the little tuft that had previously stuck up at the back. "Man, to have a piece of that—*ow*! Quit throwing shit at me."

"*Your turn*." Dick turned to Tyrone for support, unsurprised to find that he, too, was distracted.

Tyrone reclined in his chair and bit his lip. "Is that a bullwhip? I like a girl who values a good bit of BDSM. Even more so when we can play with toys."

"How about this?" Dick's impatience reached its peak. "You guys flush me out of cash, and you can pursue the pretty lady. If I clean you out, you can pursue the pretty lady. Either way, gentlemen's code, let's finish this goddamn game before the cock crows."

"My cock's already crowing." Arnie arrived back at the table.

"So is Connor's. Check him out, going straight for the home plate."

Dick finally submitted to the distraction and twisted in his chair toward the bar where Connor's tall frame hid the woman's outline. The most Dick could make out was a crop of brunette hair and the bullwhip's silhouette at her waist.

Same as every other bimbo in this city. Well, minus the whip. It's usually something metallic with more firepower.

After another nudge, Jake played his chips, and Tyrone followed. They reached the end of the round and Dick pulled more chips toward him, surprised that his dud hand still earned him cash. As he scooped them up and arranged them into their towers, he caught a snippet of Connor's conversation with the stranger.

"What you gotta carry a bullwhip around wichoo for? When it comes to security in Atlantica, you need cold hard steel. I reckon it ain't nothing but an aid for a bit of kinky foreplay."

"You got me." Her voice was soft like velvet. She spoke with a confidence that carried in every syllable. "Although, it's more for nights like tonight where there isn't anything big enough that interests me. A girl's gotta take control of her pleasure, know what I mean?"

A ripple of laughter passed around the spectators at Connor's foolish attempt. Connor laughed it off. "Barkeep, another Budweiser for me, and whatever the lady wants. On my tab, darling."

The barkeep's gruff voice added, "What's your flavor?"

"I'd like this skinny creep to leave me the hell alone and for someone to point me in the direction of a Mr. John Chambers." A short pause. "Please."

Dick's stomach fell. Nothing good ever came of someone hunting him down in a seedy bar. Couldn't he have one night of peace? His eyes narrowed as he shuffled and dealt the cards to the table.

"No John Chambers here." Connor sounded a little dejected. "You got the wrong place."

"I don't think so," the woman replied. "I have it on good authority that John was in this establishment less than an hour ago. One of you should be able to point me in the right direction, surely?"

Tyrone glanced at Dick. "'Fess up, lover boy. She don't know she ain't looking for John. She's looking for Dick."

Dick glared at Tyrone unblinkingly. Tyrone snickered, then raised a hand and pointed at Dick. "Your lover boy is here, sweet-cheeks." He stood and flexed his chest. "You're going to have to go through me to get to him, though. I'm all the dick you need."

"Sit." Dick shortly followed his command with a sigh of resignation.

"Or what? You're in the concrete jungle now, baby. The alpha dog takes the woman. You want her, come and claim her." Tyrone's voice lowered as he added, "You may be rinsing me of my cash, but you ain't taking my girl."

Dick's patience snapped. He rose and kicked his chair back with the heel of his boot. It skidded along the floor and crashed into the wall.

The woman fixed him with a keen look. "John? John Chambers?"

John tore his eyes away from Tyrone and looked straight at the woman, getting his first full view.

It was no wonder the gents were fired up. She was the eye candy that all others set their bar to. Her skin was the color of warm caramel. Her dark hair was tied back in a ponytail, and her emerald green eyes caught the light and twinkled. She wore a grey halter top and khaki combat pants, with the fabled bullwhip fixed to her side. A variety of pockets that could have contained anything covered the pants, and on her hands were something akin to boxing hand wraps. On her feet were black walking boots, and on the other side of her hips was a holster where a pistol might sit—if she had one.

Dick looked at the dark faces staring at him and chuckled. "What was your first clue?"

Without the slightest tremble of doubt or fear, the woman moved closer to Dick until she was an arm's length away. She offered a hand. "Santana Sokolov."

Dick took her hand and shook it.

"I have a job offer for you." She turned back to Connor and looked at him with mild disgust. "A *platonic* job, if that suits."

"You know how to get a man's attention," Dick responded with a hint of sarcasm.

Santana looked past Dick to the poker table and noted the situation with the chips. "I'm sorry if I've disturbed your game. It can wait."

Dick, whose curiosity was now piqued, shook his head. When was the last time a client had hunted him down and tracked his movements? More than that, when was the last time a stunning woman had taken the risk of walking unaccompanied into a backwater bar and forsaken all other gentlemen for him?

"It's fine." Dick picked up his cards and tossed them into the center of the table. "Game's over, boys. Time to turn out your pockets and pay up."

One quick look at Tyrone told Dick all he needed to know. The man's nostrils flared. A vein in his throat throbbed. A sick grin painted his face as he shook his head and said, "We can't do that, I'm afraid."

Dick noticed then that the others had risen and created a small circle around him. The barkeep was nowhere in sight.

Dick sighed and turned to Santana. In a soft voice, he muttered, "You best lay low for this. Wouldn't want to mess up that pretty little outfit of yours."

"I'm quite certain I can handle my—"

Before she could finish, the first punch was thrown.

CHAPTER TWO

Dick shoved Santana out of harm's way, which sent her into the wall. She caught herself on her hands and expertly rose to her feet as a punch landed on Dick's shoulder blade.

Tyrone leered at Dick with a predatory grin as he went for him again, and used his momentum to turn his left jab into a right cross.

Dick was too quick for him as he ducked out of his trajectory and spun to hook underneath Tyrone's bicep with both hands. He yanked the man's arm down and drove his knee up, which bent the arm against its usual position and sent a spike of bone bursting through the skin.

Tyrone howled in pain while his eyes grew as wide as china plates. Dick was aware that more men were coming, spurred on by the sudden rush of adrenaline around the bar. He shoved Tyrone away, planted a foot in the middle of his back, and sent him forward, where he crashed into a nearby table and spilled the drinks of a rough-looking couple into their laps.

Wood splintered beneath him. The couple cried their protest and left the bar with angry glances back at them.

A cry of rage came from Dick's right, and he caught Connor's fist with his open hand, but barely. The grab sent a jolt of pain up his right arm into the shoulder joint. Dick used his left hand to jab Connor in the nose, which caused the nasal passages to erupt with blood. Connor's head flicked backward, and Dick stabbed at the man's throat, hoping to jab his fingers in his airway.

A great hulk of flesh charged at his side, rammed into Dick and lifted him from the waist. Caught off-guard, Dick could do nothing but let his new companion carry him until he was thrown onto the poker table's top. Chips flew in all directions. The table snapped in two. Arnie landed on top of Dick and almost knocked the wind out of him.

"All of this because you don't want to pay up?" Dick wheezed. "Would you rather I take an IOU?"

Arnie growled. "All of this because you're a cocky, self-righteous prick."

"I always had myself down for cocky, but self-righteous is a stretch." He glanced at the behemoth of a man picking himself up off the floor. "Top points for expanding your vocabulary, though. I didn't know gorillas could learn new tricks."

Arnie's face darkened. He picked up a wooden chair in one hand and arced it over his head. Seeing this maneuver long before it came, Dick grabbed the neck of one of the few surviving beer bottles and hurled it at Arnie.

The glass smashed as it hit his face. Shards sprayed in all directions, forcing him to shut his eyes and shake his head. The forgotten chair bounced off his head before it hit the floor, where one of the legs snapped off and skidded toward Santana.

Seizing the advantage, Dick pushed himself to his feet as he grabbed another bottle in one hand, and a handful of peanuts in the other. He lazily tossed a couple of nuts into his mouth, then threw his arm out to the side and hurled the rest in Jake's face.

Jake, who had been going for the second charge, pawed at his eyes while blinking stupidly to eradicate the pain from the salted coating dissolving in his tears.

Meanwhile, Arnie turned to Dick with a face covered in lacerations and twinkling glass embedded in his skin. His eyes darted to the bottle in Dick's hand, and as Dick moved for the strike, Arnie caught his wrist.

"I never fall for the same trick twice." Arnie grinned.

Dick raised an eyebrow. "Is that why your ex cheated on you three times?"

All humor left Arnie's face. "You son of a—"

Wood splintered behind Arnie's head. A mask of confusion fell over him as he released Dick's wrist and moved his hand to his massive dome. He patted his head, then examined his hand, now stained red with blood.

Arnie dazedly spun to find Santana behind him with the wooden chair leg clutched in front of her with both hands.

"What're you going to do? Hit a lady?" Santana's voice wobbled slightly.

Arnie looked as though he couldn't understand what day of the week it was. His lip curled up, and his eyes rolled toward the back of his head. With a slight nudge of encouragement from Dick's foot, Arnie collapsed onto his knees, then fell flat on the floor, his head tilted clumsily to the side.

A moment of stunned silence passed over the bar. Dick's eyes met Santana's. "So, you say you have a job?"

Santana nodded.

"Shall we get out of here?"

Her nods increased in eagerness.

Dick knelt at Arnie's side and rifled through his pockets. He found his phone, held the fingerprint identifier to Arnie's thumb and the screen lit up. He flicked across to the Satiata Cash app and thumbed in an estimated amount for his winnings that night. Then he bumped his phone against Arnie's and a small notification rang to confirm the transfer. "Ah, how technology has made our lives all the easier. Sorry, big guy. A win is a win."

Dick rose, tossed the phone, then stepped over the mountain of a man and joined Santana. As they strode past the others in the bar, they felt their eyes burning into them. They had barely made it past the bar when the sound of a shotgun cocking drew their attention.

"Relax, Marty. It's over, okay?" Dick soothed. "Nice work on defending your bar, too, by the way. Who keeps their firearms hidden upstairs in Atlantica?"

Marty turned the shotgun's barrel on Dick without a word.

Dick nodded as resignation came over him. This wasn't the first time he had lost the privilege of entering one of the dingy establishments set up along the outskirts of Atlantica, and it sure as hell wouldn't be the last. The modest island floating off the East Coast of the United States had a copious amount of these quaint backwater bars, and the way Dick saw it, these carbon copy bars were like burner phones—great until their use expired, then you tossed them away and found another one.

"Yeah, I get it. I'm not welcome back." He turned and waved a hand behind him. "Let me know when the place changes hands again, will you, Marty?"

Night had fallen over Atlantica, but it was almost impossible to tell the difference from any other time of day. The ever-permeating veil of fog blocked the stars and reduced the full shining moon to a fuzzy orb in the sky.

Cars revved their engines at the stoplights. It was an inspiring array of some of the finest vehicles the world had ever seen—Mercedes-Benz, Jaguars, Lexus, BMWs, Bentleys, Teslas, and many custom vehicles manufactured for some of the wealthiest individuals to grace the Earth. Although cash bought them their dream cars, it didn't buy their owners' patience. Despite all that money thrown at top-drawer parts and ludicrous horsepower, there was nowhere on the island to open the throttle and let the ponies gallop.

Such a waste. We're in the year 2027, and they still haven't figured out a way to safely propel cars at breakneck speeds through the streets.

A lot of life was different in Atlantica. While the world still couldn't believe that the hidden island had been found floating around in the Atlantic Ocean almost a thousand miles east of New York City, it hadn't taken those who discovered it long to claim it as theirs and grow its notoriety. Atlantica had a reputation for welcoming the rich, the powerful, and the successful, and it didn't matter whether you were good, evil, or somewhere in between. If you had money and the right contacts, you could make a home for yourself here.

Dick fired up a cigarette, cupping the flame from his Zippo against the wind. He took a long drag and exhaled into the air. Santana watched him intently, her face a slightly paler shade than it had been in the bar. Sirens called in the distance.

"You said you have a job for me, Miss Sokolov. If it's of some importance, I'd recommend spilling the beans sooner rather than later. As I'm sure I demonstrated in there, I'm a man of little patience, and although you have my attention now, who knows what shiny object could take it from you?"

Across the street, a woman emerged from a block of luxury apartments. Her red dress dropped to barely below her ass, and she strutted as though she owned the place.

"I see what you mean," Santana scoffed as an understanding grin touched her lips. "Mr. Chambers…"

"Please, call me Dick."

Santana considered this. "I'm not going to do that."

"Enjoy the connotations too much?"

"The opposite."

Dick exhaled from his nose, then took another drag of his cigarette. "Come. Let's walk and talk."

"Where are we going?"

"Away from the place we just destroyed."

Santana's mouth fell open. "*You* destroyed."

"You mean that Arnie isn't unconscious because you belted him over the head with a table leg?"

Santana's mouth flapped open and closed.

Dick grinned. "That's what I thought. Tick-tock, lady. I don't have all night. I've got places to be."

Santana looked as if she was going to contest that notion, then thought better of it. "Mr. Chambers, a mutual friend recommended your services. I need someone who can…locate things. Missing objects, stolen treasures."

"Why don't you call the AJS?"

The sirens grew louder. Dick turned to see two cars appear back down the street and pull up curbside at the bar. The vehicles were a sleek black with angry red cherries spinning their lights on top. The AJS crest decorated the sides of the cars.

Speak of the devils.

Dick had encountered the Atlantica Justice System on more occasions than he cared to admit in his eight years of residence on the island. Having lived most of his life in the United States, with a brief spell of his early years in the UK, he hadn't believed the rumors that the laws and codes of ethics on Atlantica were so severely different from the rest of the world until he had experienced them first-hand. He was still getting his head around the do's and dont's of the island.

Atlantica has its way of dealing with lawbreakers, and that shit is as confusing as a Chinese puzzle box.

Dick increased his pace and turned left at the crossroads, passing a series of high-end diners and restaurants.

Santana fought to keep in step as pedestrian traffic increased. Three men barred her way, and she curved around them to catch up with Dick. "You know as well as I do that the AJS doesn't do shit about residential conflicts. As far as they're concerned, you can do whatever the fuck you want in your house and get away with it, but…"

"…take it into the streets, and they'll come down on you like a guillotine. I know the drill." Dick turned up the collar on his thick tan coat and brought the cigarette up for another drag. "Is there a point to all of this?"

Santana—who was now somewhat breathless—ran in front of Dick, grabbed his arm and pulled him into the shadows of a nearby alley. The smell of grilled steak and thick-cut French fries filled the air.

Dick frowned. "Look, Miss Sokolov, if this is some elaborate ruse to get me in the sack, I have to tell you that I don't carry that kind of cash on me. You want a quickie; it's gotta be a freebie, then I'm on my way—"

Red-hot pain rose on Dick's cheek as Santana's slap echoed down the alley. He moved his hand to his cheek, then looked at her. There was no malice in her eyes, only pained curiosity.

"You slapped me."

"Yes, and I'll do it again until you listen to me. I need you, Mr. Chambers. I'm a busy girl, and I don't have time for this. I need you to help me locate something." She drew a folded piece of paper from her pocket and passed it to Dick. He unfolded it to reveal four individual pages, each with a different printed picture on the front.

The first page showed a pendant on a gold chain draped across a walnut dresser. The locket lay open. Beside it was a torn piece of paper with a section of a map printed on the front, and a separate piece of paper with writing scribbled in a language Dick had never seen before.

The remaining three pages were enlarged images of each item, big enough so that Dick could see the contents more clearly.

"You photographed your evidence?" He kept his eyes fixed on

the images, angling them so that the nearby streetlamp shone its light on them.

"Then destroyed the digital copies," Santana stated.

Dick fixed her with an impressed stare. "You are thorough."

"I'm not stupid, Mr. Chambers. I know how the filth and scum of this city work. Keeping anything stored as a digital record is the same as plastering the front of your house with neons in the shape of the words, 'Rob this place, I'm carrying valuables.' It's suicide."

"The AJS keeps the city safe," Dick returned dryly. "Justice may be unorthodox on this island, but that doesn't mean it doesn't prevail."

"Okay, two things." Santana held up two fingers to illustrate her point. "First off, don't lecture me on Atlantica justice. I was born on this island. My parents excavated it and led a series of archaeological digs in the mountains. I've seen enough of what goes on here to know that justice isn't a word that is often honored, and I know the types of scumbags who reside in this place."

Santana nodded toward the building directly across the road. While the structures on either side kept a contemporary design-frame in mind—looking not too dissimilar from luxury apartments Dick had seen in New York City—the building wedged in between was experimental, to say the least. Enormous black glass panels were countersunk into the building's terracotta façade and looked like colossal squid eyes. The outside of the block bent and warped, and looked more like a Salvador Dali painting than anything you'd imagine from a city-center architectural triumph.

"People have money here," Santana continued. "A Mrs. Garcia owns that building; built it from scratch. The plot of land cost more money than you could imagine, and the building's construction wasn't much less."

She pulled her phone from her pocket, tapped the screen a few times, and showed an ancient Hispanic lady's image. "Mrs. Garcia, ninety-three years of age. Looks sweet and innocent, right? But everyone around here knows she runs a human trafficking ring in Uruguay. It's a hands-off business, but profits pour into her account on the daily. What does the AJS do to prevent this? Nothing. It's not a problem operated within the island, so it's not under their jurisdiction. She's protected." She spat angrily on the floor.

Dick sighed wearily. "Number two?"

Santana looked at Dick as if remembering her train of thought. "Oh, and point number two: why are you defending the AJS when you're infamous around here for going behind their back and getting shit done? Because of the laws imposed on the island, no one can touch you inside your home—except for in a few rare cases—but that doesn't stop you, does it, Mr. Chambers?"

Dick studied her for a few seconds. "So, you want me to find you a stolen piece of jewelry and some paper. That about it?"

Santana shook her head. "There's more. The pendant was given to me a week ago by a stranger who found me in the street. A man tracked me down, shoved me into an alley not unlike this one, and placed the pendant into my hand. He called himself Erik Burgess although who knows if that's true or not. My mother… Well, my late mother—she's been dead for years now—he claimed that he knew her, although I'd never seen this man before in my life. It seemed important that he'd found a way to give it to me, as if there was some greater purpose involved. He gave me his address and said to find him if I had further questions, then he left.

"I examined the contents, found the map and the code, and destroyed the digital trail of breadcrumbs. I kept the locket safe until last night when I came home to find that the pendant and all the clues were gone."

"An opportunistic burglar, no doubt." Dick took one last drag of his cigarette, then screwed the stub into the ground with his toe to extinguish the embers. When he looked up, Santana's face held a strange determination. "That's not the end, is it?"

"I went to find him, Mr. Chambers. I followed the address, and he didn't answer. I began to believe that maybe he had stolen the pendant back, and I banged on his door until a neighbor came out of their apartment to see what was going on. She told me that the AJS had already been and taken him."

"He had already been arrested?"

"No." Santana drew a calming breath. "He had been murdered."

They fell quiet. Nearby, the chatter from passersby filled the air alongside the gentle hum of traffic. More sirens wailed in the distance but grew fainter as they moved farther away.

Santana took a step closer to Dick. He smelled the sweetness of her perfume. "Mr. Chambers, you come highly recommended, and I can tell that this case has caught your attention. Allow me to sweeten the deal with a number that should satisfy you." She held up her cell phone with a number placed on the Satiata Cash app.

Dick's eyes lit up. "Find the pendant, find the man who killed your friend, get paid. Sounds like an easy enough job to me."

Santana smirked. "And watch my back, please. If this guy was already on Erik's scent, then there's a chance he'll be out for me, too."

"Women always assume the bad guy is a guy," Dick scoffed.

Santana took the phone that Dick had pulled from his pocket and bumped them together to transfer an advance to his account. She also keyed in her phone number, and took his.

"You need anything more from me?" Santana asked.

Dick held up the papers. "Mind if I hold onto these?"

"All yours. I have my own." Santana walked out of the alleyway. As she emerged under the full glow of the lights, Dick got one last look at her and took a second to admire her frame. His eyes lingered on her ass as she called, "When I said to watch my back, I didn't mean watch me walk away, Mr. Chambers. I didn't pay you for that."

Dick grinned. "Just doing my job, Ms. Sokolov. And, for the record, I'm happy to watch it from this angle for free."

Santana waved a hand, which turned into a middle finger and disappeared into the crowd.

CHAPTER THREE

Dick exhaled a mouthful of smoke into the pocket-sized apartment. "I need a name, Jimmy. Anything you got."

Atlantica's residential district was densest on the eastern side of the island. Although the majority of residences were financed and developed by the wealthiest men and women in the world, it hadn't been long before one keen philanthropist created an entire plot of apartments that allowed the eager and the desperate to add themselves to the island's population.

The development was controversial from the start, with many of the island's founders and residents protesting the build. However, money talks and the income brought in by individual tenants was enough to warrant filling the powerful's pockets with a healthy amount of cash.

Not to mention the philanthropist's pockets. Yeah, even the generous had motives in this city.

It was such an apartment that Dick found himself in now—a squat little thing on the thirteenth floor that was large enough for a single bedroom, a bathroom, and a living room-slash-kitchenette. The view outside wasn't anything to brag about, with grey brick and more windows a few feet from Jimmy's.

Jimmy rubbed his temples. "What do you think I am? You think I carry the name of every criminal in this city? Think I track everyone's movements and monitor everything they do? Come on, Dick. You know better than that. The AJS would be on my ass in a second." He leaned in conspiratorially. "The AJS can hack a digital trail in seconds. Why do you think I stopped watching porn on my PC?"

"Because you learned the emptiness and shame that comes with jacking off alone in your apartment?"

Jimmy looked out the window to the apartment across the thin alley. An elderly woman stewed something which spouted out steam from a saucepan. "I'm never alone." Jimmy grinned. "Not while Mrs. Hooverman watches."

Dick pinched his eyes and tried to remove the mental image that had appeared. "Give me a name."

Jimmy carefully selected a mug from the mountainous pile heaped on the table. Some were still full of a molding green and brown liquid, but some were simply stained. He took the least stained and crossed to the refrigerator, where he poured a measure of Coke inside.

Whether it was entirely soda or not, Dick didn't know.

"Tell me, Dick. Don't you have anyone else you can bother at this time of night? I have my daughter's violin recital at 9:00 a.m. tomorrow. I don't need this shit."

"You don't have a daughter."

Jimmy held Dick's stare, then glanced at the floor. He spoke almost to himself. "Damn, should never have given you access to my Facebook page." He held up his hands as if in surrender. A splash of Coke spilled onto the carpet, but Jimmy didn't acknowledge it. "I haven't heard anything about a locket, okay? Whatever the deal is with this piece of jewelry, I ain't your guy."

Dick impatiently tapped his fingers on his thigh. Jimmy's eyes darted to Dick's gun.

Jimmy leaned back against the counter and took a long sip.

"I'm telling you, man. It ain't me. It ain't one of my guys. We don't deal in jewelry anymore. Too many playing out in that game. Jewelry is easily tracked these days—at least if you're smart enough to protect it. You want to find some jewelry, find a jewel thief."

Dick rose to his feet, accidentally jolting the coffee table and knocking a couple of mugs onto the floor. Neither of them paid attention to the brown sludge staining the carpet.

He wandered over until he was a few feet from Jimmy, then stopped. Jimmy met his eyes. After almost a decade on this island, Dick had gotten pretty good at detecting the lies hidden behind people's eyes, but Jimmy was squeaky clean in this case.

Dick's voice was low. "You still in touch with Jackson?"

Jimmy searched his brain. "Jackson? Jackson...oh, her?" He grinned and shook his head. "Man, you really do want to tug on some dangerous threads, don't you?"

Dick advanced while frowning.

"Okay, okay, tough guy." Jimmy set his mug on the counter and gently nudged Dick back. "Last I seen, she was working Louie's Florist, down by the docks. What's the opposite of moon-lighting?"

"Being employed?"

"Yeah, that. Knocked into her as I walked past, managed a quick hello before she darted back into the store. Maybe she's making a break at being clean? Who knows? Every day at least a fifth of the population here starts afresh."

Not that it ever lasts.

Dick gave a stern nod and picked up his jacket. He pulled his collar up and made for the door, then opened it and paused. "The day I meet someone who successfully made it clean in this city is the day Godzilla devours us all. In all honesty, I can't wait for that day to come. Atlantica might be the only island that contains so much poison that it makes Godzilla sick. Take care, Jimmy."

"You too, Dick." As the door closed behind him, Jimmy added a quick, "And don't tell her I sent you!"

Dick waited until morning rolled around to sit on a metallic bench across the street from Louie's Florists. He had never understood where the flowers were cultivated or if they grew here. Perhaps Atlantica had set up a trading deal with the US or its partners in Europe or Asia. Maybe they were taken from the wilds that bordered the city and led into the mountains and ruins beyond. Either way, it wasn't his business to dive into the world's trading regimes.

It was his job to find things and fix the problems the AJS couldn't even if that meant treading on a few toes from time to time.

When 7:30 a.m. rolled around, an elderly man with a thick gray mustache strolled down the street and approached the store. He unlocked the door and stepped inside.

Dick waited.

And waited.

And waited some more while the man—presumably Louie, if the store name was anything to go by—set up the stalls outside and populated rows of shelves with flowers of all shapes and sizes.

At 8:30 a.m. the old man turned the sign from CLOSED to OPEN, and the store was open to the public. The streets grew busier as the sky lightened above them in a strained haze of pinks and oranges.

Dick buried his hands in his pockets and watched the store intently, his eyes only leaving the storefront to examine the passersby as he looked for Jessica Jackson. She wouldn't be difficult to spot—with her cotton-white hair and her curious displays of fashion, Jessica would stand out like a rose among thorns.

By 10:00 a.m., Dick grew bored and decided to change tack. He slowly rose, stubbed out his latest cigarette with his toe, then crossed the street. A bell chimed as he entered Louie's Florists, and the elderly man looked up with a surprise that Dick had expected. After an hour and a half of trading, Dick had yet to see a single customer walk inside.

"How are you on this glorious morning, sir?"

Dick glanced out at the hazy street. Despite the sky's best efforts to illuminate the city, car headlights were still lit. The haze demanded it.

The elderly man beamed at him. Dick couldn't understand how in a filth-ridden city like this there could still be a few rays of sunshine found among all the trash.

The man nudged him. "Are you buying for yourself or a loved one?"

"Neither. I hoped you could point me in someone's direction." Dick opened his jacket and flashed a golden badge. "Jessica Jackson is an employee of yours, is she not?"

The man's smile slipped from his face. "She was."

"Was?"

The old man sighed. "Jessica handed in her notice last week. As of yesterday, she's no longer an employee here." He shook his head, his face grown glum. "It's a real shame. The customers loved her. I always called her my 'little flower.'"

Dick tried to control his gag reflex. If this man knew what he knew about Jessica, perhaps he wouldn't have such a rose-tinted view of her.

"Do you have any idea where she might have gone? An address, or a new job?"

The old man tapped the tips of his fingers together and fell deep into thought. The numerous wrinkles on his head grew in number as he racked his brain for anything useful.

"You know, nothing comes to mind. She said something about needing to take a job, and something about the Southern Docks, but…" he laughed, "…you know what an old man's memory is like. Sometimes it's difficult to kick the old gears into motion. You can forgive an old man, can't you?"

He looked up at Dick in earnest, his eyes still bright and keen for a man of his age. Dick nodded and drew a business card from his pocket, then slid it along the table toward him. "If you hear or see anything, please let me know."

The man picked up the card. Dick couldn't help but notice there was a slight tremble in his fingers. His breathing had increased slightly, and there was a gentle flush in his cheeks.

"Of course, Mr…Chambers." The old man's voice rose a touch in volume at the mention of Dick's name. "I'll report anything I see."

Dick nodded and turned to leave. When he reached the door, he rested one hand on the glass and turned the sign around with the other.

The man grew rattled. "Excuse me, but what do you think you're doing?"

Dick spoke over his shoulder. "Enough bullshit, old man. Save us both the embarrassment. Tell Jessica I'm here and want to speak to her."

The man looked like he was about to protest, then deflated rather quickly.

"Wait here, Mr. Chambers."

Dick narrowed his eyes. "I don't think so. I'm coming with you."

When the old man opened the door, Dick wasn't surprised to find the white-haired Jessica sitting on a couch in front of the TV. Although the back of the chair blocked the rest of her body, he knew it was her at once.

The woman lazily waved a hand. Sarcasm laced her sultry

voice. "Nice work, Louie. I knew I could count on you to keep me hidden."

Louie lowered his head and wordlessly left the room.

Dick placed a cigarette between his lips and fished in his pocket for his Zippo. "Strange turn of affairs, using an old man like that to hide your whereabouts. Almost had me at first, but once you've learned the tells of one liar in this city, you've learned them all." He lit the cigarette and exhaled a cloud into the room. "Why are you hiding, Jackson?"

A small ribbon of smoke rose from Jessica's lips. She took another drag on her cigarette and added her contribution without turning around. "What do you want, Chambers? I'm a busy lady."

"I can see that. Regis re-runs? It's like happy hour at the retirement home, here."

Jessica slowly stood and turned toward Dick. His heart rate involuntarily increased as she stood before him in a long red satin gown with a black lacy negligee beneath. Her long white legs were the same color as her artificially dyed hair, and there was a red flush across her chest.

Dick cleared his throat. "What's going on, Jess? You banging the old guy?"

Jessica gave a small chuckle. Her smile brought a twinkle to her ice-blue eyes. "Jealousy is not a nice color on you. Don't worry, I've never forgotten about the time we spent together. No man has ever quite managed to," she glanced at his crotch, "stand up the way you have."

She approached Dick, her bare feet padding across the floor. Through the haze of cigarette smoke, Dick caught notes of her perfume, a scent as sweet as flowers.

Jessica placed a hand on his chest and the other around the back of his neck. She stood on tiptoe, allowing Dick a view of her chest as she whispered into his ear. "You can have me now if you want."

Dick swallowed and closed his eyes. His hand wrapped around her wrist, then with sudden firmness, he locked eyes with her. "I'm here on a job, Jess. You want me; you have me on your own time." He gave Jessica a gentle nudge backward, and her entire facade slipped.

"Should've known you'd always pick your job before you pick a woman. That's always been your caveat, hasn't it? We can fuck, as long as it fits on your schedule."

Dick gave a wry smile. "And yet, no one has ever quite 'stood' up to me."

"Oh, please. Don't think so highly of yourself."

Dick waved a hand in the air. "I know, I know. I never invested too much thought into it. It's one of your primary distraction techniques, is it not? Get the man's thoughts moving from his head to his cock so you can slip out the window and run away. Well, I'm sorry, but I need help finding something, and you're the best lead I have right now."

Jessica grabbed the edges of her gown and wrapped them tightly over her slip, but not before allowing Dick one final glance at the goods beneath.

I should get a damn medal for this. Or at least a pay raise from Santana. The lengths I go to help others...

Jessica dropped back into her seat and crossed her legs. "You sure know how to make a girl feel special."

Dick came around and took a seat on a tattered couch beside her. "Let me cut to the chase, Jess. I'm in the market for a jewelry thief. Well, I'm looking for something a thief might have stolen. It was suggested that you might be the best person to point me in the right direction."

Jessica stared long and hard at Dick before answering. "You know it doesn't work like that. There's not a Craigslist of items thieves have stolen and who worked the gig. Hundreds of sentimental objects get stolen across Atlantica every day, and you're trying to track only one?"

Dick held Jessica's stare while doing everything he could not to get distracted by her smooth porcelain skin.

"You know people, Jess. Give me some names. Give me some people to track. I know you're not as innocent as you make out to be."

Jessica bit her lip. "All I heard in that sentence was 'make out.'"

Dick frowned. "Jess…"

Jess held the playful look on her face a moment longer before sitting back in her chair. "Give me the date the item was stolen, and I'll tell you what I know. But, Dick…if I give you what you want, you have to give me what I want."

Jess rose from her chair, and her gown fell open again. She crossed to Dick and straddled his lap.

CHAPTER FOUR

Dick awoke from his nap a little later that afternoon. A quick shower washed Jessica's scent off him. As his mind tried to replay the hour they had spent together, he forced himself to focus on the case ahead.

She had given him three names. He was familiar with two of them, having either encountered them directly before or at least heard of them through his AJS hacker, which directed a constant feed of upcoming cases to his home computer. Thanks to a series of VPNs and an entire labyrinth of decoy servers, he had protected himself pretty well from detection, but he knew that it wasn't entirely foolproof.

A quick search through his computer yielded little to help him with his case. The thing to know about thieves and criminals was that the good ones rarely remained in one place for long. If you were smart, you moved. It was always harder to hit a moving target than a stationary one. That was a lesson our Neanderthalic cousins knew, that hadn't made it down to some of their less intelligent descendants.

"Ramone Kelly," Dick muttered as he scrolled through the

various windows and searches. "Seven counts of thievery, five of trespassing, and a whole load of charges for dealing in the streets." Dick scoffed and brought the glass of whiskey to his lips. "A-hole. Everyone knows you can deal in your house and you're safe. What idiot takes his dirty work into the street?"

That was the million-dollar question. If people were safe and allowed to deal drugs in their home, commit adultery, hell, even murder within their four walls, why would anyone ever take to the streets to work the lines?

Idiots. Idiots and boneheads who love the rush of the chase. Oh, and don't forget the tourists. Some queef-bags are so used to their hometown laws they forget the intricacies of Atlantica justice. More fool them.

After a few more minutes of searching, Dick had an address of Ramone's last known location. He then searched for a woman named Evelyn Trelawney and found a clip of CCTV footage of a sharp-featured woman in a jewelry shop from the previous day. An hour later, an item was reported stolen. Dick traced her journey on the CCTV feeds to a residence on Main Street and jotted down the address on a small pad of paper.

Although technology had advanced tenfold in the twenty-seven years since the second millennium hit, Dick found something satisfying in reverting to manual processes. It helped him think.

The final perp was a name he hadn't seen before. There was limited information on William "Bill" Grunch, other than a few online articles detailing the celebrations of a spelling-bee champion from the Southern District. The most recent document Dick could find was a small clipping. It showed a sullen-looking Grunch with his hands in cuffs after he attempted to break into a high-rise condominium complex in the colloquially named Crime Time Quarter—a small section of the Eastern District which famously housed some of the world's greatest crime lords who were guarded by AJS law.

"Interesting." Dick scrolled to another window and found the late-night CCTV footage of a man disappearing down the side alley into the darkness, minutes before the break-in was reported. He followed a series of other camera feeds and found several reels in which Grunch was smoking on the steps of an apartment building a mile away from the crime scene.

"Worth a shot," Dick muttered, then drained the contents of his whiskey in one. He rose from his chair, pocketed his pad, and left his apartment.

Dick drove in his 2024 sedan along the streets of Atlantica. His search took him to the Eastern District, where he staked out the outside of Ramone Kelly's apartment. While he waited in the car and kept an eye on the window on the seventh floor, he used one of his many in-car burner phones to contact his informant inside the AJS.

Terry Yayonavich spoke in a hushed whisper. "Dude, are you crazy? It's the middle of the night."

"It's 3:00 p.m., Terry. Wake up."

"Maybe for you. I was on the night shift. You know I hate being disturbed from my beauty sleep."

Dick chuckled. "No amount of sleep is going to fix that mess. You look like someone threw raw mincemeat at a brick wall."

"Charmed."

Terry asked what Dick wanted, knowing that it would be something that could jeopardize his job. Dick explained that he was after information on three possible perps and asked if Terry had anything on them.

Terry yawned. Through the line, Dick heard him rise from his bed and move through his apartment. "You know I can get in deep shit for helping you with this."

"Do you really need to say that every time?"

"I thought it was worth mentioning."

Out of the corner of Dick's eye he saw the apartment building's front door open and close as an obese woman in heels stumbled down the stairs. His lip curled. "Is it worth me mentioning that you said you owe me? Your sister wouldn't still be around if I hadn't tracked down and removed the assassin who put a hit out on her. How is Lisa, by the way?"

"Oh, you know women. They never learn. She went clean for a few months, but I'm pretty sure she's back on the glass." Terry sighed. "Not a lot I can do but wait for her to want to change. Sucks to bear witness to, though."

Dick gave an empathetic grunt.

"Ah," Terry exclaimed. "Here we go. So, your friend Ramone Kelly. Looks like he's been clean for a few months now. Got him registered as an employee of the downtown mega-mart. No current issues, looks squeaky clean."

Dick stared at the window and shook his head. "Damn."

Terry continued. "Erm… Evelyn Trelawney is currently in custody with us. Turns out she's been trying her hand at something new. Ooo, this is interesting. She's packed in the jewelry heists and turned to street walking. Our guys picked her up on the corner of Fifth last night, high off her tits and screaming at a Merc as it sped on down the street." Terry chuckled. "I thought they had apps for that kind of shit now. Who stands on the corner of a public space at 4:00 a.m. hoping to get fucked these days? Isn't everything digital?"

Dick's mind flashed to his conversation with Santana. His hand moved to the scanned photographs in his pocket. "Not if you're smart."

Terry's laugh faded. "I guess. Okay, your last request. William Grunch." Terry shuddered. "What a horrible name. Sounds like an STI. *Grunch*. Okay, I've got it here that there have been a few charges of petty theft and an attempted break-in, but he's been quiet ever since." A pause. "Nope, nothing more suspect than that,

I'm afraid. A credited employee at Tamwell's Accountants—he's the janitor there. Otherwise, that's it."

Dick rested his head on his fist. "You got an address for him? I need something to go on here."

"You got reason to believe he's in the shit?"

Dick remained silent.

"Thirty-four Croswell Street."

Dick tapped the same address on his paper. He scribbled down, "Tamwell's Accountants," thanked Terry, and hung up.

A quick drive took him five blocks down toward a wider street with two lanes on either side. He found a small corner to park and waited outside the accountants. If Grunch was working, as Dick suspected he might be, all he needed to do was wait and follow him.

Sure enough, at 5:00 p.m., a scrawny, rat-like man scurried down the stairs and into the streets. He wore a thin jacket and shouldered a tatty backpack. His pace outmatched most of those around him, and once he turned the corner, Dick blinked his turn signals and followed him home.

<hr>

He parked outside Grunch's apartment and waited. He checked the clock, made a note to wait an additional twenty minutes, then resolved to head over and buzz for his apartment.

To pass the time, Dick tuned in to the local radio and closed his eyes. East District FM was in the middle of its jazz segment, designed to calm drivers during rush hour, and he listened to the smooth melodies of the saxophone and brass instruments play their jam.

When he opened his eyes, fifteen minutes had passed. He sat up straight and prepared to exit his vehicle when he noticed Grunch skittering down the street and around the corner.

Dick twisted the ignition, pulled the car away, and followed

Grunch down several quiet streets toward a warehouse situated between two car dealerships. Grunch disappeared inside for around an hour before he re-emerged in a fresh set of dark fatigues. He'd swapped his backpack for a satchel, and as he exited the building, he stared at the darkening sky as if trying to find something through the fog.

His interest caught, Dick followed Grunch another five blocks until he disappeared down a tight alleyway. He waited a few moments before pulling up in line with the alley and peering through the darkness.

Grunch was nowhere in sight.

"And so the plot thickens."

Dick waited another minute before stepping out of his car. The street was almost empty. High-class vehicles littered the curb, which indicated the type of people who lived nearby. He waited a second at the alley entrance, then placed a long, flat cartridge between the walls at its mouth. Satisfied, he shuffled down the alley, treading carefully not to raise the alarm, until he found himself at a blank steel door.

Dick reached toward a small keypad on the wall where a strange metal box covered the numbers. A red and green light alternated flashes on top.

Dick dug into his pockets and pulled out a Swiss Army knife. He found the flathead screwdriver function and peeled away the box's outer casing to reveal several wires and cables within. Next to them was a wireless transmitter jammed into the alarm to prevent detection while hacking into the system.

Dick drew the transmitter from the housing case and clipped the shell back on. He held the transmitter in front of his eyes and admired the craftsmanship. There was a power cell inside, which would have been fueled by the network of wires drawing power from the main lock until fully charged.

Dick had seen such a device before. "Ringo, I may have to

have some words with you. I thought we agreed you'd stop producing hacking devices for low-life scum."

After placing the transmitter in his pocket, Dick rested his back against the wall. He knew he'd have a few minutes to spare, so he lit another cigarette and listened to the sound of city traffic around him.

By the time his cigarette was an ashen stump, he heard a disturbance on the other side of the door. The lock clicked, and, sure enough, out popped Grunch, so lost in his movements that he didn't notice Dick until he'd bumped straight into him.

Dick grinned. "Nice night for a stroll, isn't it?"

Grunch froze where he stood. The shadows in the alley made his rat-like features harsher, and his nose twitched. One hand clutched his satchel, while the other held the strap. The bag looked considerably heavier than it had when the man entered the building.

Grunch's eyes darted from Dick to the alley entrance. He suddenly broke for it, but Dick kicked out his leg, which caused Grunch to stumble and fall. Grunch tried to scramble back to his feet, but Dick was in front of him and blocked his way.

Dick tapped a cigarette from his pack and offered one to Grunch. "You smoke?"

Grunch shook his head, the movement so miniscule Dick almost missed it.

Dick placed the pack back in his pocket. "I want to talk, okay? A quick chat between men. You can do that, can't you?"

"Look, prick, I don't know who you are, but I'm in a bit of a hurry, here—*ow!*"

Dick stood on Grunch's back and pressed him into the ground. He knelt and unzipped the satchel's main compartment, which revealed a wad of gold and silver chains, necklaces, rings, and watches. Many of them were encrusted with diamonds. Underneath them, lining the bottom of the bag, was a bed of blue Atlantican cash notes.

Dick nodded, impressed. "Not a bad haul for a night's work. You'd think apartment blocks would take better care of their tenants, wouldn't you? The guys in that building have some serious connections. They're not going to be happy to discover a petty thief came in and robbed their asses." He nodded at the keypad on the door. "Still, with the right technology, you can make it as though you were never there. That's a signal blocker, correct? Doesn't just unlock the door for you, but helps hack into the alarm system, too. A pretty clever piece of kit. That can't have been cheap."

Dick removed his foot, and Grunch got to his feet. He clutched the bag to his chest, a desperate look in his eyes. He glanced back at the door as if expecting half a dozen security guards to be racing toward them. "Please, man. Let me pass. This ain't for me."

Dick interjected, "Oh, I never expected it would be. Thieves don't steal jewelry to wear the items. They steal to make cold, hard cash, right? What time are you supposed to meet your client?"

Grunch cautiously checked his watch, as if lifting his eye off Dick would cause serious trouble. "Twenty minutes." He eyed him suspiciously. "You some kind of cop?"

"If I were a cop, you'd be in cuffs by now. I need you to answer a question for me."

Grunch's bravery seemed to grow with the knowledge that Dick wasn't with the AJS. "Look, man, let me the fuck past. Why should I help you when you're putting me in real shit right now?"

"First, you put yourself in that shit. I didn't make you rob from Savachi Guchi, did I?"

Grunch gasped. "How did you…"

"Call it a hunch. Man, he's going to be pissed when he finds out you robbed from his stash. I guess it wouldn't help your case if the alarm were to ring now, would it?" Dick pulled the transmitter from his pocket and shook it in front of Grunch.

Grunch's face dropped. He turned back to the jammer and saw the piece looked whole. "You're bluffing."

"This here is the transmitter to your little piece of kit. I worked with Ringo on these at one point, trying to understand the tech used to break into security systems. Helps me understand what I'm dealing with in my line of work. Did you know that this little black switch right here blocks the transmitter and sets off the alarms for the entire system? Yeah…one little flick and the AJS will be hot-tailing it to our location in less time than it takes for you to jack off into your flannel."

Grunch began to sweat. He grew itchy on his feet. "You wouldn't."

"Try me."

Grunch held Dick's gaze for a long moment before exhaling. "What do you want to know?"

Dick drew the scans Santana had given him from his pocket and held them up to Grunch. "I'm looking for someone who might know where to find these. It's for a client of mine who wants her mother's locket back. These look familiar?"

Grunch made the mistake of answering too quickly. "Never seen them before in my life."

Dick sighed and held up the device, thumb hovering over the button.

Grunch waved his spare hand. "Okay, fine! Fine. I've seen it, okay? It wasn't for me, though. I was hired. Never understood what the value was for that piece of shit, but he paid me well for it. You should tell your friend to get a better security system. Breaking into that place was easier than diving into an air-bath."

Dick moved closer to Grunch and leered down at him with a hard stare. His heart pumped with adrenaline.

"And you killed the son of a bitch who gave it to her, too? Why?"

For the first time, Grunch's face screwed up in genuine confusion. "I didn't kill nobody, man. I swear it."

Dick's eyes bore into Grunch. "Give me a name."

Sirens in the distance caught their attention. Although Dick knew they wouldn't be for them, it still made Grunch's sweat increase. "I didn't get a name, okay? All I got was an alias."

Dick took Grunch's shoulders in his hands and shook him. It was like a bear shaking a weasel. "Give me something."

"Everest! His name is Everest. That's all I got, I swear. I swear..."

Dick tried to hide his surprise. He knew that name, knew exactly where to find him. But what did Everest want with the locket?

Dick shoved him away. Grunch stumbled but remained on his feet. "Thank you. Was that so hard?"

Grunch frowned and clutched the bag to him again. He glanced over his shoulder at the door one last time before Dick told him to scram.

The weasel shoved his way past Dick and was halfway to freedom when he called over his shoulder, "Piece of shit detective. Filthy asshole scum, fucking man-handling me. You're dead, detective. I know people. I can shut down your shit and have you killed in an hour. Watch your back, there's already someone aiming their sniper at it."

Dick grinned. "What did you say?"

Grunch stopped about twenty feet from the alley exit. "I said your ass is grass, cheap shot. No one fucks with Grunch."

Dick laughed, then raised the transmitter once more. "You must think I bluff, kid."

Grunch's eyes widened as the alarm was triggered and a banshee shriek filled the alley. He turned on his heels and fled the remaining distance. Only, his foot caught the metallic cartridge Dick had set up at the mouth of the alley, which triggered a paralyzing electrical pulse that sparked through Grunch's system and brought him to the ground where he flopped like a fish.

Dick made his way toward him and carefully trod over the

spasming man before curling his lip. "Enjoy your time in jail, Grunch. Always a pleasure to meet new people."

He casually crossed the street and entered his sedan. By the time he turned off the thoroughfare, three AJS cars had pulled up and trained their pistols on Grunch.

CHAPTER FIVE

Dick ran a hand across his tired face as he strolled down the street and toward Ricardo's Pawn Brokers. *Park two blocks away, that's the rule.*

He cut through the alleys behind a series of Korean, Thai, and Italian restaurants. Large dumpsters overflowing with food waste lined one wall. A group of vagrants rifled through bags, tore them open and hunted for scraps while throwing pieces of chicken into their mouths and gnawing on bones. They hardly looked up as Dick passed.

The hairs on the back of his neck stood up as the alley narrowed. He felt eyes on him, but when he turned, there was no one. Even the ravenous homeless made no time for him. When he reached the end, a chain-link fence blocked his way and forced him to the right, toward a rough-looking gate.

The night sky was still. The smell of hot food filled the alley. Dick dug his hands in his pocket and caught the first *crunch* of a boot on the gravel behind him.

He didn't turn. "Dammit, Val. You need to stop doing that shit. It's creepy as hell."

Behind him stood a woman in a blood-red trench coat with

her collar pulled high over her neck. A fedora that sat low across her brow shadowed her face, except for her bright red-painted lips.

"Nothing ever changes, does it, Dick?"

Dick spun on his heels and exhaled smoke into the air. "You're telling me. Have you even changed your outfit since we last saw each other?" He looked past Valentina's shoulder to check that no one was watching them. "I heard a rumor that you were dead."

"If it were up to my enemies, I would be." Valentina smirked. She was confident—he had to give her that. He would be too if he were one of the most notorious and elusive mercenaries in Atlantica. Both the AJS and criminal organizations had tried to find a way to exterminate Valentina Winter on many occasions, and they had failed each time "Now and then, it's worth laying low and keeping out of trouble. Gives the Feds a chance to forget you. Allows new scum to push you out of the spotlight."

"I don't think anyone has forgotten you."

"You charmer."

Dick peeled his eyes away from her lips. "You've been hibernating?"

Valentina moved closer and removed her hat to reveal a curtain of sleek dark hair. "Not exactly. Hibernating would imply that I stopped." She winked.

Dick nodded, his face straight and grim. There was something about the woman that pulled at his chest. She was beautiful, but it was a dangerous beauty. Dick had once been the fly, and she the Venus flytrap. He scratched his beard, eyes deep in thought. "I'm going to go ahead and guess that our meeting here isn't a coincidence."

"Is it ever?"

"Not as far as I can remember." He scanned down her body and breathed her in. "What's the job?"

"Always work with you, isn't it?"

That's not the first time I've heard that tonight.

Valentina reached inside her jacket pocket and withdrew a card. She placed it gingerly into Dick's hand and planted a kiss on his lips. Her lips were warm and soft like he remembered. "You know where to find me."

Dick studied the card. The front showed a black background with a red "V" that curved into the shape of a heart. On the other side was a single line with an address and a time written in elegant cursive.

Dick chuckled. "You think it's that easy? Nothing for years, then suddenly you…" He glanced up and realized that she was gone. He rotated the card between his fingers, then pocketed it. "Damn spooky assassin…but crazy in bed. Maybe it's the imminent threat of death that makes it so hot?"

Dick opened the gate and left the alley, the smell of Valentina's perfume lingering in his nostrils.

Dick paused outside Ricardo's Pawn Shop. The twenty-four-hour sign blinked as the neons began to crap out, and the glass was a noticeably thick, bulletproof affair.

"Good to know." Dick gave a resolute nod and headed inside.

The store was cramped. There was hardly space to walk down the aisles between the various items displayed. He sidled past shelves of jewelry, video games, and retro and modern tech. Dick reached the counter and rang the bell.

A man shuffled through the rear door and paused halfway into the room. There was a flicker of something in his eyes. *Fear?* As he caught Dick's stare, the strange look faded and one of eager excitement replaced it. "Jonathon Chambers. How long has it been?"

John grimaced.

The man comically threw his hands in the air. "Sorry! It's John, I know. I know."

"If you know it, you best remember it. Got that, Ricardo? You know as well as I do that I have enough dirt on you to fill a quarry."

Ricardo gave an exaggerated laugh and slapped the desk. He wore a white short-sleeved shirt with a faded logo on the chest. His arms were slim and his fingers long, each digit strangled by rings. Half a dozen chains hung around his neck, and metal had replaced three of his teeth.

The pawnbroker rested both hands on the counter. His comical demeanor faded as he exhaled and deflated. "What are you here for, Dick? You in the market to buy, or are you tracking something again? I'll tell you as I always do, nearly everything in this store has a story. I don't know every detail of what comes my way, but I'll share what I can." He raised a hand. "For you, of course. Not if it's going to aid those AJS pricks." Ricardo spat on the dust-covered floor. "Damn pricks knock on this door every other day and try to bully me into speaking. They don't realize the position I'm in, you know? A rock and a hard place. That's what I wanted to call this shop once. Had the art picked out and everything. Damn Sheila convinced me to call it after myself, and where's that bitch now? Off in some hole shacking up with—"

Dick rested his hands on the counter. "Ricardo."

Ricardo looked as though he had come around from a coma. "Yes?"

"You blabber when you're nervous." Dick leaned closer. "Let me ask you a question. Why so jittery?"

Ricardo gave an awkward laugh and rubbed his arms. "You know how it is. I'm in the middle of the shit, Dick. Rock and a hard place. I told you."

Dick grabbed Ricardo by his shirt and dragged him closer. "Rock and a hard place? Would that be a little mountain by the name of Everest?"

A flash of something cold came across Ricardo's face. His eyes narrowed as he grabbed Dick's wrist and pulled himself free. His breathing quickened, and his eyes darted to the door.

"No one else is coming, Ricardo. I have no backup. I only need information. Where's the pendant?"

"What pendant?"

"Don't bullshit me."

"I'm not."

"Rick."

"It's gone."

"To whom?"

"I can't say." Ricardo's forehead beaded with sweat.

For a man who sits on the fence between criminals and justice, this guy has the cojones of a dung beetle.

"Give me a name. That's all I need."

Ricardo held Dick's gaze for a few seconds, then looked at the floor. "This is bigger than you, Dick. Trust me when I say that the less you know, the better. I'm doing this as a professional courtesy. If you go digging down this hole, you're not going to find your way back out. Let it drop, and we'll pretend that nothing has happened. Nothing was said."

Dick shook his head. "You know I can't do that. I'm paid to find things. I've never failed. I'm not going to let you be the reason I lose my five-star rating on P.I.s for Hire."

"Is that a thing?"

"Of course, that's not a thing!" Dick snapped. He noted Ricardo's hand had now returned to the counter and placed his on top of it, then quickly manipulated his grip until Ricardo's finger was bent and strained almost to the point of snapping. "Give me something. Anything."

Ricardo complained and twisted toward the counter. His head hit the cold surface. "Okay! Okay!" He pulled his hand away from Dick's grip. "Okay, I'll tell you, all right? I'll tell you what you want to know. Just know that once I tell you, you can't be untold." Ricardo stroked his finger. "I like you, Dick. I don't want to see you hurt."

Dick remained stoic while staring at Ricardo.

Ricardo slumped. "Follow me."

The back room of the pawnshop contained a litter of boxes and plastic packaging. There was a door at the back wall leading into darkness. A computer occupied one corner, and there were two chairs at crooked angles nearby.

The smell of weed was in the air

Ricardo took a chair and offered the other to Dick.

"It's all in here." Ricardo bent forward and reached beneath the desk drawer for a key taped to the underside. He crossed the room and unlocked a reinforced cabinet and slid open a deep drawer, which he then rifled inside.

A clicking sound came from inside the cabinet, and a sudden *thrum* of electricity surged around the room. Dick turned behind him, alarmed to discover that the door they had walked through now had latticed bars that prevented him from leaving. When he turned back to Ricardo, he stared into the wide-eyed double-barrel of a vintage-looking shotgun. Two men wearing thick woolen balaclavas and stinking of vodka appeared through the door behind him, their fists clenched and eyes narrowed at Dick.

Dick shook his head and drew a deep breath. He rose to his feet and pulled a cigarette from his pocket. "Do you really want to do this, Ricardo? I thought you liked me?"

Ricardo's hands shook, but he kept the gun trained at Dick. "Oh, I do, John. The problem is, I value my life more. I told you, this whole thing is bigger than you—it's bigger than both of us."

The thugs standing behind the pawnbroker grinned.

CHAPTER SIX

Adrenaline surged through Dick and caused every hair to stand on end.

They were big. There was no question about that. Maybe not as big as Arnie, but they benched like soldiers. The only difference between soldiers and these two was the multitude of tattoos that covered their arms, as well as their tight man-buns coiled at the back of their heads.

"On ves' tvoy, parni."

Russian?

There was a perverse glee on Ricardo's face that Dick hadn't seen before. He supposed it was right for a low-life to enjoy the battles of greater men.

Dick cracked his knuckles and assumed his stance. "Okay, boys. Which one of you do I have to take down first?"

There wasn't a single flicker of understanding as he spoke. The Russian on the left walked with a slight limp, which Dick noted. The one on the right had a scar which touched the top of his upper lip. He cataloged that, too.

They both advanced.

"Both of you it is." Dick turned to Ricardo. "Then I hope you realize I'm coming for you."

The cockiness on Ricardo's face slipped. He slid his chair back and pushed himself closer to the wall.

Limpy came at Dick, using what he thought had been a moment of distraction. Little did he know that Dick had purposefully misdirected to initiate combat, counting on one of the guys to try and catch him off-guard.

Limpy's fist sailed over Dick's head. He ducked and returned with a swift uppercut that caught his chin. Limpy cried out as it pushed him off balance and knocked him into the wall beside him.

Lip-scar shoved Limpy the remaining distance aside, their bulk filling the room enough that movement wasn't easy to accomplish. He jumped at Dick, gaining more height than Dick would have anticipated from such a large man, and knocked him backward into a pile of cardboard boxes.

Metal *clinked* as various pieces of jewelry that had been waiting to be valued slid across the floor. A few earrings pricked into Dick's head.

Lip-scar grinned with glee and pressed himself to his knees as his ham-sized fists flew at Dick.

Dick dodged the first but felt the second. The copper taste of blood filled his mouth, and for a moment he saw a flash of white.

When the next punch came, Dick twisted sideways and threw his head forward. It caught Lip-scar in the face and opened his lip scar. The light bead of skin that had healed ripped open and gushed with blood.

Lip-scar's eyes flashed. Dick leveraged the moment and threw another headbutt, this time catching his forehead. That one was far more painful for Dick since his skull bashed against the Russian's dense bone.

I need to get out from beneath him before he crushes me like a boul-

der. Dick frantically searched around and found a glass bottle of some liquid within arm's reach.

He brought the bottle to the Russian's face and smashed it against his skull. The liquid instantly became gaseous as it combined with the air and as Lip-scar took a deep inhalation, his eyes grew heavy.

Crap, that made it worse. I'm going to die getting crushed beneath a tranquilized rhino.

Dick pushed the Russian to the side with a hefty shove, where he rolled to his front and remained still, nose pressed to the concrete floor.

Dick rose to his feet, pawing away at several small shards of glass which had fallen near his eye. He was certain that a little of the gas had made its way into his system since he became light-headed on his feet.

Limpy saw him sway and staggered toward him. He grabbed the back of Dick's neck and drove his face toward Ricardo's desk. Dick brought his hands out in front of him and narrowly avoided the collision, then kicked behind him, being sure to hook his heel around Limpy's crotch.

A strange *whooshing* sound came out of the Russian as his thighs clamped together and trapped Dick's foot. Dick looked up, expecting to see Ricardo still sitting there, but he was gone, the door to the back left open behind him.

Typical. The mouse goes and hides in his hole while the cats do all the work.

A glint of silver caught Dick's attention. He grabbed the key and shoved it into his pocket.

He freed his foot and turned on Limpy, then sat on the desk as Limpy doubled over and held his balls. "I know, I know," Dick soothed, "it's a cheap shot. No man should ever go for the other man's balls because he knows what it feels like to have his bashed in. It's a difficult feeling to describe when you think about it. Like a dull ache in the pit of your stomach that somehow spreads up your body like wildfire."

A groan came from Lip-scar, although he didn't move.

Dick drew a cigarette and lit it. He took a deep inhalation and blew the smoke at Limpy. "How would you describe your pain? On a scale of one to ten?"

Limpy looked up with a thunderous expression on his face. His face was dark beneath the ledge of his brow. "Ya ub'yu tebya, pridurok!"

Limpy moved his hand to his waist, where the glint of steel winked at Dick. Before he could draw the knife, Dick hopped up and kicked the man's shin as hard as he could.

The man yowled in pain and fell on his ass as he clutched his splintered shin.

"My Russian isn't great, but I picked up some key words over my time here. Strange to think that Atlantica has yet to create a universal language. We have a population that's probably thirty percent Russian, thirty-five percent American, and twenty-five percent European, and only the smart learn to speak the languages they might be missing."

Dick wandered over to the open back door and closed it. He drew the key and found it fit, then locked the door and trapped them all inside once again.

"But, here's my guess. Somewhere in that mix of Russian butchery, there was a hint of the word 'fucker.' I'm ninety-nine percent sure of that." Dick filled his lungs and slowly exhaled as he spoke. "I don't take kindly to name-calling. It's cheap. Well, maybe not as cheap as a swift kick to the balls, but you do what you got to do to survive here."

He knelt and took Limpy's knife and held it up to the light to see the blade's keenness. "Sharp. Man, you guys know how to take care of your weapons. If I were to lose my life to a swift stabbing, you better bet I'd like to be stabbed by something like this. One small prod and..." he stabbed the air a few times "... you'd be gushing like a leaky faucet."

Limpy hissed between clenched teeth. His eyes were blood-shot and filled with malice. "Tebe luchshe bezhat', idiot. V tu minutu, kogda boss uznayet ob etom, ty mertv."

Dick nodded politely with the knife pointed at Limpy. This time, he held his phone screen-first to the Russian as the speaker picked up the speech and translated it to the room: "You better run, idiot. The minute the boss hears about this, you're dead."

"The boss, huh?" Dick shuffled closer to Limpy. He touched the blade against a thin crease of skin that had freed itself from his shirt in his fall. "Now we're getting somewhere. See, I'm clued up enough to know that Ricardo isn't that much of an idiot that he'd set henchmen on me without there being some kind of chain linking all the way to the top. Your boss placed you here to protect him. Or maybe to keep an eye on him. But why, I wonder? What's the big link that ties you all together? What is it about that pendant that has you guys sitting in the back of shit-eater's store, waiting to protect him from curious folks like me who want to see a piece of jewelry put back into the hands of the person with whom it belongs?"

He waited for Limpy to answer but got nothing but a blank stare. He laughed when he realized the problem, then glanced at his phone. "Sorry, I forgot to hit 'Translate.'"

He tapped a button, and the phone reeled off his speech in a thick, Russian tongue.

Limpy replied, his face as sour as ever. Dick played it back and shook his head.

"If you're determined to keep your secrets, you leave me little choice but to take matters into my hands. That kick to your balls will be minor compared to what I can do with this rather impres-sive knife."

Dick glanced up as Ricardo's face appeared behind the glass of the locked door. His eyes widened when he saw Dick look his way, and he disappeared once more.

One thing at a time, Dick. Prioritize your threats.

Lip-scar groaned again and shuffled slightly on the floor. Dick picked up a telephone from Ricardo's desk and hurled it toward him. The phone landed on the back of his head and knocked him unconscious once more.

Dick spotted the glass shards on the floor. *I wonder what that liquid was.*

He returned his attention to Limpy. "Okay, Slick. Last chance. What's it going to be? Give me something I can work on. A name, an address, anything you got. Know that I'll find whatever's going on and I won't stop. You can either live to see me succeed, or die and I'll still succeed." He lowered the knife toward the man's crotch and pressed the tip of the blade against the fabric of his trousers. The blade slid through without resistance. "Or, third option, become a eunuch and watch me succeed."

He tapped the button on the phone, and the translator relayed his message. The Russian fought internally for a few moments before he growled and shouted something at Dick. Dick pressed the blade further. Its point disappeared into the material, and the Russian instantly shut up. He leered at Dick, then grumbled two words that translated to, "Paper Doilies."

Dick cocked an eyebrow. "Is this you being funny?"

The Russian shook his head as a small squeal came from his throat. *Funny how even the biggest among us can squeal like pigs when the right part of our anatomy is threatened.* Dick held his stare, determined that he was telling the truth, and withdrew the blade. There was the faintest trace of blood on the end of it.

Dick held the blade to the light. "I'm going to keep this. Not because I want to clone you or take your DNA, but because I don't trust you not to stab me when my back is turned.

He rose to his feet and sat at Ricardo's desk. He reached under the table and found a button that unlocked the shutters on the exit door when pressed. He was halfway through stepping over Lip-scar when he changed his mind and made his way to the back room. He pointed the blade at Limpy. "Stay put until I'm gone. There's a good boy."

He glanced at the clock on the wall, hyperaware of the time. *Shit, only thirty minutes to get halfway across town. She hates it when I'm late, too.*

With a final exhalation of smoke, he left.

Dick half-ran and half-jogged to his sedan. His lungs protested as he gasped for air. He went along the main streets this time, keen to avoid the alleyways. If two Russians had been stationed here, then who was to say more wouldn't be located nearby?

The neon of the street signs blurred by, and he wasn't sure if it was his general lack of cardio fitness or the remainder of that bottled concoction that made him lightheaded. He rounded the corner and squeezed through a group of rough-looking men in a stand-off, and almost crashed into the woman standing and watching the group.

"John?" The woman looked him up and down, then folded her arms. "Well, I'll be damned."

"Terra? What are you doing here?" He looked back over his shoulder at the rival gangs and realization dawned. "Another stand-off?"

"Happens every few nights," Terra replied. She looked sharp in her AJS uniform. Her crop of dark hair spilled over the collar, and her ice-blue eyes focused on the men ahead. "Perks of Atlantica. They know they can't attack each other in the streets, especially with AJS present. My job is to stand sentinel and keep an eye on them. I'm essentially an overpaid babysitter to thugs."

"Oh, I know for a fact you see more action than that." Dick chuckled. "I still have the scar on my ass from the last gunfight you dragged me into. Funny how with only one perp left you happened not to see him at the right time, eh? See, if *I* were in that position, I'd have taken him down before he'd have taken a shot. But what do I know? I'm not the trained AJS officer among us."

Terra scowled. "*I* dragged you into that fight? You know damn well I did what I could when I needed to. If you hadn't snooped around Slovakian drug lords' apartments, then we wouldn't have been in that situation in the first place."

John laughed. "However you choose to see it, Kris."

"That's *Officer* Kris to you."

John eyed her through narrowed lids. "I don't think we're quite there yet. Maybe once we've played together a bit more."

"You mean when you're not busy trashing local taverns?" She smiled at the look that came over John's face. "Yeah, word spreads fast in Atlantica. How does it feel to be banned from yet another public house? The Armada was one of the nicer ones, too."

"I don't know what you're talking about."

Terra grinned. "Of course, you don't. I bet you don't know anything about the apish giant we now have in custody, do you? His face was covered in glass, believe it or not. Glass. As though someone smashed a bottle upside his head. Brutal attack."

Dick stared placidly at Terra. "Could have been anyone. You know this city as well as I do—maybe better. Every day is a day to bring scum back into order and sweep the shit from the floor."

A commotion broke out behind them. Dick glanced over his shoulder as two figures from opposite sides of the group walked toward each other until their foreheads touched. One of the men's hands hovered over his pistol. Nearby citizens walked on as if nothing was happening, too wrapped up in their conversations.

Dick looked at Terra. "Looks like you're up."

Terra walked past Dick and bashed into his shoulder as she did. Dick laughed and watched as the gangs' eyes met hers.

"Oh, Terra? Make sure you tell Arnie I said hi, okay?"

Terra didn't turn back, but Dick saw her shoulders tense.

Dick glanced at his watch. "Shit. Best get a move on."

CHAPTER SEVEN

Dick flashed an ID card that didn't have his face on it against the security scanner—a little perk he'd picked up throughout his interactions with the AJS over the years. The doors slid open, and he slipped inside the Crown Hotel.

His shoes clicked against the marble floors. The lobby was a wide-open affair with potted plants and a wishing fountain in the center. He strode past the receptionist without a second glance and worked his way up through the elevator.

When he was alone, he flipped over Valentina's card in his hands and re-read the number. Thirteenth floor, room 1307.

"Can't be doing too badly if she got herself a suite in the goddamn Crown."

The doors chimed open, and Dick found the room. He gently knocked on the door and turned to his right, where a glass panel gave a view of the city.

It was no wonder the Crown had one of the highest per night rentals in Atlantica. That view was killer.

Let's hope Valentina's not in killer mode tonight. Well, maybe in one way she could be.

Dick waited a few moments, but no answer came. He knocked again, and still no reply. He triple-checked the card, then glanced at his watch. He was eight minutes past time. That could be enough to lose him the opportunity for a night to remember.

"Damn."

He turned and made for the elevator, but only managed two steps before the door clicked open and allowed him a view inside.

There was no one to greet him. Dick peered inside the massive luxury hotel room with its island kitchenette and lounge suite. The entire back wall was made of glass and towered two stories high. Here the view was one of the best he had seen, although the fog only allowed him to see so far.

He closed the door. "Val? You here?"

No answer came. Dick grinned and chuckled, then cupped his hands and lit a cigarette. The minute the lighter sparked, a hand slapped it away.

The lighter rolled along the floor and disappeared under a chair.

"No smoking for you, Dick. You already smell like a chimney sweep." Valentina's arms wrapped around him from behind.

"There are nicer ways to ask."

"You know I have a penchant for the dramatic. It's kind of my thing."

Dick stroked his hands along the smooth skin of Valentina's arms. The scent of her filled his nostrils and made him light-headed. He felt the warmth of her body against his back.

Dick half-turned his head and caught the slightest glance of Val's naked shoulder. "How do you always manage to get the drop on me?"

Valentina ran her hands down Dick's body. "It often helps to be naked. The human body is a weapon, its flesh designed to tread the floors without a sound." A pause. "You're late."

"I got caught up. I'm sorry."

Valentina kissed his neck. "I expected nothing less."

Dick turned and drank in the sight of the mercenary wearing nothing but the flesh she was born in. "How about I make it up to you by testing your theory and becoming a weapon myself?"

Valentina gave a coy smile. "Now we're talking."

Their lips pressed against each other's before Valentina took Dick's hand and led him to the bedroom.

Daylight illuminated the bedroom. Dick blinked, unaware of where he was for a moment until he saw the empty side of the bed and memories of the night before flooded back.

He let out a small laugh, his body aching from a combination of his fight and the wild night of love-making. He tried to sit up but found that he couldn't. She'd tied his hands to the bedpost.

He grinned. "Ha, ha, Val. Real classy. Leave a guy strung up like a pig waiting for slaughter."

No answer came. Dick leaned as far as he could to the side and found no trace that Val had ever been there. No clothes, no luggage, no anything. The only way he knew that last night hadn't been a strange delusion was the fact that her perfume still lingered on the sheets.

A memory came back to him. Valentina riding on top and kissing his neck. While Dick had been in the throes of passion, two knives had appeared in her hands. She had stabbed them into either side of the bed as she moaned in pleasure.

Where the hell had they come from? She was naked, for God's sake.

Dick tested the bonds by straining his muscles against them. They were Velcro cuffs, so easy enough to undo if you had a spare hand. Otherwise, it was a no-go. Unless.

Dick twisted his body and raised his toes to the strap. It was firmly secured, but he managed to get a slight grip on one corner.

As he began peeling the Velcro, a cough came from the bedroom door.

"Practicing your Kama Sutra positions?" She cocked her head and leaned against the doorjamb. "I can't say it's much of a turn-on from this angle."

Dick brought his leg back down as his cheeks colored with the faintest hint of embarrassment. "You going to stand there, or are you going to let me go?"

Valentina's mouth twisted to the side as she cast herself into theatrical thought. "I haven't decided yet. What's in it for me?"

She sauntered over to the bed and placed two coffees on the table. Her red satin gown was lazily tied, and Dick could see the skin beneath. "Round three?"

Valentina bit her lip. "Oh, Mr. Chambers, you know how to treat a lady." She climbed on the bed and planted a kiss on his lips. They were soft and warm. She raised her head and stared into his eyes before shoving herself back to her feet. "Unfortunately, I have places to go, people to see. You know what they say about too much of a good thing, don't you?"

Dick flopped his head back. "Too much of a good thing is a bad thing."

Valentina winked and pointed at Dick. "There you go, sport. Now, cover yourself up and get out of here. You know this place charges by the hour?"

"I thought that was you."

Valentina ignored the comment and crossed to a wardrobe and opened it, revealing nothing inside but her famed crimson fatigues. She dressed and placed her fedora atop her head before turning to leave.

"Hey, Red Countess," Dick exclaimed. "What about me?"

Valentina raised her eyebrows. "Come on, Dick. You know that's only the nickname my enemies have given me. Do you want to place yourself on that team?"

Before he could answer, Valentina drew two small blades and

tossed them at Dick. They spun multiple times before slicing through the bonds and stopping in the fabric of the headboard.

Dick moved his arms and undid the Velcro clasps. "I suppose when you put it like that…" He looked up, unsurprised to find that she was once again gone.

He laughed. "I don't know why I expect anything less."

Flashes of the night before came unbidden into his head as Dick walked through the streets toward the Paper Doily.

She had been insatiable and worked his body in a way that only she knew how. Every part of him ached, but that wouldn't stop him sniffing out justice and getting to the bottom of this damn mystery.

The pendant was still missing. The trail grew ever longer. Usually, he'd have a case wrapped, sealed, and delivered to his client by now, but that wasn't the case here. Something was amiss. Something was off. Something was telling Dick that it would be a long journey to track down this damn bit of jewelry and return it to the delightful Santana Sokolov.

Traffic was steady and only once did he see an AJS cruiser speed past. *Must be a quiet day in paradise.*

Eventually, the Paper Doily stood before him. The high-class restaurant lay on the corner of a cross-junction, with two of its walls made entirely of glass so that passersby could see the chintzy decor within. It was here that the wealthy elder generation would often go for lunch as they sipped tea and nibbled on bite-sized cakes served on silver trays.

It was the last place Dick would ever be caught dining.

The Paper Doily. How is this place connected to the Russians?

The place was sparsely populated. As the bell chimed behind him, a waiter in penguin blacks met him, standing behind a podium where he glanced down at a screen. "Good morning, sir. Do you have a reservation with us?"

Dick glanced incredulously around the half-empty restaurant. "I don't. Should I have?"

The waiter stood straight as a note of distaste crossed his thin features. "Sir, we are a Michelin Star restaurant, accredited and awarded more times than we care to count. Guests who dine here are some of the crème de la crème of Atlantica's aristocracy. If you can't find the decency to follow protocol and book in advance, I'm afraid we can't offer you a seat."

Dick met his stare and gave a curt nod. He dialed a number and put his cell phone to his ear. The phone beside the waiter rang.

Dick spoke. "Good morning, I'd like to make a reservation for 11:23 a.m. for a Mr. John Chambers, please."

The waiter held his gaze before glancing down at this tablet and taking a few exaggerated seconds to scroll down the screen. "11:23 a.m. is currently unavailable. I can do 11:24 a.m."

Dick smirked. "Done."

Dick was led to a table in the center of the restaurant and took a seat on a chintzy chair with golden arms. The interior decor was like the palace of an 1800s queen, with hand-painted murals across the walls, gold-framed portraits, and white doilies littering the tables.

Dick ordered a black coffee and reveled in the waiter's disapproval. When he was gone, he studied the scene.

There was a litter of patrons in the restaurant, all of them exactly as Dick would have envisioned. Their hair was white as snow, many in perms. Gentlemen wore suits and monocles, and women wore dresses of varying shades of white, pink, and gold.

I'm beginning to think I've been had by the Russians.

Dick slurped his coffee and ate from a platter of mini cakes. The caffeine helped clear his head as he watched the waiter disappear into the back after hesitating a moment at the door as if to check that no one was watching him.

You can always spot the shifty ones. What's the betting that these people are plants to make the restaurant look somewhat busy? He chuckled. *No, Dick. You're acting paranoid.*

When he was fed and watered, Dick leaned back in his chair. On the table across from him, he noticed an older woman with a collar of pearls pass something under the table. Dick caught a flash of a small packet before her friend took it from her.

Dick scoffed. "You know there are better ways to drug-deal?"

The ladies turned to him.

"Keep it in your home, ladies. You'll do yourselves a favor there. What's the point in risking public dealing when it could lead to AJS intervention?"

The woman nearest to Dick twisted in her chair. There was a playful smile on her face. "What's the crime without the thrill?" She winked. "Are you with the AJS? Going to slap some cuffs on me and take me into custody?"

Dick smirked, impressed by the woman's brazenness. "Not me, I'm afraid. I won't dob you in unless someone pays me. I hope you haven't found anyone in Atlantica who's got your face on a bullseye."

The woman laughed. "I probably have more than you think. The only thing that keeps me safe is keeping away from my house. The minute I walk through my door, I know there will be a hundred red dots searching for my body. My corpse will hit the morning paper faster than you can blink, son."

Dick raised his cup and toasted the woman. "Well, best wishes to you, ma'am." She returned to her friend.

Dick waited a few moments before he wiped his mouth and dumped the napkin on the side. He rose from his chair and crossed to the back of the restaurant, then made his way into the restroom. As he neared the door, he slowed and cocked an ear toward the kitchen and the doorway the waiter had disappeared through.

Where have you gone, monsieur?

Keeping face, Dick entered the restroom and did his business. As he sat in the cubicle, he heard a quiet conversation through the vent in the wall above him. He climbed onto the seat to for better listening.

"…not our usual clientele. Something's off."

A second voice replied, laced with a Russian tone. "You think he's a cop?"

"He has that look, but I'm not convinced. He's looking for something."

"Well, what are you doing out here, then? Go in there and keep an eye on him." There came the sound of flesh hitting flesh. "Fucking idiot."

Dick hopped off the toilet and waited a few moments. He saw himself in the mirror and adjusted his collar. There was a bruise on his face from the Russian's ham-sized fist, but he seemed in decent condition otherwise.

He paused at the restroom door and slowly opened it. He peeked outside and spotted the disgruntled waiter at his table looking around. He shouted at the other patrons, "You were supposed to keep an eye on him!"

Dick slipped out from the restroom and quickly dashed for the door the waiter had used. As the restroom door closed behind him, a voice cried, "Over there! Get him!"

Dick opened the door as the smattering of patrons rose to their feet. They trained pistols his way and took shots, but not before Dick worked his way into the room beyond and shut the door. He clicked the lock shut from his side and booted off the handle with the heel of his shoe.

He turned, flinched as each bullet *thunked* into the wood on the other side, and found himself at an immediate set of stairs.

The smell of cake and tea dissipated quickly, replaced with

the scent of dust and mold. Dick ran up the stairs, treading softly until he reached a hallway above. Somehow, he had found his way into the apartments above the Paper Doily.

Movement from his left. Dick ducked behind the wall as a man and woman came out of their room and headed toward a set of stairs on the hallway's far side. They paused enough to hear the commotion in the restaurant below, then shook their heads. "Honestly, it's always drama down there."

They carried on.

Dick waited for them to disappear, then crept along the hallway, pressing his ear against each door as he passed.

The second door on the left was quiet, but for the gentle grumbles of a man talking to himself. A TV played in the background. Dick tried the handle and was pleasantly surprised to find that it was unlocked. He teased the door open and peered inside.

The room was dark and hazy. The curtains were closed, and there was a strange smell in the air. Dick eased inside, then tiptoed until he stood in the doorway behind a man in a cushy upright armchair.

Dick spotted the gun lying by his feet. He drew his pistol and cocked it.

The man turned, and his eyes widened with alarm.

"Make one move toward that gun, and you won't have enough fingers to count to three," Dick warned.

The man paused mid-crouch as his eyes darted to the weapon. He jittered, then went for it anyway. Dick ran at him, jumped on the guy, and grabbed his wrist. They clattered backward and smashed into the TV stand. The TV fell to the floor and shattered with a *thrum* of spent electricity. Dick kept his grip and twisted the man's wrist until the gun dropped from his hand.

"I learned that from one of your guys," Dick explained as he pressed the mouth of his pistol against the man's throat. "Nice guy. Big. Had a hell of a swing on him. Not saying that all

Russians are related, mind, but it seems like a strange coincidence, don't you think?"

"Engliyskaya sobaka Vy ne znayete, s chem vy stolknulis'."

Dick punched the man in the face. "Cut the dumb act, Slick. I heard you speak English through that vent shaft." He pointed at a box of slats on the wall beneath a grimy fish tank. "You want to keep an eye on your business? I'd recommend changing apartments. Who knows who could be listening to our conversation through that tunnel?"

The man's eyes narrowed. He scowled. "Fine. You want to talk, let's talk. You can tell me what you're doing breaking into my apartment and disrupting the family business."

Dick grunted agreement. "I'm going to remove this gun from your throat now. If I see so much as a whisper of a movement toward yours, I will shoot you in the heart. It will hurt. You will likely die."

The man nodded, then pushed himself to his feet. Dick kept the gun trained on him as he sat in his chair.

The man crossed his legs and stared at Dick. "Are you going to tell me what all of this is about? Breaking and entering is a criminal offense, you know."

"So is murder and theft," Dick replied. He flashed his badge. "Hence why I'm here."

The man's eyes betrayed him as he glanced at floor. The gunshots had stopped, but they heard hammering on the door below.

"I'm guessing that's something to do with you?" The Russian raised an eyebrow.

"Actually, that leads to my first question," Dick started. "Why do you have plants with weapons set up in a restaurant when you're running a respectable business?"

The man stared evenly at him. "I don't know what you're talking about."

Dick sighed and raised his gun. "Don't make me get my friend involved again. I have a feeling that time may be running short, and since I'm currently in a residential apartment, I'd rather be clear by the time the others barge in here. I always dreamed that if I were to die, it would be from chain-smoking these bad boys, not from getting riddled with bullets in a lowlife's apartment."

The man held his tongue. Downstairs, the door smashed open. Dick raised his gun again. "Where is the pendant?"

A flicker of recognition crossed the man's face. He swallowed and stared down the barrel of the gun. Heavy footsteps trod the stairs.

"Where is it!" Dick shouted, his patience waning. He fired a shot at the ceiling. Dust and debris rained down on the man, who yelped and covered his head. "Tell me!"

The Russian whimpered. Silence followed the shot.

Dick grabbed a fistful of the man's hair and pulled his head back. He placed the cool steel of the gun's barrel in his mouth and towered over him. "Last chance, fucker. Where is the pendant? I know you know something."

The man coughed and nodded eagerly. He muttered, "Thirteenth floor, second door on the right," before Dick punched him in the mouth.

"Thank you. Was that so hard?"

He could hear the others running down the hall toward them. Dick fired a shot through the open door and gave them pause. Then he glanced up and saw that he had loosened a tile in the ceiling. Without care for the Russian, he clambered onto the chair, grabbed the ledge, and pulled himself into the gaps between the apartments.

Those outside waited for only a few seconds before they rushed into the apartment. The waiter crossed to the Russian, knocked out cold on the chair, and examined his face. He had a split lip and blood leaked down the side of his neck.

He turned to the others, the elder plants who had been in the restaurant, and shouted, "Well?"

A man with a sweeping mustache emerged from one of the side rooms. He noticed the ceiling tile. "He's gone."

The elderly woman with a fuzz of white hair who had been dealing beneath the table smiled. She muttered to herself, "Good for him. He's one of the good ones."

CHAPTER EIGHT

Dick worked his way to the ventilation shafts. The crawl spaces would have been difficult when he was younger and thinner, but now they were worse. "I need to make a note to lose a few pounds when this is all said and done."

When he made his way into the metal chambers, he was able to breathe fully. He had no idea where he was. He only knew that he needed to move fast. Every shuffle inside the air shafts felt like someone was beating a drum inside a cavern, but somehow, he avoided detection.

He climbed higher, sweating a little with the exertion and the heat, until he found a slatted vent and could see through.

The hallway was empty. That had to be a good sign, right?

He teased off the panel and emerged in the hall. Voices were audible downstairs as the group continued their search for him. He snuck across to the stairwell and placed a replica of the detection box that had momentarily disabled Grunch when he tried to dash away from the alley. The legend Paraly-Z was written on its side.

Satisfied he had some kind of barrier, Dick read the numbers on the doors. He had climbed five stories of the building and was now on the eighth floor. The Russian had said the room he was looking for was on the thirteenth floor.

Five to go.

Dick trod up the stairs with extreme caution. He placed another Paraly-Z box at the top and made the left down the corridor. Large potted plants were brown and drooping, and a number of the doors were ajar.

That slowed Dick down. He peered inside to ensure that they were empty or anyone inside was otherwise occupied before he continued to the next stairwell. Only once did he come across someone in the open rooms. A small boy no more than six years old looked at him with wide eyes.

Dick brought a finger to his lips.

The boy stared.

Dick gently pulled the door closed but elicited the boy's fearful shouts as the door clicked shut.

Dick ran. He made it to the twelfth floor and could almost make out the wail of the first victim of his traps. They must have been thorough about searching the rooms, probably knowing that the only way out of the building was back the way Dick had come.

"A problem for later," Dick muttered. His heart beat with excitement as he neared the final stairwell.

As soon as he thought he was clear, a voice called from behind.

"Freeze."

Dick paused and turned on the spot. A large Russian woman with a braided ponytail hanging over the front of her shoulder trained a sawed-off shotgun at him. Her clothes were far too expensive for what this rundown shithole had become.

She squinted through near-closed eyes. Dick realized that she held a bundle in the crook of her arm. A baby wrapped in white cloth began to wriggle. "You shouldn't be here."

"Should any of us really be anywhere?"

The woman cocked an eyebrow while giving it some serious thought. "You are American?"

Dick nodded. "You are Russian."

The woman remained silent, but Dick took that as a yes. She studied him with hungry curiosity.

Dick lowered his hands. "I'm sorry, but I have somewhere I need to be. Not that this isn't fun and everything, but I'm kind of on a tight deadline here."

The woman turned her head slightly at the sound of shouts from down below. "You are a troublemaker?"

"I am a peacemaker." Dick flashed his badge, hoping to draw on the woman's sympathy. She wouldn't shoot anyone while holding a baby, right? Imagine what the sound would do to their eardrums. "No AJS. Simply a detective. I'm looking for something for a client."

The woman's eyes flashed at the sight of Dick's badge. He'd clearly made the wrong move as he saw the intent in her face. She pulled the trigger, and the bullets screamed into the space where Dick had been a millisecond earlier. He now crashed through an apartment door and fell into an empty hallway.

The baby burst into tears.

"Damn. I should've known these guys will do anything to protect their own." Dick thought briefly of his family, people he hadn't seen in years. "I wonder what that feels like."

Knowing he had to keep moving forward, Dick placed his back against the wall next to the door and prepared his gun. He counted to three, then drew a small silver ball from the inside pocket of his coat. He crouched and rolled the ball into the hallway and heard the woman utter something in her native tongue.

Dick pointed his gun at the ball, then shot it. Smoke exploded the instant the bullet kissed the metal, and Dick took his chance to dive through the doorway and up the final set of stairs.

The smoke followed him and provided the cover he needed.

He emerged onto the final landing and met a single door. This one looked better kept than the other apartments, and Dick knew he was in the right place.

He knocked on the door, then drew a second ball and set it off. He tucked his back against the wall beside the door and waited for someone to come out.

Voices came from inside. A woman's voice cried, "I'm going! I'm going!"

Dick was now unable to see, but he could hear the door opening. As the door swung toward him, he grabbed hold of the edge. Before the woman could warn those inside about the smog in the corridor, he shoved the door at her and sent her sprawling into the room.

Dick stepped around the door, cloaked himself in the smoke, and entered the apartment.

Voices shouted from all around. Several shots were fired at the door, but Dick tucked out of the way. He kept close to the walls, disadvantaged by the fact he had no idea of the apartment's layout. He accidentally knocked into a dresser that housed several jewelry displays and instantly, his eyes searched for the pendant.

A man lunged out of the darkness, surprised to find Dick standing there. Dick quickly reacted by ducking out of the way of his fists and returning a hook to his stomach. The man wheezed and folded over. He charged at Dick and trapped him against the dresser. Dick drove the butt of his gun onto the man's head, and he let out a violent wail.

"They're over this way!" another voice pitched in.

Dick threw the man away from him and tried to find a new hiding spot. The sound of enemies came from everywhere, and all Dick could do was try to creep past. If he could find a way to incapacitate them all, perhaps he'd stand a chance of getting to the big boss.

There's always a big boss somewhere.

Dick fished into his pocket once more and found what he was looking for. Two slightly orange-tinged earplugs were in his palm. He pressed them into each ear and found a device that was no bigger than a keyring.

He pulled a toggle on the gadget's chamber, and the room filled with the banshee squeal of an alarm. Those around him cried in protest, and Dick used the opportunity to work his way back through the room.

They tried to fight him off but were unprepared for the noise. The shriek pierced their minds and made their eardrums throb in pain. One of the Russians he came across had a few trickles of blood leaking from his ear canal. Dick grabbed the body of his rifle and shoved it back into his face before he slammed his boot in the center of the man's chest and propelled him back into a refrigerator.

Another came from behind with determination etched on his face. Dick doubled over and tossed him over his back. The man tried to recover, but Dick kicked his skull. The man blinked stupidly, then lay still.

Dick relieved the first man of his rifle, then swept through the apartment, which had begun to clear of the smog.

He retraced his steps as he ran back to the door and slammed it shut. Cries of annoyance and rage met him as he caught a meager glimpse of the waiter and those who had hunted him. He locked the door and took a step back. He expected bullets to rip into the door, but none came. Dick surmised that the kingpin's followers wouldn't blow holes in his apartment door.

Dick turned with the rifle ready. Men groaned in the rooms off the main corridor, but Dick ignored them, now focused only on his walk ahead.

With the smoke no more than a hazy mist, he crept onward. Part of him admired the glitz and glamor that decorated this apartment. While the others had been shacks and hovels that reminded him of the slums of New York, this apartment lived and breathed Atlantica. The rich coveted themselves and lived in abundance while their followers cowered in squalor.

Where are you?

Dick twisted left, and the kitchen came into view. He saw the refrigerator he had knocked the enemy into and the man lying still on the floor. He was still breathing, which was a relief. Not that it would matter now that he was in someone's house. The rules of Atlantica were bent, and Dick was hyperaware of that.

On the right was a game room, complete with a pool table and VR space. Headsets lined the walls, alongside famous faces in photo frames. A man with thinning black hair, fat cheeks, and the scars of an old burn wound across one half of his face accompanied each celebrity.

I'm starting to get the picture. But who are you?

Dick turned a corner and encountered a wide-open lounge area. Bean bags scattered the room. Multiple television sets lined the walls, high-value items sat in glass display cabinets…

…and in the far corner of the room, surrounded by three topless women aiming automatic rifles at Dick, was the fat man in question.

The man grinned and sucked from the end of a cigar. "Now, then. I think we have a problem here, don't we?"

After that, all went black.

CHAPTER NINE

Dick blinked stupidly as his consciousness came back.

It took a while for the woman to come into focus. Dick's body ached, and the first thing he became aware of was the smoke lingering in the room.

"Rise and shine, sweetheart," a soft, melancholy voice crooned. "You've been asleep for some time."

Dick peeled his eyes open and nearly choked at the sight of the woman. Her skin was dark, and a translucent sarong wrapped around her waist. Her breasts were perky, if a little asymmetrical, and her perfume was the only thing that seemed able to permeate the smell of cigarettes.

"Where am I?"

Dick tried to lift his head, but it seemed impossible.

The woman replied in a voice that Dick would associate with a nymph or a character from a children's cartoon. It was perky and bright as if the visceral feeling that he was in danger was only in his imagination.

"Silly! Don't you remember? You're in the Guardian's tower now."

She left a trail of giggles as she darted away from him and

vanished somewhere out of sight. Dick tried once more to lift his head and found that some of the weight had lessened. He blinked and discovered that his right eye was throbbing. If it weren't for the rough bonds tying his hands behind the chair, he worried he might fall to the floor and cause more damage.

A fight. Yes, there had been a fight. Dick remembered the fat man sitting comfortably in his bean bag chair and puffing on his cigar. There hadn't been an ounce of fear, despite Dick bringing a firearm to a fistfight.

Then what happened?

Dick glanced around the room that was little more than a storage cupboard. Empty shelves were high above him, and a painfully bright beam of light came from the naked bulb that shone overhead. A door was in front of him, but it was closed. It would have been within reach, but he learned that his legs were tied to the chair.

Dick sat up straight. His head wobbled on his shoulders. He strained against his bonds, but there was no give. The rope felt like the kind you'd find on ships, thickly wound with prickly hairs fraying from the coils.

He closed his eyes and recalibrated, trying to shift the fog in his head.

The girls. They gave me something...I think. Dick remembered sudden sleepiness washing over him as he stared into the fat man's eyes. Something sparkled like gold dust, and when he turned to see the source, a beautiful woman was by his side, her cheeks round from blowing a palmful of...something, into his eyes and respiratory system.

After that, everything came in strange bursts. The fat man had moved at an alarming speed. His fists were thick and powerful. An image of the man's—the *Guardian's*—rage-filled face inches from his overpowered everything.

And now he was here, tied up and abandoned. The woman who had awoken him had disappeared, and that was now his greatest pain. To be woken without cause and left by a beautiful woman was no way to spend a day.

Dick tugged against the bonds which bound his wrists. He rubbed them against the back of the chair but only ended up making his skin raw.

Fuck.

There were voices outside. The women were talking. There was a man's voice, laden with a Russian accent. The voices grew heated and the sound of gunfire was followed by silence. A door slammed. After a few seconds, the women began talking among themselves once more.

"What the hell is this place?" Dick asked no one.

His haze lifted as adrenaline coursed through his body. He was still fully clothed—at least that was a saving grace—and he began to rock left to right to see how much leeway he had with the chair they'd tied him to.

Someone had made a half-assed effort to bolt the seat's front legs into holes in the floor, but the screws were loose. With each gentle rock, they wobbled and turned a fraction in their moorings. Dick kept his eyes on the door as he swayed back and forth, vibrating the chair until one of the screws came free.

He continued for another minute, and the second one rolled on the floor.

Dick's heart leaped. Now he could rock the chair backward and slide his ankles out from the ropes tied around the legs. He kicked the screws back into the corner of the room and was about to stand when the door handle jostled, and one of the women called back, "I don't care if it's his cousin. He gets in the way; he pays the price."

Dick rested his legs against the chair's and hoped the woman wouldn't see the ropes were loose. The door opened, and he once again saw a beautiful topless woman. Her face turned from furious to enchanting in a heartbeat as she closed the door behind her and straddled his lap. Dick noted the knife strapped to her hip and felt its sharp edge graze his thigh.

"Comfortable?"

Dick's mouth went dry. "I've been worse."

She wrapped her arms around his neck. The heat of her body made its way over in waves and made Dick's heart race. "The Guardian is almost ready for you, Mr. Chambers. He's been sorting out preparations for your trial."

"My…" Dick stammered. "What do you mean he's ready for me? What trial?"

The woman leaned back and gave Dick a full view of her body. She theatrically chewed her lip and mused, "Well, you see, the thing is that the Guardian doesn't take well to strangers storming his tower. Less so when that someone murders members of his family in cold blood. And what for? That's what I want to know."

"Cold blood? They were going to kill me."

"They were protecting their own."

Dick scoffed. He shoved his hips forward, hoping to knock the woman off-balance and send her sprawling to the floor, but instead, she held on tight and bucked back while releasing an entertained, "Ooo, easy cowboy."

"My advice," she continued, "is tell the truth and surrender yourself. There's only one way you'll get out of this alive, and that's by answering questions like a good boy, and not fucking around. You got that?"

"I think so." Dick thrust his hips forward again. "No *fucking* around?" He slammed a foot on the floor, and the sound filled the room.

The woman giggled as her face flushed red. "Mr. Chambers, you're awful." She leaned toward his ear and whispered, "And a thousand times better looking than our Guardian. Who knows? Maybe when this is all over, I'll be allowed a new plaything."

"Here's hoping," Dick breathed.

The woman giggled again as she departed and left Dick in silence, his heart racing.

Dick waited until she was sure to be out of earshot, then glanced down at the floor. A wave of relief spread over him. His hip thrusts and foot slams had dutifully performed their job of freeing the knife from the woman's strap and masked the sound of it clattering to the floor.

Dick shifted his weight and forced the chair to topple, doing his best to control the movement so it wouldn't draw too much attention. His head hit the wall, and a throb of pain exploded behind his eyes. He balanced his head and used it to slow his fall until he was sideways on the floor, his tied hands scrambling for the knife.

After a few moments, he found the blade's keen edge.

Dick grinned and got to work.

* * *

Vladimir Petrov watched his minions scurry around the penthouse suite from the comfort of his favorite chair. His face showed no hint of a smile.

For thirty years, he had lived a life of squalor. He had been the butt of his family's jokes, the source of their twisted pleasure, the one they dumped on when they had nothing better to do.

Well, look at me now, Ma.

Atlantica had been a risk. After his drug empire had grown beyond measure in two years, Vladimir had pulled together his resources and applied for a visa to live in the fabled city. He had taken only those he had fathered with him and bought the quaint restaurant and its accompanying apartment block.

The restaurant was a front for money laundering. The apartments were for those who remained loyal. He shed his skin and eradicated those who had tormented him, and instead, chose only those who doted on him hand and foot. His four wives were examples of that, the beautiful ladies who had flocked to him after egregious displays of wealth and power, and who would give their lives to maintain a certain lifestyle.

Vladimir had always wondered how those who were older than him kept the family under their thumb. It turned out the equation was simple: money plus power equals respect.

Yet, despite his deranged feelings toward the family that was now dead and forgotten in the distant land of Mother Russia, he couldn't help seeing himself as something of a savior. He had brought his family with him—cousins, sons, daughters, grand-daughters—and all he thought of now was the protection of his bloodline.

From the moment he had crossed the threshold above the Atlantic Ocean and seen the first glimpses of Atlantica appearing from the sea like a solitary cloud among an endless blue sky, he had become the Guardian.

"He is awake." Menora roused him from his pensive thoughts.

"How is he?"

"Groggy, but he has his faculties."

Vladimir grunted. "Is everything in position? Is everything in order?"

Menora glanced at the women and men operating behind her. They were still clearing up from this man's intrusion, sweeping shattered glass, and finding a place to store the bodies until they could figure out what to do with them. There would be a cere-mony of some kind, but an acid burning in the bathtub to destroy the evidence would likely follow it. The last thing they needed was the AJS sniffing around their operation.

Menora followed the progress of one of her sister-wives, then nodded. "Almost." She saw the concerned expression on his face. "Do not worry, my love. There is nothing this Chambers can take from you. You are the king of this empire, the head of this idol. Your family is here to serve, and that is something we will do until the day we die."

Someone dragged a limp body along the wooden floors. Menora seemed to realize the irony of her words. "Forgive me. I meant no offense."

Vladimir silenced her with a wave of his hand. He opened a container beside him and removed a cooked chicken leg. He held the bone like a club and gnawed on the juicy skin. Herbs and spices filled his mouth and got his saliva working. Small reams of dribble trickled down his face and toward the folds of his many chins.

"Tell them to hurry up," he managed between mouthfuls. "An intruder must pay for his crimes, and thanks to this inbred city for its ridiculous laws on justice, he is now in a house without bounds or limits." He picked up Chambers' badge and studied it for a moment. "We will make this investigator squeal, no matter what it takes. The world will hear him scream and will be powerless to stop it."

He released a full-belly laugh, and his folds of fat wobbled excitedly as his body moved more than it had in an age. Flecks of chicken sprayed toward Menora, who did well to hold in the disgust she felt when looking at her husband.

She left before he had finished and relayed his commands. The Guardian wanted the pace to increase. He wanted the PI to pay. There were no limits to the coming interrogation, and that was how the Guardian liked it.

The final strands of the rope severed. Dick's arms sprang apart, and a strange feeling ran through his wrists as the blood rushed back into his hands.

He lay where he was for a moment, relishing the feeling of being free before he heard an increase in the clattering on the other side of the door.

Dick grabbed the knife and thrust it into the folds of his

jacket pocket. Although he was free, he became aware it might not be a great position for him once they discovered it. He took what remained of the rope and loosely bound it around his wrists, repositioned his chair, and did his best to make it seem as though nothing out of the ordinary had happened.

Just in time, too. The woman with darker skin opened the door as he placed his feet into position. She afforded him an uncertain glance, then turned back to the room beyond Dick's vision and called to the others that she was bringing him.

How many others there were, Dick had no idea. The woman knelt by Dick's feet and untied his ankles. "Don't get any ideas, Chambers. You kick me or lash out, and you'll face the wrath of our family. There are many more beyond the door, which you'll see for yourself soon enough."

"When you free me?"

The woman chuckled, impressed by Dick's brazenness. "Play nicely, and he may spare you. Although after the way you entered this abode, that option is slim to none."

Dick stared at the woman curiously. "Your English is better than the others. You're not a blood relative? You've never been to Russia, have you?"

The woman smiled. "You are quite the PI, Chambers. No, I'm not. I am but a wife to the Guardian, and a native of Atlantica." She moved behind Dick, and he hoped to God that distracting her might make her overlook the small cuts of rope he'd thrown into the far corner of the room. "He is a great man, a savior to many. It is because of him that I have been blessed with life. He saved me as he plans to save us all."

"Save you from what? High rates of cholesterol?"

He expected the woman to laugh, but instead, she punched the back of his head. "He is a great man. You'd do well not to mock him openly, especially to his kin." She dragged him to his feet. The chair wobbled, but she paid no attention. "Come,

Chambers. It's time for you to see how great a man the Guardian is."

Yeah, sure. A morbidly obese Russian lording his position at the top of a tower surrounded by multiple wives and a restaurant that's a front for a money-laundering scam. Oh, let me bow before thee, oh mighty one. I am indebted to your greatness.

CHAPTER TEN

Reverent silence filled the room.

The woman had led Dick forward and pushed him to his knees in front of the blob of a man. A ring of men and women waited patiently behind him, and blocked all exits should Dick try to make a quick escape.

Not that he wanted to, of course. Dick wanted answers.

The Guardian stared at Dick through narrowed eyes. The only signs of movement were him devouring an endless line of chicken wings, and the dabbing handkerchief of one of his many wives. Beside the fat man was an array of metallic instruments. None of them looked in the least bit inviting.

"Speak."

The command came out of nowhere and caught Dick off-guard. He said nothing for a moment until the fat man repeated his instruction.

"What do you want, like, a CV? A joke? I have this great line I picked up from a Christmas cracker last year. Where do snowmen go to dance—"

The Guardian rose to his feet in an impressive display of speed. Dick remembered the hazy vision he had under the influence of whatever that gold dust had been and was kind of glad to discover that it hadn't been an illusion. The Guardian could move pretty fast.

The Guardian stopped, but his fat continued to jiggle. He stared at Dick with a thunderous expression, his face dark and contorted. "You *dare* to enter the Guardian's abode and fill the silence with jokes and bullshit talk? Do you have *any* idea who you're dealing with here?" He pummeled his chest with a bowling ball-sized fist. "I am the Guardian. To disrespect my family is to disrespect me, and the only thing keeping you alive right now is the fact that I've yet to discover your motives behind your intrusion. So speak to me, worm. Tell me what you seek. Then I can break you piece by piece and send you back out into the world in blood-soaked parcels."

Whether he was going for intimidation or downright fear, Dick didn't know, but he held his ground and showed no sign of distress. Dick drew a breath, then nodded at the pile of his things, which had been collected on a small table nearby. His phone, his gun, and a stack of papers sat untidily on top of one another.

"You know what I'm after," Dick growled. "If you've had the wherewithal to examine my things—and I think you have—you know what it is. The pendant. Where is it?"

A smile crept onto the Guardian's face. "You'd risk so much over so small a thing?"

"I've risked a lot more for less." Dick shrugged. "My currency is cash, and I seek what others pay me to find. I'm pretty good at it, too. Got myself here, didn't I?"

The Guardian cocked his head to the side, a note of intrigue in his eyes. "Kneeling before the man who will soon end your life? That's hardly a position to brag about, now is it?" He stomped toward Dick and grabbed a fistful of his hair. He pulled him to his feet and stared into his eyes. "Strange. You lack something the others all have. It's disturbing."

"Nasal hair? I trim regularly. You never know who might be looking up your schnozz."

The Guardian narrowed his eyes. "No, not that. It's fear. You lack the fear that many hold in their eyes before they meet their maker. It's the sign of a serial killer, I've heard. Only a true psychopath refuses to allow their body to yield itself before the moment of their death."

Dick gave a thoughtful nod. "Well, then, one of two things is going on here. Either I'm a psychopath, or the reality is that you're not going to kill me." He twisted in the Guardian's grip and studied the crowd behind him. At least ten witnesses, and four of them the man's wives. "Although let's be honest, you calling me a psychopath is very much the pot calling the kettle black. You're doted on hand and foot by your minions, and you have no qualms about killing a man in cold blood."

Sudden rage overcame the Guardian. He tossed Dick back on the floor and towered over him. "*You* killed my men."

"*They* fired first!" Dick combatted. "Self-defense, my man. I might have knocked some of your guys out cold, but I didn't shoot until I needed to survive."

"It doesn't matter. The result is the same." The Guardian clicked his fingers, and two men grabbed Dick's arms and resumed his position kneeling before the fat man's plush throne.

The Guardian squatted back in his seat and tore at a piece of chicken like a hyena stripping a zebra corpse. "Andre, Pasha, Menora, get to work."

Dick's eyes widened as the pair twisted Dick's arms behind his back. The smell of incense and perfume wafted by him as Menora carefully selected from the tray of instruments and sauntered over to Dick. She knelt before him with a coy smile and whispered, "I warned you. You didn't play along."

Dick grunted in pain as the pliers clamped around his thumbnail. Pressure built as the woman pulled and he cried, "At least tell me what I came to know. The last justice you can give a dying man is to grant him a final request." He glanced up through blurry eyes. "Please."

The Guardian laughed, a real all-body laugh that made Dick queasy. How this man had so many beautiful wives was beyond his understanding.

"You think that's how this works? You think that after all you've done, I'm going to soothe your slow and painful undoing by giving you what you seek?" He laughed again, and this time the others joined in. Dick flushed red with anger.

Dick gritted his teeth. "Is that your final answer? No closure for a dying man?"

The Guardian leaned forward and chomped on a succulent piece of chicken flesh. He chewed with an open mouth and grinned, his teeth mostly black or stained. "That's my final answer, vermin. Now suffer the price for your insolence."

Dick sighed and lowered his head. Menora had lifted some of the pressure on his finger. "Very well, then. You leave me no *choice!*"

As he spoke his final word, Dick tore his arm from his captors' slackened grip. He rose to his feet and elbowed Pasha or Andre in the face before he spun and kicked the other in the crotch. Before the others could react, he grabbed the knife from his inner pocket and hurled it at one of the men in the back. Dick had noted that he was the only one with a firearm on display, and the knife found its location in his shoulder.

The man fell to the floor, all thoughts of the gun abandoned. The woman standing beside him gasped as she recognized the knife's hilt and glanced uneasily at the Guardian.

Dick kicked Menora and sent her sprawling backward, instantly feeling sorry for the woman. He turned to face the next imminent threat—*priority is the key to victory*—and his entire field of vision filled with the Guardian as the man barreled toward him.

Dick braced himself, but it wasn't enough. The mammoth

man smashed into him and sent him flying toward the wall. Dick's back cracked from the impact, and he gasped in pain.

There was no time to slow down, however. His element of surprise was fading.

There was a glass cabinet beside Dick, filled with ornate blades and knives with decorated sheaths. Dick smashed his elbow into the glass and caused it to fracture. Pain jolted up his arm as the Guardian howled with laughter.

"Puny detective."

Dick gritted his teeth and prepared for the pain as he smashed his elbow against it again.

The cracks grew, but the glass didn't break.

Dick scanned nearby and found an animal skull high on the wall behind him. It looked like a buck or a goat. He tore it from the wall and drove down with everything he had, satisfied when the glass filtered to the floor.

Without a pause, he grabbed two of the blades and took them from their sheaths. They were blunt and a little rusted from years hidden in their cases, but they would do the job.

He ran with his momentum as two men came at him. They were cautious and dodged his slashes and blows, but he caught them in the arm and hip respectively before he kicked them out of the way and moved toward the exit.

"Don't let him escape!" the Guardian shouted, his face red with rage. The remaining men and women tried to maneuver into Dick's way, but Dick had other plans. While they ran around him, he ran toward the Guardian but stopped by the man writhing on the floor in pain. Dick dropped the knives in favor of the pistol and aimed it at the Guardian.

"Go ahead," the giant man sneered. "Make my day."

Dick hesitated as the Guardian stared at him. He could run—grab his things and get the hell away. Would they find him again? Maybe. But did that mean he had to kill a man in cold blood?

A tiny voice gnawed at the back of his mind. *You still don't have your answers, do you, Dick? He's still holding onto info you need.*

"This is your last chance," Dick warned. "Tell me what you know about the pendant. Where is it? Then we can let all of this go."

The Guardian's eyes darted past Dick for the merest of moments. The next thing Dick knew, someone tapped his shoulder.

The flickering glance was all Dick needed to prepare himself. he reached back and grabbed Menora's wrist without turning, and steadied the glittering powder in her hand. He spun her around and threw her toward the Guardian, then slapped the dust into the air.

A cloud enveloped the pair, and they both choked on its contents. Their pupils dilated almost instantly, and they began to move as if they were underwater, stuck in slow motion.

Satisfied they were no immediate threat, Dick turned his attention to the rest of the room.

The other three women were crouched near the shattered glass cabinet collecting knives for themselves. Dick fired three shots at the wall between them. "Move another muscle and the next bullets find their way into your skulls." He twisted to fire two shots at the five men blocking his path out of there. "Same for you, fuckers. That door behind you so much as opens without my permission, I'll mow you down without question." Dick backed up and slowly picked up his missing objects from the table. He picked up the gun last and kept in his other hand, now able to point at both parties.

Behind him, Menora and the Guardian drunkenly laughed and fumbled. Dick heard them kissing passionately, but refused to turn around.

"Over to the door," Dick instructed. "Uh! Nope. Away from the knives, bitches. You think I was born yesterday? That's better." He gathered them together and guided them back into the hallway. He found the cupboard he'd been held in and packed them all inside. They hardly fitted together, but he managed it. They glared at him, but before Dick shut the door, he shot out the single light bulb. "There we go. Safely tucked away, and I don't have to stare at your ugly mugs. No offense, ladies."

Dick locked the door from the outside and drew a deep breath. His elbow throbbed, and he was pretty sure it was bleeding, but there was no time to worry about that yet.

He almost vomited when he arrived back in the main suite. At first, he was confused, but then he identified the rolling boulder of flesh for what it was.

Menora and the Guardian were furiously making love. Menora emitted pleasured squeals while the Guardian grunted and panted, his whole body covered in a sheen of greasy sweat.

Dick rolled his eyes and approached them, fixating on the woman's beautiful figure over the Guardian's blob. He shoved her off indelicately, and they both protested. Menora eyed Dick and crawled toward him. He aimed the gun at her face, but she showed no sign that she'd seen it.

"Come join us," she crooned. "The more, the merrier, hmm..."

The Guardian, on the other hand, had begun crying. Great, blubbering, salty tears of emotion dribbled down his face as he struggled to push himself to his feet. His arms shook under his weight, and when he stood, he rocked about on his heels like a toddler.

Dick warily approached and took his arm. He batted away the grasping Menora, who had begun to stroke his trouser leg, and guided the Guardian to his plush throne.

The Guardian dropped inelegantly to his ass. His head and eyes rolled back. Dick grabbed a chicken leg and wafted it under his nose. He hungrily grabbed it and chowed down.

"Guardian, look me in the eyes," Dick commanded.

The Guardian showed no signs that he heard, his eyes screwed shut in ecstasy.

"Look at me," Dick boomed, then grabbed his cheeks and directed his gaze. The Guardian stared square into his eyes, and a flicker of recognition passed over him. "You…" His dilated pupils shrank a fraction.

"Tell me about the pendant. Where is it? It's here, isn't it?"

The Guardian cast a lazy smile and laughed. His saliva pooled and bubbled in his throat, giving the impression he was choking. Menora had reached Dick again and tugged on his belt.

The Guardian collected himself, his head lolling as if in a drunken stupor. "Go to hell, American." He closed his mouth, and Dick heard the distinct sound of crunching. When he opened it again, a tooth was missing.

Dick's eyes widened at the realization of what the Guardian had done. "No! No! Tell me!" He clutched the man's collar and slapped his face, but he was too far gone into the throes of death, the cyanide pill making its way into his digestive system and shutting down his organs. "The pendant! The pendant!"

Dick kicked the woman, who had managed to undo his belt. She sprawled on the floor and laughed. He shook the Guardian, but it was pointless. The man was gone.

"Shit. Shit…"

Banging on the door indicated that his captors were trying to escape. Dick's main lead was dead, and a woman was doing whatever she could to try and make love to him. He fled, running from room to room to find anything that might be beneficial or at least lead him to the next checkpoint.

"Son of a bitch, you had to have a record, surely? Some clue that…"

He stopped when he reached a room filled with electrical gear. A laptop sat on a desk in the corner. Various wires and plugs connected it to towers and servers.

Dick rubbed a hand over his face. "Better than nothing, I suppose."

He ripped the laptop free of its connecting systems and

debated heading back out the apartment door. He wondered how many of this man's family were waiting outside as backup, ready to jump in and help if ready, and chose instead to go for an alternative route.

Dick headed back into the main suite and found Menora curled up in the Guardian's arms, fast asleep. On the far wall were shutters that Dick opened to allow light to enter the space, and found what he was looking for.

He picked up the pistol and fired half a dozen shots at the window until the glass shattered. He scraped away the jagged parts from the edge of the window and climbed out onto the fire escape.

With the laptop clutched tightly under his arm, he made his way down, wishing that it was night and he had more cover. Before the Guardian's remaining family could break through the door, Dick had hopped in his sedan and was several blocks away.

CHAPTER ELEVEN

Dick hopped out of the shower and checked his security. His entire apartment was under the ever-blinking eye of CCTV cameras, and motion sensors could be activated by an app on his phone.

He'd drawn his curtains, and the apartment was in a dull gloom. The only source of light came from a table lamp in the corner. He had been in the shower for barely more than three minutes, but if history had taught him anything, it was better to be safe than sorry. That was more than long enough for someone to break in and do some real damage—as Dick had proven.

He flopped on the couch and poured himself a glass of bourbon. A towel wrapped around his waist, and he had hardly bothered to pat himself dry. He rested his arms on the back of the sofa and flicked on the TV to get his daily hit of Atlantica news.

It was the usual pile of chaos: residents missing, shots fired, a drug ring busted. But the ticker tape showed a headline that caught his attention and caused him to lean forward.

A blonde woman in a skirt much too short to be appropriate for prime-time television stood outside the chintzy little cafe where John had been only hours before. She held a microphone to her mouth with the legend "APCN," Atlantica Premium City News' call letters, written on its base.

"…shots fired inside the premium apartment listing, several of which, it is reported, happened inside the Paper Doily itself," the woman explained.

"Premium listing?" John remembered the state the building's Russian inhabitants had left it in. There was nothing premium there, only a building that had the potential to be stunning but was filled with cigarette smoke and a family unable to clean up after themselves.

The woman continued. "AJS arrived on the scene a short while after someone called in the initial gunshots, hoping to catch the criminals in the act while they were inside the café and under commercial jurisdiction. However, when the events moved into the residential property above, all they could do was watch."

A smug smirk appeared on the woman's face. John was familiar with APCN's work. The media outlet constantly argued that Atlantica should fall under the same jurisdictions as the rest of the world. That justice shouldn't be restricted to public properties.

"Unfortunately, it's the rich who make the rules on this shoddy island," John grumbled. He sipped his bourbon as the ice *clinked* against the glass. "Money talks louder than people." He shook his head. "What a sad state of affairs."

Dick switched the TV to mute as the camera panned toward the window where Dick had made his escape.

A voice came from behind him "You're lucky they didn't catch your ass sprinting out of that apartment. You're getting sloppy, Dick."

Dick rose and whirled so quickly that his towel fell from around his waist. Valentina Winters smirked and tilted her head with her eyes fixed on Dick's junk.

Dick breathed a sigh of relief and didn't attempt to cover

himself as he drained his bourbon. "Should I be surprised that you were able to penetrate my security system?"

"That's the million-dollar question, isn't it?" Valentina crooned while leaning against the back of the sofa and staring at the screen. "Is any security system impenetrable these days? All it takes is for someone to reverse engineer even the tightest measures and boom, you have an instant skeleton key that'll have you breaking into any system within that network. I'm telling you, Dick, no one is immune."

Dick shook his head, then busied himself pouring another glass of bourbon. Every fiber of his body ached, and he was more than aware of the cuts and bruises that were breaking out over his body. He felt Valentina's eyes on him but thought nothing of it. If anyone were to devour his flesh, he prayed it would be her again. He raised the bottle toward her. "Can I offer you a nightcap?"

"None for me, thanks." Valentina vaulted over the back of the couch in one fluid bound and took a seat where Dick had been. "Oh, come on, Dick. Dry yourself before you sit. This is practically primitive." She removed her red velvet fedora and frisbeed it onto the coffee table.

John chuckled. "I didn't know I'd be expecting company."

Valentine scoffed. Her chest flushed between the lapels of her jacket. "*You* invited me, remember? And judging by your state, you should have contacted me earlier. I could have saved you some of those bruises." She waggled her eyebrows. "Maybe replaced them with some of mine."

"I thought you didn't get involved in other people's business?" Dick reached down to grab his towel, but Valentina kicked it away.

"Yet, here I am." She crossed her legs and grinned.

Dick thought about trying for the towel again but instead settled for putting his bare ass on the coffee table in front of Valentina. "I hardly thought that number I had for you would work. It only rang once before it disconnected and shrieked in my ear."

"Oh, good. It works then." Valentina nodded in approval. "Technology is something of a strong suit for me. If you know how to play with the digital, you know how to become invisible in the digital."

"Which is why I called you," Dick segued. "I have a favor to ask."

Valentina rose and crossed to Dick's windows. She poked two fingers between the blinds and peeked out at the city. "Always want something in return, don't you? I've yet to meet a man who doesn't require a quid pro quo to enjoy his company."

"As I recall, it was you who was the last to hold your end of the bargain." Dick winked. "You wanted *me* for something, remember?"

Valentina smirked. "Fair enough."

Dick got to his feet and quickly took the opportunity to grab his towel. He tied it around his waist while Valentina looked out at the city, then picked his glass up once more. He admired her from afar, the curves of her body, the sleek red of her hair. There was something so enticing about Valentina that he couldn't quite understand. Perhaps it *was* the danger about her, the possibility that at any moment she could snap and end his life.

I'd like to see her try.

"Are you going to tell me what you want, or are you going to perv on me all evening?" Valentina caught Dick's eyes on her ass, and he turned away. "I'm a busy lady, you know. Things to do, jobs to perform. I can't put the world to rights if I'm here waiting for you to unstick your tongue from the roof of your mouth and remember what you invited me over for."

"Is that what you call your work? 'Putting the world to rights?'"

"We all have our occupations, Dick." Valentina's eyes narrowed.

Dick moved over to his desk and opened the laptop he had stolen from the Russian's apartment. Strange digital letters and characters filled the screen, but even he could tell it was a universal landing page to log in. "I need to find a way to access this computer."

"Breaking and entering? Most uncharacteristic of you," Valentina crooned.

Dick raised his eyebrows. "We're in my apartment, aren't we? Nothing illegal going on here."

"What's so special about this laptop?" Valentina asked, her interest piqued as she joined Dick at the desk and rested her palms on the cool glass top.

"I hope it'll glean some information for a client. I'm in the process of returning a family heirloom, and so far, all I've managed to do is piss off some Russians and kill their leader." John noticed Valentina's judgmental look. "Okay, let me rephrase that. He killed himself. Cyanide pill. Still, he was the end of my rope, and now he's gone. I couldn't even question the bastard. All I have is this computer and a pounding headache."

Valentina chuckled. "Are you sure the headache isn't connected to your drinking problem?"

Dick smiled. "It's no problem. Look..." He drained the bourbon, then swallowed and showed her the empty glass. "See? No problem."

They laughed. Dick returned to the bottle of bourbon and poured himself another glass. The warm, sour beverage did wonders for helping his body forget the pain from his apartment raid. This was his fifth glass since he had returned to his apartment, but it certainly wasn't anywhere near a personal record for the highest quantity consumed in the shortest time. How many times had he been warned about the volume of liquor constantly coursing through his system? Yet, had it ever crippled him or slowed him down?

Maybe on one occasion... I still don't know how I ended up in that cemetery, body coiled and covered in toilet paper.

Even that had been a one-off. Dick prided himself on his booze control. There was something inside him—whether it was adrenaline or genetics, he didn't know—but under pressure, the alcohol lost its fuzzy edge and sharpness returned. While it dulled awareness in others, it sharpened his, so was it a wonder he'd stocked his cupboard to the brim with the stuff?

That familiar warmth spread through his body as he sipped again and closed his eyes. He arched his head back and savored the taste. "Yep. No problem."

"Done," Valentina called.

John turned to her. She was leaning back in his chair, a smug grin on her face as the screen illuminated the contours of her features.

"Done?" he repeated.

Valentina rolled her eyes. "Are we copying each other, now? Come on, Dick. Get your head in the game. Breaking into this system was easier than the Rubik's cube I solved at four years old."

"Got hold of the algorithms, did you?" Dick nodded at the Rubik's cube he had on a floating shelf on the wall. A thin layer of dust coated the top. "They're easy to solve when the internet tells you how."

"That's cute," Valentina mocked. "Mine was a ten by ten, and my mother wouldn't let me use the internet until I was at least six."

"You're kidding."

Valentina stared levelly at him, no suggestion of humor on her face. She pointed at the screen. "Are you going to check out the files on here, or do you want me to lock it all back up again? I'm on the clock, you know."

"Got a wolf to hunt on Wall Street?" Dick waited for a

response but got none. "Fine, let's see what we're dealing with here."

He pulled up a secondary chair when he realized that Valentina wasn't going to move out of his. He commandeered a mouse he had plugged into the system and worked his way through the files on the machine, methodically moving step-by-step through the communications and data that might glean some hope of where he could look next. He hated being in a position where the way ahead was dark, and everything relied on finding the right nugget of gold in the coal mine, but here he was. The only way forward was to keep his head down and find something—anything—that an idiot like a man who named himself "the Guardian" might leave behind.

Luckily for Dick, there was a structure to the machine's operating system. Although most of the files and organization were in Russian, he was able to navigate toward the email cache and get into the system files.

"How's your Russian?" Valentina asked.

"Da. Zavtra spasibo," Dick replied.

Valentina laughed, the sound as beautiful as her face. "You said, 'Yes. Tomorrow, thanks.'"

"And I meant every word." Dick tried to hide his grin. "How's yours?"

"Well," Valentina started, then drew in a deep breath that made her chest rise and fall, catching John's attention. "Khvatit pyalit'sya na moyu grud."

She said the words in a sultry tone, the r's rolling off her tongue with a gentle purr. Dick swallowed. "What did that mean?"

"Stop staring at my breasts."

Dick smirked and returned his attention to the screen. "So you know enough to help me navigate these files?"

Valentina chewed her lip in thought. "I'm surprised the great John Chambers doesn't know enough Russian to hack his way into the system. Aren't you supposed to be the city's greatest private investigator?"

"I'd be doing a bad job if the entire city knew about me," John quipped. "And I'm fine in my knowledge that Russian isn't the greatest tool in my toolkit." He held his phone in the air and shook it. "Luckily for me, technology has come far enough that translators do most of the hard work. If you weren't here to lend me a hand, I could simply do this." He clicked a couple of options on the computer, and a pop-up appeared. John clicked a box with a green tick next to the Russian writing, and all the text on the system converted into near-perfect English.

John leaned back in his chair in satisfaction. "I'm surprised you didn't know about that."

Valentina rolled her eyes. "I'm surprised it took you so long to do it."

John started at the email inboxes, searching for anything that contained the keyword, "Pendant." A half-dozen messages sprang to the top of the email client, which Dick read through eagerly while Valentina strolled around the apartment, examining Dick's things.

"There's a string of messages here from an unknown user. He's asking Vladimir Petrov about the pendant's location." Dick cocked his head to the side. "Huh. Guess that must be the Guardian's real name. It says here that he's willing to pay whatever it takes to get the pendant, and will offer his services to aid in the coming war."

"Coming war?" Valentina asked. "What kind of war are we talking?"

Dick shook his head. "I don't know. Could be anything with these guys. Turf, drug, arms, there's always some kind of war spinning out between the clusters of families and gangs in this city." He continued reading the emails. "Okay, we're on the right track. He mentions Ricardo by name, says that he's provided sufficient leverage to commission Ricardo to redeem the pendant."

"He the pawnshop guy near the string of cultural restaurants and takeaways?" Valentina asked.

"The very same," Dick replied.

Valentina chewed her lip. "This case does have legs, doesn't it? Makes me wish that I'd gone into PI work instead of… Well, you know."

"Mercenary work?" Dick nudged.

"Don't be so crass." Valentina smirked. "I merely engage in high-stakes missions for premium clients. Consider me a PI in my own right."

Dick spun in his chair to face her. "Some people might say you're a glorified Bassett hound with weapons."

Valentina looked at him thoughtfully. "Funny, I've heard people say the same about you. Sans weapons. Also, less of a Basset hound, more of a scrawny Chihuahua."

"Maybe there's a reason our favorite position is doggy." Dick cocked an eyebrow.

Valentina couldn't help her small laugh. "Don't get distracted now, Dick. We're on the clock, remember?"

Dick shook his sleeve and checked his watch. "Not for much longer. I have somewhere I need to be in half an hour." He held her gaze. "Maybe that's enough time for…"

Valentina crossed over to him and kissed him, which took his breath away. Her lips were soft and warm and familiar in a way he couldn't describe. While Dick knew that the nature of their encounters was nowhere in the arena of traditional romance—Dick had been there before and why the hell would he want to go down that route again—there was something about her. As though they were puzzle pieces and they just…fit.

Dick leaned into the kiss, only for Valentina to pull away and take his head in both her hands. With gentle firmness, she turned his attention back to the computer. "Finish your work. I have places to go, people to see."

"Fine." Dick tried to hide his smile. "Okay, so we have a link back to Ricardo, but that doesn't bring us any closer to finding out who killed Eric. Grunch stole the pendant, but where the hell could he have stolen it from?"

"Unless this Grunch was the murderer?" Valentina offered.

Dick tried to imagine it while remembering the scrawny thug he had encountered and easily trapped in the street. After nearly a decade of PI work in Atlantica, Dick liked to believe he had learned to read the shitbodies of this city, and it seemed unlikely that Grunch would engage in something as heinous as murder. Stealing jewels was one thing, but taking another human's life took a whole other level of skill and courage.

Dick sighed. "I've got to go back and question him. He's got to be able to give me something. It's either that or chase down the unknown sender of these messages. Then, how the hell am I supposed to tap into this person's account and figure out where to find them?"

Dick rested back in his chair and reached for this bourbon, surprised to find the tumbler now full. Last he remembered, he'd nearly finished the drink.

He smiled and spun in his chair. "You always were an excellent stalker. Silent as a…" Dick trailed off as he realized that the apartment was empty. The only remaining sign of Valentina was the lingering scent of her perfume. "Okay, sneak off before I get a chance to pay you back for helping me."

His phone vibrated in his pocket. Dick took out the cell and opened the message from the unknown sender. **Sadie Turnberry. Apartment Eighty-Seven, Monarch Boulevard. Be careful.** He turned to the computer screen in confusion, wondering if the message was somehow related to his question. His confirmation came a second later with another vibration. **Don't worry about payment. I could ask for money, but frankly, I don't** need it. **A warm body I trust not to stab me in the back? Priceless.**

A third message from another number. **Until next time. VW.**

Dick shook his head, still not quite able to believe how good Valentina was. When he spun back to the laptop, he received a final surprise. The screen was completely black, apart from a pop-up box which contained a red V that curled into the shape of a heart. A message read, **I've copied the contents of this laptop to my offshore cloud server. If I find anything else of note, I'll let you know.**

Dick closed the laptop and sat a moment in the quiet of his apartment. Outside, the cars drove by, speeding through the streets. AJS sirens sang gently in the distance, a permanent feature of the city's nightscape. Dick checked his watch, then emptied his bourbon down his gullet in one. He gasped after swallowing, then put on some clothes, ready to enter the city again.

He had a game to win.

CHAPTER TWELVE

"There's one in every district." Dick's hands were buried deep in his pockets, and his collar turned up against his neck. The night was dark, even the sodium arcs unable to penetrate the soft creep of fog that layered the city. He could make out the back-alley tavern across the road by the warm orange light that stared at him like a giant's glowing eyes.

Dick headed inside.

The place was busy, but not too crowded. Groups of questionable-looking men and women hung out around the wooden tables and the booths that lined the left wall. On the right, a long bar made its way along the length of the room. A bald meathead served customers and gave a throaty laugh while he poured his drinks. A girl who looked as though she couldn't have been the legal drinking age took the rest of the bar, failing miserably to avoid the ogling stares of the creepy patrons who leaned against the bar and whistled for her attention.

Dick's lip curled in disgust. "Animals."

He snaked his way through to the bar and waited to be served.

A few minutes later, the girl came around to him, thankful to finally tear herself away from the dozen or so lads who couldn't peel their eyes away from her white tank top and jean shorts. A dirty towel poked out of the waistband like a scrubby tongue. "What?"

Wow, where's the warmth? Where are the manners?

Dick chose to ignore her short address, understanding how a girl in her situation must feel having to deal with these dickheads daily. "Blue Moon, please."

The girl's eyebrows lifted. "Wow, a man with manners. That's a rare thing in these parts." She turned away and bent to grab a bottle of Blue Moon from the fridges beneath the bar. As she did, the lads elbowed each other and wolf-whistled at her. She didn't bat an eyelid, only stood and slid the beer to Dick. "Glass and ice?"

"Bottle's fine." As Dick tapped his phone against the contact-less receiver, he leaned toward her. "You don't have to put up with this shit, you know."

The girl's eyes darted toward the bald meathead. "Oh, I think I do."

"How old are you?" Dick asked.

"Old enough," the meathead growled as he moved to her side. "Now, unless you want me to knock your teeth out so that you have to drink that beer through a straw, I suggest you mind your own business, prick."

Dick raised the bottle and winked. "I'll pass. Thanks."

Dick turned away from the bar, aware of the lads laughing at his expense. He shrugged it off, knowing that at some point they would get what they deserved. He noted each of them in turn, and Dick rarely forgot a face.

He made his way to the back of the bar where three doors split off in different directions. One was marked "Occupied," and this was the one that Dick entered.

Walking into the small square room was like walking into fog, only with the added stink of cigar smoke and the faint tang of sweat and booze that lingered on the tongue. A round table dominated the center of the room, and five of the six chairs were occupied. Dick sat in the empty seat and rested his beer on the coaster.

"Sorry I'm late, gents," he addressed.

A cough came from his left.

"And ladies," he clarified.

The woman beside him, Connie Broughton, studied Dick with emerald eyes that caught the faint glow of the light above them. She wore a thick coat made of an animal fur Dick could only guess at, and long, silver fingernails that reminded Dick of claws decorated her fingertips.

Connie's lip curled in disgust. "We worried that you weren't going to make it, John. And what good is a poker game with only a handful of players? Honestly, you could show a little decorum. Perhaps notify us in advance if you're experiencing difficulties. We were almost at the point where we were going to have to bring in a new player."

"Why didn't you?" Dick's stomach curdled at Connie's pathetic attempts to establish herself as an upper-class civilian. As far as he was concerned, she was a filthy, rotten pig trying to jazz herself up and create a new persona by painting herself with lipstick. "Would've increased your odds at winning, surely?"

A grumble made its way around the room. The gentlemen on the other side of the table—an eclectic mix of a stout man with one eye, a stick-thin man with a v-neck cut so deeply you could almost see his bellybutton, an old man with the deep frown of a frog, and a man who revealed a gleaming set of gold teeth when he smiled—tapped their knuckles impatiently and told John to get on with it.

John gave an affirming nod to the old man, who looked as though a long pink tongue would launch out between his dry lips and snatch a fly from the air at any moment. He held the deck of cards in his hands, and at John's cue, dealt them to the players.

As the game got underway, the temperature in the room

rose. The plain wooden beams captured the heat, and John soon removed his jacket, showing off muscular arms that strained against the mesh of his custom black tee. Scars decorated one arm, and a thick nest of dark hair sprang from the skin.

Occasionally the girl from the bar would pop into the room with a tray and collect their empty drinks. She'd offer more beverages, allow the players to tap their cells against the contactless terminal, then reappear a minute later with a full tray. Dick's stomach turned, but he wasn't sure if it was a result of the growing heat and smoke or the stares the guys dragged behind the girl as she left.

Meanwhile, Connie did her best to withstand the heat in her jacket, refusing to take the thick fur off. Sweat peppered her forehead, and no matter how many times she wiped it away, it mixed with her makeup. Her mascara ran down her eyes, and her blusher and concealer smudged with the efforts to remain sweat-free. At one point, Jackson Devaney—the stick-thin man who had forged his way into second place behind Dick—leaned an elbow on the table and asked, "Why don't you take it off, Connie? You're clearly boiling."

Connie's eyes sank to the table. "I'd rather not, thanks."

"What, are you naked under there or something?" Porter chuckled darkly, the wrinkles around his ancient eyes like wet trash bags.

Connie remained silent.

"Wow." Jackson chuckled. "You really will do anything to try and fool the world into thinking you're worth a damn."

"I'm worth a damn sight more than you," Connie barked. "Sitting there as though butter wouldn't melt on your tongue."

Jackson grinned. Dick had seen this behavior before. As much as they each enjoyed playing cards, the real game here wasn't poker. It was proving your status to anyone who happened to share the same oxygen you breathed. Cash wasn't the only currency in Atlantica. If you wanted to succeed, you traded in status.

"I'll have you know that I now own four jewelry stores in Atlantica," Jackson boasted. "Three on the eastern side, and one on the lower southwest. My collective quarterly revenue is almost two billion dollars. That's almost double what Tiffany's makes per quarter. I have real estate in San Jose, Santa Fe, and Cuba. In this city alone, I've built an empire that staffs over one hundred—"

"Oh, give me a break," the man with gold teeth, Cruz de Loine, exclaimed. "Quit measuring dicks, will you? We all know that's bullshit, dawg. Those jewelry stores ain't nothing compared to the Bling Factory on Seventh. And, they ain't even your companies. Your ex took them from you in the divorce. You can't pull that kinda bull. We know you, man. If you were doing so damn well in the jewelry game, what the hell are you doing wasting your nights in this sewage plant?"

Jackson held Cruz's stare, and Dick wondered whether something was about to kick off. It wasn't unheard of for a game like this to devolve into a fist or gunfight.

His mind flashed back to his trip to The Armada, the first place he had encountered Santana. He had just gotten himself kicked out of one of his favorite locals. It was a little too soon for him to get kicked out of another. He decided he needed to douse the heat a little.

"Gents, gents, gents," Dick soothed as he placed his cards facedown on the table and climbed to his feet. "Enough of this friction, okay? We came out tonight to play a nice friendly game of cards. Why don't we finish what we started, then maybe you can go into the alley out back after, pull out those cocks, and measure them once and for all?"

Cruz scoffed. "The only reason you ain't salty is because you're sitting pretty behind your tower of chips."

Jackson peeled his narrowed eyes from Cruz and muttered,

"Damn. I could've done with some of that coin tonight." He grabbed his fistful of remaining chips and hurled them into the center of the table. "All in."

John remained standing for a few seconds, ensuring that some of the heat had died. He wiped a layer of sweat from his head, then caught the girl as she entered the room with another empty tray. "Keep the door propped open, would you, please? Things are heating up in here, and it's not only my fiery winning streak."

The girl bit back another laugh and took their orders. Dick bought the next round, wanting to keep things amicable for a change. The girl returned a moment later and passed the drinks to the others around the table who scowled but kept their silence.

John raised his drink to the stout man coolly peering at him with his one good eye. "Quiet tonight, Bram. Something up?"

"Oh, leave him alone, won't you?" Connie defended. "Two of his lackeys got busted by the AJS today, didn't they?"

Bram grunted and casually tossed a chip into the center of the table. "Goddamn AJS scum. Can't keep their grubby mitts to themselves. Locking away good, honest people."

Honest? The day this guy hangs out with honest people is the day the city holds its first Sunshine and Rainbows parade.

"What happened?" Jackson asked.

When Bram spoke, there was a hint of an accent in his words. Dick had never been sure where it came from. It sounded like a mix of Italian, Spanish, and Russian all at once. "Benson and Romero were minding their own business, playing with ink in the alleyways near BonVivant, when they got jumped by some woman. They were knocked out and left to rot in the alley before the AJS came and claimed them for themselves."

"They were doing ink in the alleys?" John questioned.

Bram spat defensively. "Harming nobody. If they want to inject that shit into their bodies, they're more than entitled to. What they do with their flesh is nobody's business."

Cruz chuckled. "If they're dumb enough to be injecting ink in an alley, they're dumb enough to get caught. They had it coming, dawg."

Bram tossed his bottle at Cruz, who ducked in time for it to smash against the wall behind him. Brown liquid sprayed over Cruz's back and soaked into the floor as droplets rained onto the table.

Bram was on his feet, his single eye boring into Cruz. Now that he was standing, Dick noticed the black pinpricks in his forearm and the darkness of his veins beneath the skin. The guy was still high off his dose of ink.

Dick stood, held his hands in the air, and waved them to calm the situation. "Jesus fucking Christ, guys. We can't play a simple game of poker without it devolving into a brawl?" *Thank God they don't know about The Armada.* "Who gives a shit whether your boys were arrested, your wife left you or..." he looked at Connie, "whatever the fuck your issue is? Let's be gentlemen and finish the damn game."

Bram prodded a stubby finger at Dick. "You're only interested because you're winning."

"Well...yeah," Dick admitted. "Fair is fair, and I won't have you cheap shots back out of paying because you're caught up in some schoolyard drama." He nodded at Bram's arm. "Don't let the ink do the talking for you. Cruz is right. If your friends are dumb enough to deal and dabble in a public alley, they're asking for it. Atlantica makes it so easy to do this shit. Do it in your home, and you can do whatever the fuck you want. Why were they doing it in the alley, Bram?"

Some of Bram's fire extinguished. He shrugged. "Adds to the danger. It's never as exciting when you know you're allowed to do it."

"Then your friends are idiots." Dick turned to address the rest of the table. "Now, does anyone else have any beef they want to air before we carry on? Connie? Jackson? What about you, Porter?"

The old frog man had barely moved an inch during the dispute. He looked up at Dick with heavy eyes and licked his lips with his long tongue. He picked up a chip and tossed it in the center of the table. "I'll match." He took another chip. "And I'll raise."

Cruz laughed, which was a relief since his back was growing sticky from the beer. "You son of a bitch. Nothing stops this one from playing the game." He peeled away the shirt clinging to his back and pointed at Bram. "Another shot like that, and I'll throw you out myself."

At that moment the door opened, and the bald meathead from the bar filled the frame. "That won't be necessary. I'll toss you lot out myself."

"What did we—?" Connie protested before the barman pointed at the glass and stinking liquid on the floor.

"You break my shit? You get out." He turned his eyes on Dick. "Not least because your buddy here keeps creeping on my niece. She's sixteen, bro."

Dick lowered his eyes, then looked back at the barman with a triumphant grin. "She's how old?"

The barman's eyes flickered as the realization of what he had let slip dawned on him. "She's—"

"Not only underage for half the legal activities in Atlantica," Dick scolded, "but far too young to be working in an establishment that serves alcoholic beverages. Does the AJS know about your little extortion scheme? I suppose she accepts lower wages than the average bar person, doesn't she?"

The barman growled. "You best keep your goddamn mouth shut."

Dick gave an understanding nod. "I can do that. But the only way you'll gain my silence—any of our silence—is if you let us see this game through to the end. Can you do that for us? Can you?" Although it was a question, there was no doubt about which answer Dick expected. The barman considered this for a moment longer before someone called from somewhere deep in the bar.

"Fine. Finish your game, then get the fuck out. You're not welcome here anymore."

Dick nodded and waited for him to close the door behind himself. When the man was gone, he addressed the room. "I think I'll come back here every Friday night. What do you say, guys?"

The others scoffed and returned to their cards. An hour later, Dick left the establishment with a warm smile for the barman, a friendly wave for the girl, and a vast increase in the overall amount sitting in his bank account.

Dick slept well that night, cuddled in the warm embrace of his tipsy state. He awoke to sunlight streaming into his apartment, memories of the night before coming in short, fuzzy bursts.

Something about yesterday's poker game irked him. Dick had never been one to let injustices lie when there was something to be fixed, but he wasn't sure he could do anything about the girl in the bar. Maybe her uncle was treating her unfairly. Perhaps he had hired an underage barmaid. It was the AJS' problem to sort out issues that broke city policy and legislation.

Then why can't I shake off this feeling that I should do something?

Dick rolled out of bed, had a quick shower to wash off the stink of smoke from the bar, then stood in front of the Guardian's laptop. Illegal hiring or not, Dick had other priorities to deal with today. His near dead-end had now folded out into two possible branches of investigation, and he debated which road he should take.

On one side, he had a possible address of someone who had been in contact with the Guardian and sought the pendant.

On the other, he had an unresolved set of actions that might lead to the identification of Erik Burgess' killer. Each side of the coin weighed heavily in his mind. Perhaps that was why he had taken so fondly to investigative work—because he couldn't stand the idea of the unknown. Either way, he knew he would pursue both avenues, but which one held the highest priority?

Dick logged into his computer and looked up the address that Valentina had provided. The apartment building was about five miles across the city, while the jail cells in which Grunch was likely to be sitting were a mile along the same route.

Dick dialed a number on his cell phone and waited for an answer.

"Dick? Is that you?" Terra Kris' voice was crystal-clear through the receiver.

"Yeah, it's me. You got a second?" In the background, Dick could make out the sound of people talking and the drone of cars.

"I… Oh, hold on…" The rumble of a motorbike engine kicked into life, then cut off. "Can I call back? I'm just leaving work. Been a hell of a night, I can tell you."

"I only need you to answer a quick question for me." He drew a long breath. "You've been at the precinct all night, haven't you? Any idea if a man who goes by the name of Grunch is in the holding cells?"

Terra sighed. "Dick, you know I don't have a comprehensive knowledge of every shitbag we throw in the holding cells. Do you know what my job is?"

Dick smirked. "Looking pretty while riding a bike?"

Terra gave a dramatic dry heave. "You're kidding, aren't you? I don't know how ladies fall for that snarky charm of yours, but remember, it doesn't work on me, Dick. I see through your façade, and in all honesty, I'm fucking tired right now. A twelve-hour night shift cleaning up the scum in this city, putting my body in the way of bullets and having to deal with ink-heads and men with egos bigger than our twisted skyscrapers can wear you down, so cut the bullshit, all right?"

John waited a second for Terra to calm down. "Terra, this is important." He lowered his voice. "We're talking about a homicide here."

Although he couldn't see her, he could almost feel Terra's curiosity rouse. If there was one thing he knew about Terra Kris—besides the fact that she and Dick were like oil and water when put in the same room—it was that justice led her heart. While AJS restrictions bound Terra and she had to let slide a thousand incidences of murder, drug use, and gang war, John had the advantage of working outside the law. If there was one string to his bow that could earn Terra's attention, it was the fact that she could aid in making the city of Atlantica a little better.

Terra was quiet for a long moment. "What's the name?"

"Grunch," John repeated.

"A real name, Dick." Terra sighed.

"I don't know." John waited.

"Give me a few minutes," Terra replied. "But you owe me, okay?"

John smiled. "That's fine by me."

"You owe me a lot. This isn't the first favor you've called in." Terra chuckled. "I'm keeping a tally."

"I wouldn't expect anything less."

Dick arrived at the precinct an hour later. It was nearing ten in the morning, but the cloth of fog that hung over the city made it feel like early dawn. The sun was a milky orb in the sky, its light barely able to penetrate the city around them.

Dick gripped his coffee cup in one hand as he approached the AJS building. He drained the grainy contents and tossed the cup in the trash can. He climbed the steps and nodded acknowledgments to a handful of the AJS officers he'd come to know throughout his time as a PI in Atlantica.

Dick walked up to the desk and leaned an elbow against the wood. Through a glass panel, a young officer with the naïve glint of recruits in his eye grinned up at him. His badge read, "Custer."

"Good morning, sir," Custer offered. "How may I help you today?"

An officer walked into the building, noticed Dick, and called, "Don't trust that one, boy. He's the parasite that feeds off the whale." He turned to his colleague strolling beside him. "What're they called again?"

"You mean those little fish that chew the dead skin off the bigger fish?" the second officer asked. "Remora, or some shit, I think."

The pair of them laughed.

Dick grinned. "It's called symbiosis when one animal benefits from another. It's part of the circle of life."

The first officer scoffed. "Yeah, if the circle of life involves you digging around for our scraps."

Dick didn't rise to the bait. "Whatever you need to believe, Marconi."

Marconi and the second AJS officer laughed as they left the lobby.

Dick turned his attention back to the young officer, whose cheeks were flushed. "You know they're right, don't you?"

Custer was flustered. "Oh, you know, it's not my place to judge."

Dick leaned closer and lowered his voice. "Still, you can guarantee that there's a hell of a lot more money in my bank account than that pair have made in their entire lives." He winked, and Custer smiled. Dick stood straight and cleared his throat. "I have an appointment to speak to someone you're holding in your cells. I believe that Agent Terra Kris has cleared me for access."

Custer tapped his keyboard and nodded. "John Chambers?"

"Call me Dick," he replied.

Custer looked as though he didn't know whether to laugh or

not. Dick grinned. "I'm kidding. Hand me my badge and tell me which room, and I'll be out of your hair."

Dick waited in the stone-cold silence of the AJS interrogation room. One side's entirety was one-way glass, and Dick could only hope that the area behind it was empty.

Of course, it won't be. They know you, Dick. They're watching you like a hawk.

The door opened, and two AJS officers led Grunch into the room. The scrawny rat-faced jewel thief glared at Dick as they brought him inside. He struggled against the officers, but with his hands in chains and a frame that boasted little muscle, they easily secured him in his chair across from Dick.

"Five minutes," one of the officers instructed.

"Ten," Dick countered.

"Five," the second replied.

Dick shrugged. "Worth a shot."

When the officers exited, he was left staring at Grunch. He narrowed his eyes while examining the prick he had left in the alley for the AJS to capture. He looked worse than Dick thought possible, with dark bags beneath his eyes and red lines across the whites of his sclera.

Dick stared silently at Grunch. It was an intimidation technique he'd learned. Let the person you were interrogating believe that you were in no hurry, and stimulate their minds into concocting their worst-case scenario. After two minutes of waiting, Grunch leaned his handcuffed hands on the table and glared at Dick. "What is this, then? Huh? Wanted to see my pretty face for five minutes? How do I look? As beautiful as you'd pictured? Is this the face you'll jack off to tonight?"

Dick held his gaze. "The pendant."

Grunch let out a thin laugh. "You're kidding me with this

again." He leaned closer, eyes darting to the one-way mirror. "Yeah, I took it. But I didn't touch the man. I swear, hand to God, I never touched a single hair on his head."

"Your promises mean shit to me." Dick's lip curled. "Give me a name. Give me something. You sent me to the guy who hired you, and that trail has led to a lot of destruction already. I want the killer."

"You found Everest?" Grunch stammered. "How?"

"I've been in this game a while. You think I became a PI in Atlantica without having made a few connections? Yes, I found Everest. It wasn't that hard. I've climbed higher than Everest too, and quashed some of the guys higher up, so if you think I'm going to take shit from a worthless flea who steals shiny things from women, you best check yourself."

Grunch sat back in his chair. "I got nothing for you, man. Nothing."

Dick instantly rose to his feet, kicked the chair back as he whirled around the table, and grabbed the back of Grunch's neck. He brought his face millimeters from the criminal's and scowled. "You know *something*. I can see it in those beady little eyes of yours. Now, tell me what you know."

Dick's eyes darted to the clock on the wall. He only had sixty seconds left.

Grunch trembled. "I don't know what to say, man—"

Dick slammed Grunch's face into the table. The man yelped in pain. "Tell me!"

Grunch stared longingly at the glass, but if the AJS were watching, they showed no sign. "I don't know!"

Dick slammed him again Blood painted the table as it spilled from his nose. "I can do this all day."

Grunch put his hands up. "Fine! Fine! Okay. Fuck…"

Dick released his collar and took a step back while Grunch dabbed his nose with the cuff of his sleeve. "I don't know names, okay? You think they're going to give me the fucking identification of a stone-cold killer? No." He sighed. "If you're looking for the guy who killed your buddy, then go check the body. Find his calling card."

Dick frowned. "If there were a calling card, the AJS or the morgue would have found it."

Grunch gave a weak grin and tapped his right temple with a single finger. "Not if they don't know what they're looking for."

Before Dick could ask another question, the door unlocked. He muttered a brief thanks to Grunch for his cooperation, then was at the door before the officers could enter. He swept past the pair without looking back, leaving the AJS officers confused as their eyes found the bloody stain on Grunch's face.

Grunch raised his eyebrows. "I'll have you for this. Leaving a fucking psychopath in a locked room with me."

The taller of the two officers gave a half-shrug. "It's your word against ours. I don't fancy your chances."

CHAPTER FOURTEEN

Dick's phone dialed on loudspeaker as he drove across town.

"Yyyello?" Santana answered. "What's the word, hummingbird?"

Dick gave the phone a strange look, unsure why Santana sounded so bright. "You sound abnormally chipper."

"Let's just say that I encountered a group of wild animals, and I easily came out on top. Idiots." She drew a deep breath. "Man, I love the jungle."

Dick looked out at the city as he drove along the road. The streets were busy with the day's foot traffic, expensive show cars raced around him, and the eclectic mix of architecture towered hundreds of feet above. Dick supposed he loved the jungle, too. Only, his jungle was the concrete jungle that was the city of Atlantica.

"Why do I get the feeling you're not talking about real animals?" Dick slowed for a red light.

Santana ducked the question. "How's the case going? Got any more news on the whereabouts of my mother's jewelry? It's already been a few days. I'd have thought you'd have the whole thing locked down by now. I paid premium, after all."

Dick grinned. He sensed her teasing tone in her voice. The lights turned green, and he pressed his foot on the gas. "I've hit a few snags. I hope you appreciate the lengths I'm going through to secure a tiny piece of gold. It's more than the AJS would ever do for the common folk."

"Is that all I am to you, John? Common folk?" John made out the excited chirping of birds in the background.

"I told you, call me Dick. And, no, of course not. I treat my clients with the respect and dignity they deserve. If you knew half of the shit I've had to go through to—"

"I have time," Santana interrupted. "And I told you I'm not going to call you that. Now, enough stalling. What's the ten-four?"

Dick laughed. "Ten-four means 'okay.' I think you mean four-one-one."

"This is why *you're* the detective." Santana paused. "Well? Fill me in!"

Dick gave as much information as he was happy to. He told Santana about his leads with Grunch, and his encounter with the Guardian and his family of angry Russians. He mentioned the laptop but neglected to fill her in on the specifics of how he managed to hack the computer, even when she pressed him.

"I didn't have you down as a computer whiz," she commented.

"I had some help," he replied dryly.

"From who?" she asked.

John shrugged as he turned right at the end of the road. "A friend. It's not important. What *is* important is that we may have a lead on the pendant's actual location. I'm on my way there now, hoping to keep my head low and gather some intel. I'll let you know what the four-one-one is once I'm out and away from prying eyes."

Santana was quiet a moment. Only the rustling of the jungle canopy and the odd animal call in the background were audible.

"Thank you, John. It honestly means the world to me that you're trying so damn hard. I'd come after it myself, but…"

"The city is not your jungle. I get it," Dick replied. "Hey, let me know when you're back in the city, okay? We'll grab a drink. Talk all of this through. Hopefully, I'll have a pendant to bequeath upon you, too."

"Ew." Santana chuckled. "Bequeath? No one's died, John."

"Not yet, at least," he joked. "What do you say?"

"Sounds good." Santana was quiet a moment longer before adding, "It's not a date, though."

John scoffed. "Absolutely. Not a date. Just a client and their employee getting a chance to talk. Something tells me you're knee-deep in shit right now."

"What makes you think that?" Santana asked.

"I can smell it." Dick grinned, then hung up.

━━━━━

Dick turned onto Monarch Boulevard a few minutes later. The street was wide, the pavement clean. Impressive buildings dotted either side of the road, each one a testament to different origins of architecture. It was clear that they were premium apartment blocks, but each one bore its creator's unique stamp.

Dick signaled and turned toward the side of a building that defied the rules of traditional structure. Where the others around it consisted of straight sides and conventional corners, Sadie Turnberry's apartment building twisted along a central rod that supported the building to its impressive height. The edges bulged in and out, casting the illusion that it was a small portion of the helix-shaped structure of a giant's DNA string.

The parking lot went deep underground, each of the gleaming vehicles giving Dick an indication of the type of people he'd be dealing with when he entered the building. He parked, found his way up into the main lobby through a side door, and blinked at the dazzling array of lights in the pristine white marble lobby.

I stick out like a sore thumb. Dick dusted off the sleeves of his jacket and tucked his hands in his pockets. On either side of a walkway leading farther into the building was an identical pair of reception desks. About forty feet ahead of him, a gold-plated elevator carried snooty looking residents to their apartments.

Worth a shot. Dick pulled his jacket's collar tighter around him and strode across the lobby, beelining for the elevator. He only made it between the reception desks when a woman with a tight ponytail called to him. "Excuse me, sir. Are you lost?"

Dick shut his eyes and composed himself. He turned and flashed his warmest grin. "Not at all. I'm here to visit a friend."

She scanned his worn and dusty wear, clearly not buying any of it. Dick couldn't blame her. He was a giant black smudge against the pristine cleanliness of this building.

"And who are you here to meet?" the woman asked. Her badge read, "Annabel."

Dick had to think fast. The last thing he wanted to do was give the receptionist a name. If he did, he was leaving another breadcrumb in a trail that might in some way lead back to him. If Sadie weren't home, and the receptionist reported someone asking for her, it would only raise suspicions.

"The client didn't leave their name, only an apartment number." He held her gaze, noticing a slight tilt of her head.

"A client? I'm afraid we have a policy against that kind of... business." She crossed her hands in front of her, then nodded to the revolving entrance doors. "If you would please kindly remove yourself from the premises, it would be much appreciated."

Dick nodded politely. "Of course, I apologize." He made his way back through the revolving doors and emerged onto the street. He hadn't entered this way, but he wanted to get his bearings on the building's layout. He was going to make his way inside, with or without permission. The only question was "how?"

Dick politely waved to a security guard who studied him over the top of a pair of black shades. Then he followed the walkway around the building and ducked into the colossal structure's shadow. There was a narrow pathway leading between apartments where the dumpsters were kept to deal with the excessive amount of trash the residents threw away. The smell of cooked meats poured out from a vent at the side—presumably from the complex's diner—and several doors in the back of the building had digital panels and locks keeping them closed.

Dick kept his collar high and his head low to avoid the CCTV cameras picking up his face. Once he performed a full circuit, he made his way back to the parking lot and sat in his car. He opened the glove compartment, pulled out a notepad and pen, then quickly sketched what he remembered of his trip so he wouldn't forget it.

Once satisfied with the map he'd drawn, he closed his eyes and tried to imagine which rooms sprang off from where. It was easy to remember the gym since he'd passed a long glass window where several residents worked out. He could determine where the kitchen was by the vents, but the rest of it was all guesswork.

When he was happy with his rudimentary blueprint, he dialed a number on his cell. A man answered, and Dick delivered his instructions. The man enthusiastically agreed when Dick assented to his financial demands.

Dick waited in his car, switching the radio on and soaking in some casual jazz. He set an alarm on his phone, closed his eyes, and allowed himself a brief moment of rest.

Dick was awakened twenty minutes later by someone knocking on his windshield. In his groggy state, he imagined Valentina there, ready to meet for a rendezvous in a quiet spot out by the hills that skirted the city. Instead, he looked into the angry eyes of the security guard who had watched him outside the apartment building.

"Gotta move, sir. This ain't a park and nap kind of place." He pointed behind Dick. "You're also in a reserved spot."

Dick waved an apology and started the car. He pawed at his sleepy eyes, then drove out of the lot and found a public parking lot around the corner.

He looked at the clock and noticed he still had a few minutes until he met his dealer. He waited a minute more before finding the diner where he had agreed to meet Ringo.

The waitress led him to a booth in the corner, per Dick's request. The place wasn't packed, but it wasn't empty, either. Customers littered the tables, but the booth Dick sat in offered the most cover for the transaction he was about to make. The main solace he could take from this diner was that he certainly wasn't the shadiest looking customer in the joint.

A shadow loomed over Dick. "Long time no see, pal. How the fuck are ya?"

Dick half-turned and ushered the man to the seat across from him. He was grimy to look at, but not in the usual way that the scum Dick dealt with looked. It was a hazard of his occupation. Thick oil smudges decorated his face. Grease and dirt darkened the thin wires of his grey hair. He was scrawny, with cheekbones that almost poked out of translucent skin, and as he sat at the booth and placed a laden rucksack beside him, several of his joints gave an audible *crack*.

"You always pick the best places," Ringo commented as he glanced around the diner with an approving nod. He grabbed the menu and slid a finger down the listings. "Waffles, pastries, bacon sandwiches. I don't know where to start. All on you, isn't it?"

Dick smirked. "You really are a piece of work, aren't you?"

"A hungry piece of work," Ringo replied. "You want your gear? You have to feed me first."

Dick sorted out Ringo with a plate piled with pancakes.

Whipped cream spiraled into a peak on top. Syrup doused the whole plate. As Ringo made his way through his meal, Dick settled with a black coffee and a single slice of buttered toast.

It was impressive to watch the skinny guy across the table devour the entire plate. Dick was certain he would have thrown up if he had attempted it, but Ringo showed no sign of slowing as he scraped the final piece of pancake across the syrup-drenched plate to get as much into his mouth as possible.

Dick shook his head in disbelief. "You eat like a five-year-old."

"You say that every time." Ringo smiled. "Ready to see what I have for you?"

Dick nodded.

Ringo wiped his face clean with the napkin, then paused as the waitress came and cleared their plates. Dick ordered another coffee, then leaned forward to get a closer look.

The dealer pulled numerous strange metallic devices from the tattered rucksack. They were small, the largest being no more than the size of a grape. Each one was gleaming silver with a decorative "R" etched into the sides.

Ringo glanced around cautiously, then spoke to Dick in a hushed tone. "Every device you should need to scatter electronic frequencies, disable alarms, and enter a building undetected. Upgraded since the last time you used them."

Dick plucked one of the devices from the table and examined it closely. "Upgraded how? You told me the last time I purchased from you that they were undetectable and perfect. You said there was nothing more you could do with them."

"Don't be so obtuse, Dick." Ringo chuckled. "Technology always evolves, and so does the counter-tech department. Every device has frequencies and signals. Think of them as digital fingerprints. You have to keep moving, changing things up. Devices get smaller, too. As new technologies come out, they make the AR-34s look like TXI-500s." He exploded into sudden laughter that he tried to hide behind his hand.

Dick turned over his shoulder and saw that a few of the customers had glanced their way.

"You understand my business is in secrecy," Dick reprimanded. "Can you try and show a little more decorum? I haven't paid for your pancakes yet."

Ringo's mirth vanished. "Of course." He leaned back and laced his fingers behind his head. "So, what do you think?"

Dick examined each device with a careful eye and asked further questions until he was satisfied with what he was purchasing. Ringo reached into his bag and pulled out a device that looked like the contactless terminals used to pay for items in shops. Only this was another device with his "R" scratched into the side.

"No," Dick told him plainly.

"No?" Ringo raised an eyebrow.

Dick's lips thinned. "You think I'm going to let you use one of your custom devices to transfer cash? I wasn't born yesterday, Ringo. For all I know, you've done your techno mumbo-jumbo and made it so you have instant access to all my accounts. I'll pay you in the usual way."

Ringo smirked. "You're a smart man, Dick. No wonder you do what you do."

"And I do it well." Dick stood and took out a handful of blue Atlantican bills, which he tossed onto the table. "This should cover the pancakes."

Ringo held up a single Atlantican dollar, eyes wide with wonder. "Paper money. Who'd have thought the world once ran on this? I figured I'd have to go to a museum to see this in real life. It's bad enough your bank transfer is going to take twelve hours to process."

"You trust me, though?" Dick was clearly prepared to accept only one answer.

"Of course," Ringo agreed. "You trust me, too?"

Dick scooped the handful of devices scattered across the table into his deep pockets, then stared at Ringo. "I will, the same day you stop serving your wares to the bad guys. Skinny guy, goes by the name of Grunch. You remember him?"

The expression on Ringo's face told Dick that he did. "A customer is a customer, Dick. I don't ask what people want with the devices. I only sell them. My part of the exchange begins and ends in finance."

"I know." Dick gave a small nod. "That's one of the things I love and hate about people like you." He patted his pockets. "Thanks for that, Ringo. I'll see you around."

CHAPTER FIFTEEN

Dick returned to his car shortly after meeting Ringo and switched on the radio. He allowed himself some time to listen to the news of Atlantica before closing his eyes and catching up on some much-needed sleep.

While that would be uncomfortable for many, Dick had gotten so used to reclining the seat to a forty-five-degree angle that sleep came almost instantly. His arms were folded across his chest, and the doors locked tight. The world drifted past, unaware of the sleeping PI as he whiled away the hours in the public parking lot, waiting for what little sun was there to fade, and for night to cover the city in darkness.

When Dick awoke, it was like coming out of a bath of molasses. He sat up and pawed the sleep from his eyes. Stale coffee and nicotine lingered in his mouth, so he opened the glove box and tossed two pieces of gum between his lips. After another moment of thought, he added a third for good measure.

He righted his seat and studied the world around him. The clock on his dashboard told him it was a little past midnight, yet civilians still walked around the city. The apartment complex wasn't all that far from BonVivant Valley—Atlantica's fashionista district—so the people strolling the sidewalks were clothed in the latest fashion trends. Dick shook his head while silently judging the crazy styles that came in and out of favor, each item of clothing likely costing more than his monthly share of rent.

It was no surprise that this was where the premium apartment complexes were situated. All the residents would have to do is walk a block away to buy everything they needed to model for the front of Glamour or Vogue.

Dick climbed out of his car and walked down the street. He found the apartment building as he turned the corner and made his way onward. He paused around fifty feet from it and stared up at the massive structure.

It's a hell of a long way to the top. Should've gotten a coffee before this. Ah, well. I'll nab one after. Hopefully, this won't take long.

Dick turned onto a pathway around the back of the adjacent building and wormed his way into further darkness. He skirted the edifice and made his way to the rear of the apartment complex. When he leaned around the corner, he could make out one of the back doors.

He withdrew his rudimentary map and confirmed he was in the right location. Next, he dipped a hand into his deep pockets and found the device he wanted.

"Here goes nothing," he mumbled and pointed it at the security cameras as he pressed a small red button on top. A green LED flashed its confirmation, but there was no evidence it had worked apart from that.

Dick waited a few seconds before he slid the device back in his pocket. If all had gone well—and he had no reason to distrust any of Ringo's technological advancements, the guy was an absolute pro—the security feed would have frozen on the last image it had caught. He could then move like a specter around the back of the building, where he now found himself at a set of metallic double doors secured by a digital panel.

Beneath the panel was a single socket, small enough to be

invisible to anyone who didn't know what they were looking for. Dick found a device like the one he had seen Grunch use outside the jewelry store and inserted it like a USB pen. Once again, he clicked a button. A green LED flashed, but this time there was an audible click as the door's locking mechanism released.

"Open sesame." Dick grinned, cast a final look over his shoulders, then allowed himself entry.

Dick stepped into a back passage that appeared to be a place for the kitchens to lug their discarded materials on large wheelie bins out of the building. There was a faint odor of moldy food, and dark stains on the floor from the wheels as they had been carted back and forth in this direction.

Moving quickly, Dick made his way along the passageway. Somewhere up ahead, faint but animated voices carried toward him. *Probably the kitchen staff.* When the voices grew louder, Dick turned right and found his way into an office whose door had been left wide open.

He closed the door behind him and switched on the light. A desk took the center of the room, its surface piled high with papers. Post-It notes and corkboards littered the walls. *You'd think the office environment would have stepped up a little in the last few years. Guess technology isn't always the pathway to production.*

Next to the door, Dick found what he was looking for. There was a map that marked the procedures for evacuation during a fire. Managers were always equipped with safety standards, and this map gave a thorough blueprint of the entire floor. Dick leaned closer, then traced his finger from his current location to the closest stairwell. Only two led to the upper floors, and the closest was only a short distance away.

Must be a service stairwell for the hotel staff.

Dick memorized the route and noted that it ran incredibly close to the diner. He stepped back and was about to turn off the light when there was a knock on the door.

A voice spoke cautiously. "Janet? Mrs. Porter?"

Dick stepped back behind the door and held his breath. The door eased open, and a young man poked his head inside. He scanned the room, and the minute he saw Dick's face, he froze.

"Have you seen Mrs. Porter?" His voice wobbled a little from fear.

Dick shook his head.

They held each other's gaze for a moment before Dick reached out and grabbed him by the collar. He pulled him into the room while closing the door with the back of his foot. He placed the man on the table, lifting him easily given his slight frame, and took a step back.

The man stared at him, uncertain whether to shout or talk. Dick gave him the answer. "You say a word, and this will not end well for you." He pulled open his jacket and flashed his badge. "Before you say anything, know that I'm not a criminal. I'm a private investigator, and I'm here in the hope of finding someone who can put an end to a spate of crime that has seen people die, and items stolen."

The man's eyes lit up. Stray hairs stuck to a clammy head beneath a small chef's hat. "You're with the AJS?"

"No." Dick spat the word as though it tasted awful. "No, I'm a *private* investigator. All I need is for you to promise your silence until I finish with my business. No one else can know I'm here. Understood?"

The man considered this. He craned his head to the door as the handle turned. The door was stuck. A moment later, keys jangled.

Dick lowered his voice. "You'll be a hero. Contributing to the capture of a dangerous criminal. Can you keep quiet for me?"

The man nodded. Dick spotted a keycard pinned to his chest and snatched it away. "I'll take this."

As the door unlocked and opened, Dick slunk back behind it. A middle-aged woman with her hair in thick grey curls walked in. The careworn look on her face melted to puzzlement as her eyes fixed on the man sitting on her desk. "Truman? What the hell are you doing here?" She looked back at the doorway. "How did you get in?"

Dick held a finger to his lips, the woman clueless to his presence. She stalked closer to the man and folded her arms, which allowed Dick enough of a gap to slip out silently. He mouthed a "thank you" that he wasn't sure the young man caught as he began to defend himself and stumble over some logical reason as to how he'd made his way into his manager's office.

Dick crept along the corridor, Mrs. Porter's words fading as he marked his mental map and made his way to the stairwell. A few times along the way, he ducked into empty rooms and behind dumpsters to hide from the apartment staff. Finally, he reached a white door and scanned the card.

"Truman Herman?" He chuckled as the door unlocked and he entered. "What a name. I wonder where that freak show is from originally. Probably Atlantica, to be honest. Everything's about making a statement here."

While climbing the stairwell, Dick realized there was no chance of being quiet anymore. Each step clapped and echoed around the white-painted concrete walls. There were no windows here, and when he looked up, he could barely see the end of the spiraling stairs.

Dick sighed. "Sadie Turnberry, Apartment Eighty-Seven, here I come."

If climbing up dozens of flights of stairs wasn't bad enough, at each floor Dick had to re-use the CCTV-blocking device to mask his presence from the security team. Dick had snuck into enough places over the years to learn that there was no sense in getting panicked. Worst-case scenarios were for suckers. If he encountered a situation, he'd keep his cool, and he'd deal with it. He wondered if some of that mindset was from the days he'd spent in the army. It probably was, but he didn't like to think about that.

Halfway up the building, Dick peeked through a door and saw a golden plaque with "Apts 38–41" printed on its front. If the apartments clustered in groups of three, that left him with another sixteen or so floors to climb.

He was about to take another step when a door opened and closed down below. Two people walked and spoke in loud voices, clearly unaware of the intruder above.

"That's the problem with these pieces of shit," one of the voices, a woman's, commented. "They act all high and mighty, but the stains tell another story."

The second voice, a man's, chipped in. "You don't need to tell me. I argued with Mrs. Venebles in thirty-seven for five minutes as she tried to convince me that was chocolate on her bedsheets."

"How did you know that it wasn't?" the woman asked.

"It didn't smell like chocolate," the man replied.

The woman gave a disgusted wretch, then laughed. "These guys pay thousands a month for their apartments. They have a residential gym, diner, indoor pool, and room service, and they still don't have the courtesy to act like human beings. We might as well be cleaning up after animals."

Dick poked his head over the rail, hoping to catch a look at the pair. Their voices grew louder, and their footsteps indicated that they were coming up toward Dick. He looked around while wondering if he should risk going into the corridor by the door, or head upstairs where they'd be more than aware that someone was there the moment he moved his feet.

They were three floors below. The pair of them carried wash baskets filled with crumpled laundry.

Who has their delicates cleaned by the in-house service at night? Fucking rich people.

"I'd be careful what you say," the man managed after he finished laughing. He lowered his voice, but it carried easily enough. "Those cameras pick up sound, too. Honestly, work here as long as I have, and you know the tips and tricks of moving around this place like a ghost. You know there are passages without cameras? Old utility shafts wide enough to fit people, but unused since the building was opened fifteen years ago?"

The woman gasped. "You're kidding."

"Nope," the man replied. "Nothing in there except dust and air. Could be a great place to play hide-and-seek."

"Can't be easy to climb," the woman speculated.

"Nope," the man replied. "Not easy at all."

"How come I've never seen them?" the woman asked.

Dick had to make a decision and fast. They were right below him. Any movement would draw attention, but what was the right way to go?

He was about to take a step on the stairs and hurry upward when the door below opened, and the pair disappeared through it. Their voices trailed away as they presumably went to collect more linens to wash. Dick looked around the stairwell, imagining a hidden maze of chambers hidden behind the walls, then carried on upstairs.

He found Apartment Eighty-Seven without any further incident. After poking his head into the landing outside the three penthouse suites, Dick froze the CCTV circuits and walked up to the door. He pressed an ear against the rich mahogany surface and listened for anyone moving around inside. He hoped that Sadie Turnberry would be fast asleep.

But evil doesn't sleep, does it?

His heart thumped with excited apprehension. Convinced that no one was moving around inside, he glanced at the ceiling and found a roof panel that led to the air vents. A nearby pedestal held a vase, and Dick carefully placed the container on the floor before using the pedestal as a step to ease off the ventilation panel and creep inside.

There was some noise—more than Dick would have liked— but he moved quickly. This wasn't his first time exploiting a large building's ventilation system. When he was up, he clicked the panel back into place, and silently cursed that he couldn't put the vase back. He hoped the CCTV circuit freeze would last long enough that security wouldn't pick up this anomaly.

Dick shuffled forward on his elbows, rolling one arm in front of the other as he positioned himself above Apartment 87. He encountered air filter grates and slats every fifteen feet or so, and gained an overview of the apartment through them.

The lounge was enormous, with plush armchairs and couches all positioned around a TV set that wouldn't have looked out of place in a cinema. A kitchenette took up a quarter of the space, and still had room for an island counter with a set of gleaming utensils—including, Dick noticed, a pristine kitchen knife set.

Dick scanned the area and was pleased to discover that it was empty. Before he allowed himself inside, he drew his cell from his pocket, then fished for one of Ringo's devices.

This device he pointed into the room. He pressed a series of buttons on the side panel and opened an application on his phone. The screen flickered, and a replica of the room slowly appeared on it. Another few seconds and a series of red dots appeared in specific locations across the digital image. Some concentrated around the doorway, with others posted at intervals across the walls.

A few more seconds and some of the dots were connected by thin red lines, indicating the places where the invisible lasers were registered.

Sophisticated setup. I wouldn't expect anything less.

Exercising caution, he opened the panel and lowered himself into the room. The vent clicked gently, but as Dick's feet touched the floor's soft carpet, he ducked out of sight behind the couch and held his breath. Eyes fixed on his phone, he took note of the lasers on either side of him and positioned himself below them both. He crawled under another, then stood to his full height in front of the large glass window that paneled one side of the room and looked out into the city.

It was a shame that the fog blocked most of the view. In any other city, being up this high would grant astounding vistas, perhaps with enough vantage to make out the mountains and jungle beyond. As it was, Dick could barely make out the buildings across the street, the lights in the rooms like milky eyes seen in the darkness of a cave.

Dick turned his attention to the apartment and wondered where to begin his search. He decided to check each of the rooms off from the lounge to ensure no one was here. It never hurt to be too careful. Before he turned to the nearest door, he took a third device from his pocket and cupped it in his hand. It was round and rolled easily enough along the floor until it stopped by the front door. If anyone entered the apartment when he wasn't looking, he'd know about it.

Unless they, too, used the vents.

Dick drew a pair of latex gloves from his pocket, reluctant to leave any fingerprints, and looked around the apartment.

The first room Dick searched was a bathroom. There was nothing extraordinary about it, aside from the fact that there were no toiletries to be seen. No soaps, no shampoos, no toothbrushes. The room was empty.

Dick examined a second room and found only a utility closet.

When he came to the third room after ducking under a nearby laser by twisting his back so much that it clicked loudly, he was certain there was something wrong.

What should have been a bedroom was bare. There was no bed, no closet, nothing. There was only wooden flooring, bare walls, and a single note left in the center of the space.

Dick held up his phone and pointed the scanning device into the room to ensure no hidden traps or cameras awaited. A single window let in a glow of yellow light from the adjacent building, which enabled him to see. The device showed no additional technology. Only a faint grey rectangular shape shadowed against the wall.

Dick moved to the shadow and knocked on the wall. It gave a hollow knock back, but whatever was on the other side couldn't have been digital, of that he was sure.

Satisfied, Dick crossed the room and picked up the note. It was cut into a perfect square with neat handwriting across the front. Its message was simple and clear.

"Better luck next time. DL."

Dick let his eyes play over the note half a dozen times before he folded the paper and stuck it in his pocket.

He chewed his lip while debating what to make of it all. He had expected that whoever had sent messages to the Guardian would have some way to track Dick, but he hoped that Valentina's magic in securing an address would have given him a chance to get ahead of the enemy.

Whoever the hell the enemy is. All of this for a goddamn locket.

Dick stood by the window and lit a cigarette. The city was calm, at peace. He opened the window to allow some room to expel his smoke. Even if the apartment was empty, he had enough decorum not to stink the place out. He tried to see the street below, but it was lost in the fog.

DL, Dick thought, re-reading the note in his mind. *DL...*

The only thing he knew of any kind of "DL" was as a shorthand to the word "Download." But what could that mean in this situation? He was certain that whoever was at the heart of this was tracking him in some fashion. Perhaps they were giving him a clue. They "downloaded" something of his which had given away his position. Only one person besides Dick knew the address of this apartment.

Could it be Valentina? Dick imagined having to go toe-to-toe against the mercenary. He envisioned a situation that pitted them against each other, but it was difficult. Despite the nature of Valentina's work, she couldn't have set this up. Why would she bother sending him to break into a luxury apartment to find an empty room and a note?

He smirked and glanced over his shoulder. "If you're in here, make yourself known. I may have time for a quickie if you ask nicely enough."

No response came. He hadn't expected one.

That only left one option. Someone had hacked into his cell. He drew the phone from his pocket and unlocked the screen. Ringo was right. With the advancements of technology, everything could be hacked or taken out these days. It wasn't beyond the realm of possibility that a cellphone could be wirelessly compromised, no matter how careful its operator.

Dick dangled his phone out the window and let it fall. He waited a few seconds, wanting to hear the satisfying sound of it smashing against the curb, but the fog stole it from him.

Dick plunged both hands into his pockets as he allowed himself some time to think. A moment later, a piercing siren wailed in the lounge.

CHAPTER SIXTEEN

Dick cast a longing look out the window before moving to the doorway. He pressed his back against the wall and listened for the intruders.

"What the fuck!" a gruff voice called. "What the hell is that?"

Dick imagined the owner of the voice scrabbling around for his shrieking device. Ringo had done well. Not only did it alert anyone when it was disturbed, but now the motors within it would have kicked into action, and the ball would be speeding around the lounge like a Roomba on steroids.

Dick eased the door open and peered across the gloom. There were three people silhouetted by the hallway light pouring into the room.

"Jesus, shut that thing up!" another voice added. "She said this place would be empty."

"It's only the laser alarms. Punch in the code," the first person grunted.

The other retorted, "What do you think I'm doing?"

After a few seconds of keypad bashing, they switched on the lights. Dick ducked away, but not before he glimpsed two men and one woman who all appeared as though they'd come back from a night at the opera. The men wore tuxedos, and the woman was in a shimmering red ballgown.

Dick edged the door closed as something bounced into the wood. The shrieking grew to an impossible volume as the alarm rebounded and headed back into the room.

"What the hell is that thing?" the woman shouted.

"Get it!" another commanded.

The trio scrambled around the room while chasing the orb-shaped device. Dick took the opportunity to reassess his way out of here. It would be impossible by now to head out into the room and sneak by the others. He *could* take them on all at once, but he still had the bruises from his last scrap with enemies and decided to use that option as a backup if he had no other choice.

He looked around the room and remembered the hollow wall. He ran over and knocked on the surface with his knuckles, the sound masked by the shrieking and shouting in the other room. "Here goes nothing," he grunted as he curled his fingers into a fist and punched.

His hand met some resistance, then passed through to emptiness. He ripped his fist back through the plasterboard hidden behind the wallpaper, then punched again. After the third hole, he kicked through the wall and tore out a path large enough for him to pass.

Dick smirked. "Son of a bitch. Those cleaners were right."

There was a passageway beyond, its edges constructed from metal like the vents, but the space large enough to walk single-file. Dick headed inside to where the darkness was all-consuming and wished he'd held onto his phone so he'd have a light source.

The shouting in the other room reached a crescendo as something knocked over and broke. Someone shouted, "Got you!" Then everything went silent.

Dick threw caution to the wind and walked into the darkness, leading with his toes and feeling with his fingers. The tunnel ran twenty feet before coming to a sharp bend to the left.

"What the fuck?" The woman's voice came from the tunnel entrance. Dick spun and could make out their shapes as the three entered the bedroom.

Dick froze. Any movement would magnify against the metal.

The three were so disheveled and disoriented that at first, they didn't notice the large hole torn into the wall. They scratched their heads and examined the metal ball in disbelief.

"What the fuck is this?" a man with a thick beard asked. His shoulders were broad, his height enough to tower over the others. "I've never seen anything like this before."

"Who cares," the other man replied while drawing something from his pocket. Dick made out the small pot of ink and a single syringe. "Let's get down to brass tacks. She said this space was safe, right?"

It was then the woman noticed the hole in the wall. "Not as safe as we figured." She moved closer and peered into the darkness. At one point she looked straight into Dick's eyes, but if she saw him situated where he was in the gloom, she paid no notice. "Where d'ya think this leads?"

The closer they got and the more they spoke, Dick could hear the slurring in their words. The trio might dress like the upper-class, but they sure didn't act like it. Judging by the dark veins painting their arms, they had undoubtedly indulged in a little ink, and the dark viscous drug coursed through their systems.

The bearded man came closer to the hole, a goofy smile on his face. He cupped his hands and shouted, "Hello!"

The echo came back to greet him. "Hello! Hello…Hell…"

He chuckled. The other man repeated, "Hello!"

Dick moved his hands to his ears. Inside the metal tunnel, the sound was deafening. When the woman cupped her hands and did the same, Dick waited for the echo to fade before calling back, "Hello, there."

Their faces fell as their eyes widened. They turned to each

other as if they were each hallucinating before the bearded man asked again, "Hello?"

Dick remained quiet.

The woman swallowed. "You heard that, didn't you?"

"Yeah," the bearded man replied. "Something's playing tricks on us."

"You think it's a monster?" the other man asked.

The woman slapped his arm. "Don't be fucking stupid. No such thing as monsters."

"Well, it's something in there, isn't it?" The bearded man took a tentative step forward, then reached into his tuxedo jacket and pulled out a small pistol. He aimed it into the darkness. "Who the fuck is there?"

Dick moved his hand into his pocket and withdrew a device that Ringo hadn't given him. This one was the size and shape of a AA battery. Dick screwed a cap on the top, then rolled it toward the three. As it came into sight, small reams of smoke poured from the top.

The woman moved forward and picked up the device by pinching it between her forefinger and thumb. She brought it close to her face as more smoke kicked out from inside.

Idiot. She must be so jacked up on ink that she's in a fairy world.

Dick put his hands over his ears as the bearded man managed, "What the—"

A flash and an explosion gave Dick the chance to run. While the room disappeared in smoke, he hurtled through the dark tunnels, feet clanging loudly around him. He felt his way as best he could, but after thirty feet, the floor disappeared, and he fell.

The sensation was brief since his instincts kicked in and helped him land in a crouch. He blindly felt with his hands and pushed onward, finding himself in another tunnel the same size as the first.

If there are many more of these gaps leading to the lower floors, I'll either have the fastest escape on foot, or I'm going to knock myself unconscious and die in here.

The trio's shouts traveled down the tunnel and added to the din. Dick wasn't sure if they were following him, but he didn't want to take that chance. Throwing a little more caution to the wind, he sped up although he checked each step before he took it and found more holes where he eased to their edges before hanging from his fingertips and allowing himself to drop gently to the next level.

Darkness consumed him. After five minutes of this, he lost all sense of direction. The voices became whispers, and although he could make out their footsteps coming from the tunnel opening, it didn't sound like they were keen to follow him into the unknown.

After the sixth drop, Dick stopped and gathered his breath. There was an aftertaste in the back of this throat, and he had a sudden craving for a cigarette. He remembered he had his lighter in his pocket and clicked the ignition wheel. The tunnel lit in the flickering glow of the flame and illuminated his way ahead.

Not that it helped his internal compass. The tunnel stretched before and behind him in either direction. The only advantage he now had was that he could see the holes in advance. They dotted the tunnel at thirty-foot intervals. He navigated his way onward, trying to keep an internal count of how many floors he had descended.

As Dick walked through the tunnels, he wondered why the apartment building's owners had blocked them all up in the end. It seemed like a waste of space to have all of this property and not use it. There had to be a structural component or a hazard that blocked the whole thing up. If that were the case, it meant Dick could be inhaling something he shouldn't, or treading somewhere he shouldn't be.

Too late to worry about that. Find the exit, deal with the conse-quences later.

He could make out the distant chatter of people through the walls, accompanied by the wailing sirens of the AJS. He assumed he was near the reception area now, and hoped that the AJS sirens weren't intended for him.

Who are you kidding? You set off an explosion outside a private room in an upscale complex. Of course, they're here for you.

"Shit," Dick grumbled when he reached a final tunnel in which there were no more holes in the floor. He walked the length of it while hitting four corners, which all turned in the same direction and presumably marked the building's border, then stopped.

There was no exit.

"Damn. What to do?" Dick tapped on either side of the walls as he worked his way around the perimeter once more. He looked like a child playing airplane in slow motion as he listened for any kind of hollow that could lead to a possible way out.

At last, he found a single location that sounded different from the metallic ring of the rest. Here, he heard a dull thud as though he were knocking on brick. Guided by his lighter, he found a metal panel with corners rusted and curling from time and neglect. He grabbed one with his fingertips and peeled it back. The thin edges cut in and caused a few of them to bleed.

Dick gritted his teeth. He made out an increased volume of footsteps somewhere in the tunnels. He was sure he was alone for a while, but if the AJS were here, that meant they'd likely be making their way into the tunnels, too.

And they'd probably have flashlights.

"Come on, Dick," he encouraged as the metal ripped off its ancient screws and clattered to the floor. Large gray breeze blocks lay behind it. Dick sighed.

Only one way to go. He drew out a small disc from his pocket, pressed it against the brick until the adhesive strips stuck, then tapped a combination of buttons on either side.

A red number ten appeared in the center and began counting

down. Dick ran as far as he could while counting in his head to match the sequence. When he reached zero, he closed his eyes, pressed his hands to his ears, and crouched. The explosion sounded and sent a bright burst of light around the corner.

Dick waited a few seconds before heading back to the bomb site. It was a small detonation, only enough to blow a hole large enough to step through. He trod past the rubble and was pleased to discover that he was now in the underground car park.

"Thank God for small miracles." Dick strolled to the nearest vehicle. It was a Tesla with blacked-out windows and almost immaculate paintwork. A few scratches had appeared from the force of the explosion.

Dick moved to the driver's side and fished out a small, thin rod from his jacket. He eased it into the gap between the window and the car's bodywork and jimmied it until he heard an audible click.

He tested the handle. The door opened. He climbed inside.

Once in the driver's seat, he removed a panel near the steering wheel and fiddled with the wiring. A moment later, the car kicked into gear.

He grinned and massaged the steering wheel with both hands. *All cars are the goddamn same.* The headlights turned on, the engine rumbled, and Dick pressed his foot on the gas.

Outside the building was a jumble of flashing lights and AJS vehicles. Dick kept his head low, which was unnecessary since the tinted windows would prevent anyone from seeing him, and crept out of the parking lot. He turned right, managed to get past a small queue of cars heading in the opposite direction that had been stopped by the AJS, and with a final glance in his rearview mirror, made his escape from the apartment complex.

CHAPTER SEVENTEEN

Dick ditched the car a few blocks from the scene and walked the rest of the way home.

The night was calm once the wailing sirens faded into the distance. There was a slight chill in the air, but it hardly affected him through his thick coat and turned-up collar. He buried his hands deep in his pockets, a cigarette hanging haphazardly from between his lips, and fingered the note that the suspect had left in the room.

Someone was playing him, and if there was one thing that boiled his blood more than the unfair treatment of good people, it was someone pulling his strings. He thought back to the trail, pissed that he had gone from two leads to only one. He had hoped that he could wrap this damn thing up, catch the suspect in the act, recover the pendant, and hand it over to Santana when he saw her next—whenever that would be. But whoever was at the helm of this was sneaky, and they had clearly done their homework.

On the way back home, Dick stopped in one of his favorite haunts, a seedy bar located on the block corner that went by the name of The Trophy Hunter. The place was small and stank of smoke, although there was no visible haze in the air. Discharged firearms hung on the walls alongside the taxidermy heads of creatures that had been hunted in the forest, their beady black eyes unblinking and full of terror.

Dick thought Santana might like a place like this. Then again, it might be her worst nightmare.

Dick sat at the bar and ordered a double Cedar Ridge whiskey. His shoulders hunched, and the stink of explosives, dust, and metal tainted his skin. He scratched his face and figured he needed a shave soon since his skin was growing itchy.

Joe Statton, the only barman in sight, finished serving a customer before returning to a spot in front of Dick. He grabbed a murky glass and lazily wiped it with a cloth. "Tough night?"

Dick sipped his whiskey. "No tougher than usual."

Joe chuckled and walked over to a waiting customer. While Dick didn't make a habit of sharing the intricacies of his business, Joe had seen him in here often enough over the past eight years to know something of what he did. He knew that Dick was a private investigator, and he knew that Dick liked whiskey. That was all a man like him needed to know.

"Tell me, Joe," Dick started when Joe had finished and returned to his cleaning duties. "You live a simple life here, right? You serve fuckers, close up shop, then open again. Ain't that about the truth of it?"

Joe chewed his lip and leaned back against the counter. "I've never thought about it like that, but I suppose it is. Only if you look at it from that angle, though."

Dick waited for him to continue.

"Way I see it," Joe processed, "each day is different in its own right. I never know who's going to come through that door, I never know who's going to order what, I never know who's going to start a fight and destroy half of my property."

He gave Dick an accusing look.

"One time," Dick defended. "Three years ago. And, once again, that prick was asking for it. Who pulls a pistol on a man enjoying a quiet night with a glass of scotch?"

"You were eyeing his girl." Joe held up a finger to a waiting customer and smiled.

Dick laughed. "It's a compliment. Shouldn't have arm candy and expect others not to want to taste with their eyes." He sipped his drink. "Still, I appreciate you giving me another chance. You're the only barman who's ever given me that pleasure without the whole establishment changing managers."

Dick waited while Joe served the customer. Drink orders were simple at The Trophy Hunter. There were no cocktails, no fanfare with the liquor. Beer, whiskey, or cider were the extent of it. A spirit mixed with soda was ordered on rare occasions, which was the limit of Joe's cocktail skills.

"Why are you asking about simplicity?" Joe resumed his position across from Dick and cracked the cap off a beer. "You regretting your position? After the easy life in Atlantica?"

Dick gave a thoughtful nod. "Easy doesn't exist here. You want easy, you go to the Bahamas or retire in Cornwall. If I wanted easy, this isn't where I'd settle."

Joe glanced at the door where two patrons were leaving. "Then what's the problem?"

Dick scratched his head and sat up straight. "I'm not sure. In my line of work, it's easy to overcomplicate things. You're fed a series of clues, and you follow the trail, but you find a smattering of red herrings along the way. Each one looks like a possible lead, and it's impossible to follow them all. I've found that often it's the simplest things you miss that lead to the greatest finds."

Joe chuckled. "You're stuck?"

Dick met his gaze. "I'm in the process."

Joe drew a deep breath, unsure of what to say for a moment. "Dick, I'm not going to pretend I know anything about your world, but the one thing I will say is this. Sometimes all you need to do is flip your perspective. Put aside what you know, and eventually, something will click into place. You should know that better than anybody."

A customer called Joe's attention. He waited a moment while staring at Dick. Dick tipped his whiskey to Joe. "Go. Customers wait for no man."

Dick emerged from The Trophy Hunter sufficiently tipsy at some time after midnight. His apartment was only a block away, and before he knew it, he was sitting on his couch in the dark, a glass of bourbon in hand.

He pressed the glass to his forehead and stared into the dark while letting the cogs of his brain turn. He always thought best in the quiet, his body coursing with an unhealthy mix of alcohol and blood. He closed his eyes, and in the darkness, he saw a flashing image of Valentina sitting on the coffee table in front of him. One minute she was there, the next she was gone.

Frustrated, Dick stood and paced around the room. His jacket lay discarded on the couch, and his unbuttoned shirt allowed the cool night air leaking through the window to caress his skin. Sadie Turnberry had been a forced dead end, but he still had one train of investigation he could ride. Grunch had spoken of Erik Burgess' apartment. He said that there could be something there.

What does that little punk know? Dick was convinced the convict still hadn't given him all the answers.

Without thinking, Dick reached for his cell phone in his jacket pockets. After a minute of turning up nothing, he remembered he had dropped it from the upper floors of the luxury apartment complex.

How the hell was he supposed to contact Santana now? He needed an address, and his only options were to track down the jungle-raider or pull on his AJS contacts to find out the crime scene's location.

He debated calling the AJS precinct and asking for Terra Kris, but he knew it would be useless. The murder had happened in Erik's apartment. There would be no casework on that one. The closest Dick could get to any identifiable information would be through the city registry or the goddamn morgue.

Dick wandered over to his computer and opened his browser. He opened the Satiata Cash site and perused his accounts. Thanks to Santana's advance, they looked pretty healthy. Add to that his winnings from his last few poker games, and he wouldn't need to do any work for a good few months after this was all over.

Not that he'd sit still in a city that constantly spewed out problems to solve.

Dick clicked on the transaction that Santana had sent him and read the information. He gleaned a few account numbers and a reference line from the content on the screen. He had hoped there might be more, but this one would take a little more deep-diving.

He leaned back in his chair and drank his bourbon. The edges of his vision were blurry, and if it hadn't had been for his nap in the car earlier that day, he might fall asleep where he sat. Instead, he scrolled over to an app on the bottom of the screen and double-clicked. "EnkryptoVid" appeared on the screen, and Dick searched through his contacts. From what he knew about the platform, it was highly unlikely that his activities through this one would be hacked.

Still, you never know.

Dick decided to make his call brief.

"JC," a modulated, unrecognizable voice greeted through the monitor. A blank avatar filled the screen with no other information provided.

"I need a job done," Dick explained.

"Shoot." No bullshit, to-the-point.

Dick told them what he wanted. The voice replied, "Consider it done."

"How long do you need?" Dick asked although the line had gone dead.

Dick turned in his chair and looked out the window. He looked tired and careworn in the reflection. He was still young, relatively speaking, but Atlantican life took its toll.

He swirled the bourbon in his glass, then drained the contents. When it was gone, he headed to his bedroom. He stripped to his boxer briefs, lay on top of his duvet, and stared at the ceiling as he let his mind process it all. Although he firmly believed that sleep wouldn't come, the world went dark before long, and Dick drifted into slumber.

CHAPTER EIGHTEEN

Pounding on the door replaced Dick's alarm.

He wasn't used to being woken up. Most of his Atlantican life he had lived and slept on his schedule, after learning that the best alarm clock he could find was his internal system. When the pounding came, Dick was deep in sleep and unsure where the sound came from. For a moment, he wondered if it was his head until he opened his eyes and realized where he was, and a voice followed the banging.

Dick opened the door through squinting eyes. Terra stood with her hands on her hips, kitted in her steel-blue AJS uniform. It was a sleek, form-fitting build with hexagonal structures woven into the fabric to make it look like a honeycomb. Dick knew the outfit served a greater purpose than a decorative item —although he couldn't help but notice it amplified Terra's gentle curves. The uniform had the latest in nanotechnological defenses to deflect bullets and keep the wearer free from harm in many extreme circumstances.

"Are you going to invite me in?" Terra demanded with an edge to her voice. Her eyes darted awkwardly to Dick's boxers.

Dick looked past the AJS officer and into the hallway,

checking that no one else had been alerted by Terra's cacophony and had decided to stick their nosy beaks out their doorways.

Dick chuckled. "Are you a vampire?"

"I'm polite," Terra replied, a waiting expression on her face.

Dick thought of pointing out that banging relentlessly on someone's door was anything but polite, but thought better. "Why? Are we changing the terms of our arrangement?"

A look of disgust crossed her features. "I'd rather stick a claymore up there and count to ten."

"That's an image." Dick grinned.

Terra rolled her eyes and barged past Dick.

Dick called after her, "I guess that politeness went out the window?" He closed the door and muttered, "Technically not illegal, though." He turned and found Terra by the coffee table. "I suppose you have a good reason for your visit?"

Terra dipped her hand into a satchel by her hip and tossed the contents onto the table. Small fragments of a cell phone littered the glass surface.

"Rude," Dick commented. "You're cleaning that up."

Terra shook her head in disbelief. "Unbelievable. You spend the evening causing chaos in one of Atlantica's most high-profile spots, and yet I'm the one who's always cleaning up after your mess."

Dick raised his hands. "Now, always is an exaggeration. Besides, that's not mine."

Dick's eyes darted toward the cell phone, instantly recognizing a few of the fragments.

"Don't bullshit me, Dick." Terra shook her head before tossing a piece of gum into her mouth. "I've just come off a twelve-hour shift, and in an investigation exploring why the upper floor of the Hanton Apartments spontaneously exploded, I found this little piece of evidence in the streets below. You know how I know that it's yours?"

John remained stoic. "Fingerprints."

"Exactly," Terra replied. "All over the fucker."

"It's a phone," Dick commented. "Of course, they are."

Dick's computer pinged behind them. Terra turned as the screen flashed with a message. When she turned back, she ran her fingers through her hair, her eyebrow cocked. "It's a phone that's linked to the crime scene. You need to be more careful."

Dick turned from Terra and selected a fresh tumbler. He poured a measure of bourbon and downed it in one before refilling it. "You're talking like I leave a trail all across Atlantica. You know I'm a private investigator. It's my duty to be careful and leave no tracks where I tread. Sometimes I slip up." He pointed at the cell. "But that thing would never connect me to the crime scene. It may arouse suspicion, possibly pull some questions, but I'd have a super tight alibi, and besides, the explosion was in residential quarters. The AJS has no jurisdiction."

"The AJS got jurisdiction the moment residents reported the explosion, and you opened a hole into the building's public spaces," Terra explained. "That hidden relic of a tunnel remains a public concern. Now the AJS is searching for a terrorist dealing in small explosives."

Dick smirked. "Sounds exciting."

Terra scoffed. "A simple thank you would go a long way."

Dick nodded. "You're right. I'm sure it would."

Terra waited expectantly, but Dick gave her nothing. She growled and shook her head. "I don't know why I expected anything else." She barged past Dick and caught him on the shoulder.

Dick rolled his eyes. "Terra, wait."

"What?" Terra whirled, face like thunder. "I've done you a favor. Now I'm going back home to get some well-deserved rest."

"You want to get a drink sometime?" Dick asked in earnest.

Terra was knocked back. "Me and you? A drink?"

"Yeah. Figure it might help remove some of our sexual tension." Dirk smirked.

Terra shook her head. "It's called friction. We're oil and water, Dick. We don't mix. Besides, I'm meeting someone else for drinks tonight. An old school friend. I believe you know her."

Dick tilted his head. "Who?"

"Santana Sokolov," Terra replied dryly. "Isn't that what your little hack machine is giving you information on?"

Dick looked over his shoulder at the computer. "You're a quick reader."

"When are you going to learn? I'm the best." It was Terra's turn to grin. "What do you need her for, Dick? I hope you're not pulling her into your bullshit."

Dick shrugged. "I'm afraid I'm not at liberty to discuss that information." He paused as a thought crossed his mind. "I don't suppose you have her phone number, do you?"

Terra leaned against the door jamb. "If you two are in contact, shouldn't you already have it?"

Dick sipped his drink. "I can either regain it legitimately from you or use my 'hack machine.' If anything, I'd rather go by the book."

"Makes a change," Terra quipped.

"I'm a changed man," Dick replied.

Terra laughed, a genuine belly laugh. An old woman stuck her head out from a nearby apartment and frowned at the pair before disappearing back inside her room.

"Here." Terra grabbed Dick's arm and scribbled the number on his forearm.

"Thanks." He examined his skin. "That's twice you've saved me in twenty-four hours. If you're not careful, you'll start making a habit of it."

Terra gave Dick a soft smile, then yawned. "You should be careful out there, Dick. Remember, I can't always be there to help you."

"And I, you." Dick watched Terra as she walked down the hallway, eyes lingering on the curves of her ass. His hand unconsciously moved to his and felt the scar from the bullet wound she had given him.

Dick sat in his sedan and took his new cell phone from its packaging. The clerk had told him that it was the latest model, complete with the most up-to-date anti-hacking technology on the market.

Dick had cocked an eyebrow. "I should hope so, at that price."

It was nothing spectacular to look at. Cell phones had long ago grown stagnant in their design. They were all the same now. The only difference was the GPU's intricacies, or the RAM, or whatever the metal and plastic casing housed inside.

Dick fired up the cell, bypassed the introduction sequences, and punched in Santana's number. It rang for at least a minute before she finally picked up, a little breathless. "Who's this?"

"Dick," he replied.

There was a moment of quiet.

"John Chambers," he reiterated.

Santana chuckled. "Oh, hey John. Now's not the best time."

"I'll keep it quick," Dick stated. "You're in the city later, aren't you? Meeting an old friend. How about we catch up before your dinner date? I need some info."

"How do you know my calendar?" Santana asked. "Are you spying on *me*?"

"Not yet," Dick replied. "The trail hasn't pulled you in as a possible suspect, but don't be surprised if that becomes an option. Let's just say we run in similar circles. Anyway, are you in?"

Santana made a considering "umm," before adding, "I don't know that I'll have time beforehand. Can we do after?"

"Only if you answer me a question first," Dick replied. "Can you give me the address for Erik Burgess? I need to do some further exploration of his place."

Something growled on Santana's side of the line. Scuffling sounded before Santana finally answered. "Sure." She gave him the address. "Although I've already snooped around and there's nothing there of note. The place is clean. I'm not sure what you hope to find."

To be honest, Dick wasn't sure either. "No offense, Miss Sokolov, but you've not been in this game as long as I have. You deal with jungle monsters, I'll take the city."

"Sounds like a plan," Santana agreed.

They secured a place to meet later that evening before Dick thanked Santana and ended the call. He looked up the GPS coordinates for Erik's apartment building on his new cell, then took off into the city.

Traffic was mild, with Dick only gripping the wheel in frustration a few times before he pulled up to Erik's old apartment. It was in the southern East Side, with the Atlantican commercial docks a mile away. On another island, the ocean views might be fantastic from the upper floors, but from where Dick stood, you couldn't make out the top of the white and gold-painted building. Its peak was lost in the fog, almost as though it had somehow pierced the sky.

Dick made his way to the reception counter. This time, he didn't need to operate in secrecy, so he flashed his badge at the reception clerk and requested access to the room.

Dick knew it was a fifty-fifty gamble whether or not he'd be allowed in. On this occasion, the clerk was in a good mood. He told Dick that another resident would move in a few days from now, and the apartment was due to be cleaned later that afternoon.

Dick thanked his lucky stars he got here when he did.

Erik's apartment was on the eighth floor. Dick unlocked the door and headed inside the modest residency. A small corridor opened into a lounge area, with a separate kitchen and bedroom off either side. A television stand occupied one side of the room, its surface covered in dust aside from a small square where a TV used to be.

Dick wouldn't be surprised if someone from the hotel's staff had looted the expensive items and sold them to the highest bidder.

From surface appearances, it was as though nothing had happened here. Dick picked up framed photographs of a middle-aged blond man standing with various family and friends as he examined the room. Erik looked like a friendly enough guy. How did he get caught up in something that got him murdered in his home?

How does anybody? Yet it's the second-highest cause of death in Atlantica.

Dick growled, his frustration at the twisted policies and rules an ever-present poison in his gut.

Exploring everything from the kitchen counters to the lounge carpet, Dick fixed his beady eye on the job. It wasn't until he entered the master bedroom that he saw where the murder had taken place.

"Clean up in aisle two," he muttered.

Sheets were thrown to the side of the bed. The closet door hung off its hinges. Although there was no sign of blood, there had been a struggle. Ornaments were smashed on the floor, and the lampshade was at a crooked angle.

Dick stood by the side of the bed and scanned the room, slowly taking it all in piece by piece. The fact that the homicide occurred in the bedroom led almost instantly to the notion that the attacker tried to catch Burgess while asleep. Although the amount of mess made and the angles of smashed things suggested that Erik had caught the attacker in the act.

Which meant that there would be forensic evidence around. No fight or scrap ever ended without hair shed or droplets of blood finding their way somewhere into the room's microfibers.

For the next hour, Dick scrutinized every aspect of the area. He swept across the obvious places before gently easing the sheets aside and looking under the bed to find any clues. Along the way, he collected a dozen samples of varying individual hairs, and in the crevice where the floor met the wall, he found a few droplets of blood.

Dick cut them out with a small pair of scissors and added them to his various samples. When he was certain that he'd examined the entire room, he stood in the doorway and lit a cigarette.

The smoke soothed his throat and helped him think. He wondered if there'd be any CCTV evidence of an intruder, and decided to try his chances with the reception clerk.

"Why, sure. You can have a look," the clerk informed Dick. "But you'll have to make it quick. Security change is at midday, and the afternoon shift aren't often as generous with their time."

A single security guard sat in a room behind reception with his feet on the desk. He was as wide as he was tall, with folds of his skin visible through the buttons which strained to hold themselves closed over his stomach. He had a one-liter drink of soda in one hand, and with the other, he scratched the inside of his ear. "Tell me the date and time, and I'll do what I can." He glanced at the clerk. "You told him we're off-duty soon?"

The clerk nodded.

"Don't worry," Dick reassured him. "This shouldn't take long."

He scrubbed through the CCTV footage at speed, searching for anyone who might come across as suspicious on tape. He checked footage from the lobby, then sped through the images from cameras on the landing of Erik's floor. His eyes kept darting to the clock, conscious of the guard change, and as his obese companion was packing up his things, Dick found it.

On the screen was a man in a baseball cap, the peak hanging

low over his face. He wore a jacket with an upturned collar that hid his features.

The guard looked at him suspiciously. "Hey, he looks like you."

Dick moved a hand to his neatly combed hair. "Don't get any ideas. I'd never wear a baseball cap. Messes up the 'do."

A bell rang. Two guards appeared in the door.

"Didn't realize it was bring a friend to work day," a woman with brawny arms and a low-set brow commented. "If that's the case, I'll get my Mary-Anne to join us for the afternoon. Maybe we could have a picnic."

Dick committed the man's image to memory, noted the strange way he walked, and the large golden studs that decorated his earlobes.

The chubby guard chuckled and picked up his bag. "Ain't nothing like that. This is John Chambers, a private investigator working on Mr. Burgess' homicide case. He's doing some snooping to find out what happened."

Newfound respect crossed the woman's face. She gave an approving look to her colleagues. "About damn time, Mr. Chambers. This mystery's been playing on my mind since we first discovered the body. You know the frustration we have by not being able to investigate people's residential quarters? We offer security to residents, but our boundaries end where theirs begin. Half the shit going on in this building would be considered illegal halfway across the world, but we gotta watch on the sidelines like guests at a zoo marveling at the animals." She shook her head.

"I guess you're not from around here," Dick commented.

"Detroit, Michigan, sir," she replied. "Been in Atlantica two years. Thought of switching back a few times. Go to a place where I can make a real difference."

Dick frowned. "Why don't you?"

The guard let out a soft laugh. She rubbed the tips of her fingers together. "Paper, sir. Cash. I'd never get a paycheck like this on the mainland. People in Atlantica splash the cash, and for me, that works just fine."

She nodded to the monitor where the video was playing a loop of the suspect. "If you need more time, you can have it. I don't think any of us will object to you scrubbing a tiny stain off the moldy counter of this city."

The other guard shook his head while the chubby guard said his goodbyes and slipped out of the room.

John shook his head. "That won't be necessary. I've seen all I need to see for now. Although if possible, I'd love a copy of this part of the tape." He handed over a business card with an email address at the bottom. "Could you send this my way? I have other business to attend to."

The guard examined the card before taking a seat in her colleague's chair. "More murders to examine? Sexual assault? Drugs? Trafficking?"

Dick shook his head and grinned. "A hankering for coffee and some pancakes."

CHAPTER NINETEEN

Dick wiped his sticky lips with a napkin and sat back in the diner booth, content and full.

He had gone through two black coffees and was now on his third. The waiter gave him a judgmental look as he set down his third cup, but Dick ignored him. He had gotten used to the disapproving comments and nods about his behaviors. Gambling, drinking, and smoking were a young man's game, but in Dick's mind, you only stopped being young when you gave it all up.

He sat for a while, watching the diner's patrons and trying to imagine each person's lives. He'd never learned to understand why so-called "normal" people lived in this city. The crime rate was high, the ratio of drug barons and criminal overlords to regular civilians was astonishing, and there were incidents in which the AJS got involved every day. Dick's only logical conclusion was that, despite outward appearances, no one here was actually "normal."

During the day, in a little diner such as this, the illusion was cast. But at night, when the lights were out, and the darkness consumed, the animals ran the zoo.

Dick emerged onto the street a short while later. He dug his hands into his pockets and felt around for the samples he'd taken from the apartment to ensure they were still on his person. Then, since the weather was warm and the milky sun was doing its best to break the fog, he decided to walk to his next destination.

He needed these samples analyzed.

The pharmacy was five blocks away from the diner. It was an innocuous thing that didn't draw the eye. Anyone who didn't know it was there could easily miss it.

A bell rang upon Dick's entry. He crossed straight over to the counter where an irate man shouted profanities at the woman behind it. She was cute, a little plain-Jane maybe, but with her hair pulled back into a tight ponytail and her white lab coat on, her features held a natural beauty even with her face contorted in a mask of fear.

The man pressed his hands to the counter and leaned across. He jabbed a finger in the woman's face. "...give me that shit. I know you have it. You dabble in that shit. Where the fuck do you think it comes from in the first place? Big Pharma makes it, and you dish it down to the little guys. Don't tell me you don't have any. I can tell you're lying, bitch!"

Dick silently moved toward the man. His hair stood at odd angles, and his face was unshaven. He wore a filthy short-sleeved shirt, and red marks decorated his scrawny arms.

Fucking inkers.

The woman turned her eyes to Dick and looked as if she were about to shout something, but he placed a finger over his lips. She swallowed hard and returned her attention to the customer. "I told you, sir. It doesn't work like that. We don't stock that kind of stuff here."

As she finished her sentence, Dick grabbed the man by the arms and slammed his face into the counter. The man yelled in surprised indignation, profanities pouring from his lips. Dick put him in an arm lock and pressed his face down until his cheek squished against the glass surface.

The man looked up at Dick with fierce rage, and a horrible sound came from his nose. He coughed, then coughed up a loogie that he tried to aim at Dick, but it got nowhere near. Instead, it trailed along the counter and hit the cash register, leaving behind a murky brown streak of saliva and phlegm.

Dick checked the clerk. "Are you okay, ma'am?"

"Yes. I think." She sounded breathless and unsure of what had happened. Dick pegged her at around twenty years old.

Dick leaned toward the man. "Let's get you out of here, buddy. Back out with the rest of the trash so you can leave this poor lady alone." He straightened. "Where do you take your garbage?"

The woman pointed at a side door locked by a number pad. She thumbed in the code and allowed him through. The man wriggled in his grasp, but was weak and frail, and could do little against Dick's strength.

He threw him into the alley. The man traveled five feet through the air before landing on a pile of refuse sacks. He scrubbed himself down, then clambered to his feet, eyes ablaze. The woman remained behind the door while Dick held his position. The inker ran for him. Dick punched him in the cheek. The man pivoted, eyes rolling into the back of his head before he landed on the concrete.

Dick cast a pitiful look at him. The veins in his arms weren't black, but they were darker than they should be. "Bless him. Coming down from a high. Any fucker would be desperate to get more of the good stuff."

He scooped the man off the ground and put him in a fireman's carry. When he neared the closest dumpster, he nodded for the woman to open the lid. She came to his side and obeyed, allowing Dick to toss the man inside. He closed the cover and clapped his hands.

The woman scrutinized him. "You speak as if you've had experience with ink. Have you?"

"Nah." Dick popped his back and neck to stretch out the tightness of his muscles after the brief encounter. "None of that for me. My body's a temple."

A temple filled with scotch and nicotine.

The woman gave a short nod. "Well, thank you. You'd be surprised how often that happens."

"I guarantee I wouldn't." Dick gave the woman an expectant look.

"Gillian."

"Dick."

Gillian's eyebrows raised. "Really?"

Dick chuckled. "You can call me John if you like. You're new here, aren't you? What happened to Tony?"

They headed back inside together, Gillian taking extra caution to ensure she securely fastened the locks. "Tony is on vacation. Went somewhere out in the Andes with his wife, so Chuck hired some part-time helpers." She waved. "That's me."

Dick narrowed his eyes. "I hope Chuck informed these part-time helpers about our little arrangement?"

Gillian looked at him blankly.

Dick sighed. "Do the words 'lisinopril for Charlie Porter' mean anything to you?"

Gillian shook her head.

Dick turned his gaze to the security camera located in the corner of the room and cupped his hands to his mouth. "What are you teaching your staff, Chuck? We have a deal, remember?" Dick moved over to a white-painted door at the side of the back room. It looked like a utility closet on the outside, although when Dick knocked his fist against it, he heard someone run up a flight of steps.

The door opened. A man with shorn gray hair and glasses with lenses much larger than they needed to be poked his head out. "Ah, Dick. Always a pleasure." He shooed Gillian away. "A little private business. Back to the counter now, will you?"

Dick gently took her arm and kept her still. "You're leaving a newbie to fend for herself against the inkers and scum of this city? *And* you haven't given her sufficient information on how clients can access your services?"

"Services?" Gillian asked.

"It's nothing," Chuck commented. "Back to the counter, please. Remember, if you're in real trouble, press the red button. There's also mace under the counter."

"But I couldn't *reach* the counter…" Gillian started, but Chuck had dragged Dick through the door and closed it behind him.

Dick followed Chuck down a set of concrete stairs and into an underground room that was so harshly lit by overhead lights that Dick had to shield his eyes until they adjusted. Chuck brought his hand down. "It'll take longer if you do that. Just grin and bear it. You'll get used to it."

"I never do," Dick replied. "You want to tell me what all of that was about?" He thumbed toward the stairs.

Chuck scrambled around the room, his long white lab coat trailing the floor. His eyes darted across to many machines and storage cupboards that, on its surface, many might believe only dealt with creating the prescription meds that kept residents of Atlantica alive and kicking, but Dick knew better.

"You know how it is." Chuck busied himself by stuffing a packet of nondescript meds into a paper bag. "Tony discovered that he had rights and employee benefits and finally decided to take the five years of vacation days that he'd accrued all in one go. Now I'm stuck scrambling to find cover until he's back."

"How many months?" Dick asked.

Chuck peered out from over his glasses. "Three months. Damn European laws influencing the Atlantican council.

Anyway, I'm left trying to do half of the grunt work while he's off gallivanting in the Arctic."

Dick cocked his head. "Gillian said it was the Andes?"

"Who's Gillian?" There was no humor or irony in his expression.

"The girl you hired." Dick scoffed. "Man, things really have fallen to pot. Makes me not want to give you these." He held up the samples he'd found in Burgess' apartment.

Chuck pinched his eyes and gave an exasperated sigh. "Dick, normally I would, but I'm overrun at the minute. What with managing a fleet of youthful female temps more clued up on their statutory rights than I am, dealing with fucking inkers trying to attack my staff, and catching up on customer orders, I'm not in that game right now. I can't take the business."

Dick held up his phone screen to Chuck with a cash figure keyed into his Satiata app. "Chuck…"

Chuck's eyes widened. His face contorted as though he were wrestling with an internal decision before he finally gave in. "Fine! Fine. You speak my language, Dick. What can I say?" He took the samples from Dick's other hand. "What have we here? Blood… Yes, okay. Hair… Standard procedure." He looked back at Dick and examined his hand. "What? No semen this time?"

Dick looked down at his crotch. "Only mine."

Chuck clicked his tongue and pattered over to a large white machine that looked to Dick like a train ticket terminal, only with many more buttons and screens. While he placed the samples in various drawers and compartments, he muttered under his breath. "The shit I do for money. You keep telling yourself you're not going to be led by the blue, but the minute someone flashes the cash, you can't help it, can you Chuck?"

Dick chuckled and tapped a cigarette from the pack. He placed it between his lips as Chuck glanced back, eyes widening with sudden urgency. "What are you doing? You can't light that in here!"

Dick held his hands out in a placating gesture. "Come on, Chuck. You think I don't know that? I'm prepping for the outside. Sometimes my body thanks me for having it in my mouth, you know?"

Chuck's eyes narrowed. "It's a bad habit, Dick."

"So's popping your prescription pills every spare chance you get, dealing in underground mischief, and hacking the AJS' identification databanks." Dick shrugged and made for the door. "Give me a call when the results are in. I have other shit to take care of."

Without another word, Dick made his way upstairs. He paused in the back room and saw Gillian serving a customer through a glass panel in the door. He allowed himself a moment to breathe in her beauty before he opened the back door and made his way into the alley. As Dick passed the dumpster, he lifted a half-dozen trash bags piled up around its sides and set them on the cover, adding further weight to the lid. He imagined the shithead inker inside and laughed to himself as he pictured the dirtbag scrambling to free himself when he eventually woke.

"Let's hope it ain't bin day," Dick muttered as he took off into the city.

CHAPTER TWENTY

Dick picked up his sedan and made his way home.

The results wouldn't come in straight away. Dick didn't understand the full extent of the intricacies of Chuck's work—the way he figured it, the less he knew, the better—but he knew that it would take a couple of hours for Chuck to work his magic.

When he had first arrived in Atlantica, a little over eight years ago, Dick had only known two people. Terra Kris and Doug Nevill.

Doug Nevill had served with Dick in the military when he had first encountered the great nation of Atlantica. Both CID agents, Dick and Doug had been put on a case where they unraveled a plot in which the higher-ups of the Atlantican military were heavily involved. The power and corruption of the situation irked Dick, and he called them out on their bullshit.

After filing the final report, Dick was dismayed to discover that the officers at the center of the controversy remained in their posts, their hands slapped by their superiors. Meanwhile, Dick was excused from the CID and cast out into the big wide world by himself. Doug, who had argued with Dick not to unveil what they had found, remained tight-lipped and employed. If anything, his silence only furthered his career.

With little more than the clothes on his back and a strong desire to purge Atlantica of injustice, Dick relocated and took on his role as a private investigator.

The first year was difficult. It wasn't so much about getting people who were willing to agree to hack, lie, and dig around on his behalf in exchange for cash—those kinds of people were abundant in the city. For Dick, the greatest difficulty was in becoming familiar with the city and *finding* them in the first place.

Building his network of people he could trust was like swimming in a murky lake. It wasn't until he stopped paddling that the dirt and silt settled, and he could see the bottom of the lake to sift out the good ones.

He was still working on the "trust" part.

Chuck had been one of the good ones. Recommended by a fellow PI in the city, Chuck was an enigma to the AJS. He served the country by providing people with the medication they needed to keep their tickers healthy and cholesterol low. He kept a low profile and delivered results, and that was all Dick cared about.

Dick parked outside his building and scanned himself through the door. He climbed the stairs, the beginnings of a headache brewing in his temples. He knew that tug. His body wanted alcohol.

He was about to place his key into the lock when he froze, a prickling sensation at the back of his neck pulling his attention. Had he imagined that gentle knock from inside his apartment, or had it come from elsewhere?

Dick straightened. If life in Atlantica had taught him anything, it was to remain vigilant, err on the side of caution, and trust your instincts. Someone was inside. He could almost smell a change in the atmosphere. He glanced at the key, then drew his pistol with his free hand.

He moved to the wall and pressed his back against it. He stretched and fitted the key, then turned it until the lock clicked. He twisted the handle, then shoved the door wide open.

A volley of bullets flew out the door and found their way into the wall at the top of the stairwell. Dick gritted his teeth, not only pissed that someone was shooting from inside his apartment, but that they had terrible aim, too. Judging by the bullet holes in the wall, had he been standing in the doorframe, they might've clipped his hip, thigh, and shoulder. If anyone was to come for him, he had hoped he'd have some kind of challenge

Fuckers must either be old or high. He cocked his pistol and glanced at his watch, wondering how long he now had until the AJS knocked on his door. *Game on.*

Two people exchanged words inside. Dick tried to catch what they were saying, but couldn't understand their language. He did, however, recognize the guttural tones of Russian.

Jesus... He glanced up although he had no real belief in such a savior.

Dick waited until they'd finished speaking, then called into the room, "I'll give you one chance to come out with your hands up and end this quietly. I don't do second chances. It's one or death. You decide. You made the mistake of entering my quarters, so your life is now in my hands."

A door opened farther down the hall, and an old woman appeared. She poked her head around the corner, beady eyes magnified tenfold by her thick glasses. Dick waved a hand to shoo her away.

Mrs. Harrison. What the fuck are you playing at?

Dick eased his head around the doorjamb as the silence pervaded. The moment he got a decent glance at his apartment, a bullet tore past his cheek. He ducked back against the wall, only this time he shifted farther away. Good thing, too, considering the bullets that tore through the wall a moment later.

"You asked for it." Dick cupped a hand to his mouth. "Security access: John Chambers. Activate."

The sudden wailing scream of an alarm rang out from inside Dick's apartment. Dick hoped that activating the irritating noise would momentarily distract the invaders, and he was right.

He charged inside, finding one Russian down the sight of his pistol. He pulled the trigger, caught the Russian in his hand, and knocked his gun clean across the room. A quick turn toward the second and Dick shot the guy's kneecap, forcing him to the floor.

Dick wasn't expecting the third Russian standing behind his couch, hands clapped to his ears, but he took advantage of the moment to run toward him and use the couch's seat as a stepping stone to propel him upward. One leap and Dick kicked the Russian's chest, using his weight and momentum to knock him to the floor where he lay, winded and groaning.

Russians were tough. Dick had learned that the hard way. The scar on his shoulder was evidence of an encounter with Russian criminals four years ago. The first one, despite the hole in his palm, hunched over and ran for his pistol. As his hands reached for the gun, Dick shot and propelled it out of his grip, then took advantage of the prone Russian's position to fire at his heel bone.

The Russian cried out in agony and folded.

One down.

Dick sensed commotion behind him and whirled in time to find the second Russian pointing the gun at him. He pulled the trigger, although his shaking hands screwed up his questionable aim. The bullet caught Dick an inch or so into the fatty tissue above his hip. He grunted and clutched his hand to his side, using the cloth of his jacket and top to stem the bleeding. He wasted no time returning a shot to the man's face, which sent sprays of blood around his apartment.

Two down.

Dick glanced down at his carpet, expecting to see the Russian he had tackled, but instead found no one there. In the few seconds he had been turning the second Russian's face into an exploding melon, the third Russian had slipped off and now leaned out from around the doorframe of Dick's bedroom.

Dick threw himself backward as three more bullets came at him. He landed on his ass and managed to worm his way behind the kitchenette counter, groaning as the pain flared in his side. Glass smashed, and the scent of sour mash and bourbon filled the apartment.

"You son of a bitch!" Dick cried and peeked around the cabinets to discover that what he feared was true. His whisky collection had taken a hit, and now the liquor flowed freely into the carpet. "You never fuck with a man's liquor stash."

Adrenaline coursed through his body as Dick rose and emptied his clip at the doorway to his bedroom. He aimed for the walls and made out the sound of the Russian falling on the other side. He roared as his finger did the talking, and when the clip was empty, he stood for a moment in the fight's aftermath.

The first Russian clutched his heel with his one good hand, still trying to shuffle toward the gun, his progress painfully slow. Dick hurled his emptied pistol at the Russian and caught him on the side of the head.

The second Russian was dead, his heart stilled and the remains of his face a mess.

Dick still needed to confirm the third Russian was down.

Breathing heavily, Dick closed his front door and stepped past the first Russian. He grabbed the pistol and didn't attempt to be delicate as he trod over him and let his foot catch the Russian's stomach. He edged toward the bedroom, leading with the gun and still exercising caution until he leaned around the jamb and found what he had expected.

The third man lay on Dick's bedroom floor, the weapon a foot from his hand and chest blooming with crimson. Dick waited a few moments before he curtly nodded and left him where he lay. He had more pressing matters at hand.

Dick took a tumbler from the cabinet and found one of the few bottles that had survived the attack. Unfortunately for him, it was one of his least favorites, but at the moment, any drink would do. He liberally poured the Bronze Macaque into the glass until it was almost overflowing. There was no more room for class. He drained the whole thing in one as he sat on the sofa, then pressed the cool glass to his forehead, grunting as a fresh spike of pain caught his hip.

"I'd guess this isn't how you expected this sting to go," Dick declared to the apartment, eyes not gracing the only surviving Russian now hunched a few feet from him. "To tell you the truth, this isn't how I expected my day to go, either. Did you know that there are truly rare breeds of bourbon across the world, unique blends that are highly sought after by collectors of all kinds? Even opening the bottle can be sacrilege to collectors. Some drinks were never made to be drunk. They were created to be cherished, protected, to gather dust and appreciate in value." Dick scoffed. "Crazy, don't you think?"

The Russian glared at him, teeth gritted. He muttered something incoherent.

"That aroma you smell?" Dick continued. "One of those is an 1881 Rogue Sailor. Created specifically for the high-ranking pirates to enjoy out in the Caribbean. Only a dozen were made before the creator was murdered, and the recipe died with him— or so the story goes. I got my hands on that a few years ago, after finishing a job for a client where I saved his daughter and brought her back from the brink of being trafficked by one of the many other scummy fish that swims in this shit-stained pool we call Atlantica."

Finally, he turned his eyes on the Russian. "Do you know how much that bottle would fetch at auction?"

He waited for an answer, but the Russian only continued to stare angrily at him, chest rising and falling rapidly in anger.

Dick chuckled. "Of course not, you Russians are all about vodka, aren't you? Do you even drink whisky where you come from?"

The Russian spat on the floor. "We drink whisky, you racist fuck."

Dick's eyebrows rose. "So you *can* speak English? Good." He set his tumbler down and knelt beside the Russian. "Because I need you to do some talking, and I'm tired of pissing around with translators."

The Russian glanced away, clearly annoyed that he'd let his grasp of English slip.

Dick fixed him with a hard stare. "Who sent you?"

The Russian laughed, although the action caused him to flinch in pain. "Your mother."

Dick lashed out with a punch to his cheek. The Russian's eyes rolled back momentarily before returning, dazed and disgruntled. "You want to try that again?"

"Your father," the Russian managed before receiving another blow from Dick.

"I could do this all night." Dick shook his fist, the pain in his bones belying his words. It was something that they never taught you growing up. Punching others could be fun, but dammit, did it hurt. Maybe they should add that to the public school service announcements. Over the years, Dick had broken several knuckles by simply giving someone what they deserved.

The Russian looked as though he was about to say something, then bit the words back.

Dick pinched his eyes. "Your friends are dead. Both of them. If you don't answer soon, you will be dead. As much as I'm enjoying our chat, you're bleeding on my carpet, which will be a bitch to clean. I can either end your pain quickly or call medical help for you. The choice is yours."

"Dexter Lockhart!" the Russian exclaimed, his eyes widening as pain throbbed through him. He looked Dick in the eye, then shook his head as he grumbled something in his mother tongue before he spoke softly in English. "No... No... Forget that name. It is her. She's the cause of it, truly. She knows all about you, John Chambers. Everywhere you go, she's watching you. You underestimate her, you die. Cut the trail and move onto other things. There are greater problems in Atlantica for you to solve than a tiny bit of gold."

Dick's eyebrows raised. "The pendant?"

The Russian smirked. "You think you are safe. You think you are undetectable. I can confirm for you that she is watching. Always with you, she is watching."

"Who?" Dick sent another punch at the guy's face. "Who!"

The Russian gave a choking laugh. Dick wasn't sure if it was phlegm or blood clotting the man's throat. "Miss Turnberry. But you already knew that, didn't you, Mr. Chambers?"

Dick grew frustrated and turned his attention to the Russian's bloodied heel. "Where can I find Miss Turnberry? The last clue I had led to a dead-fucking-end." He prodded a finger into the wound's exposed tissue, and the man let out a roaring scream of pain. "Well?"

The Russian waved his good hand and relented under the agony. "She's running a game in The Warehouse tonight. Midnight."

"The Warehouse?" Dick muttered, caught off-guard. It was a venue he had heard mention of multiple times during his stay in Atlantica, but he had never managed to find the location. The Warehouse was rumored to be Atlantica's most high-profile gambling ring, a place hidden from view with its location only known to those who played. The circle was tight; the address given only to the players and the staff required to run the game. Should anyone let slip its location, not only would the snitch find themselves riding a first-class seat into Deathsville, but the entire operation would relocate.

"You got an address?" Dick knew what the likely answer would be.

The Russian shook his head; his breathing labored as he drifted toward unconsciousness.

Dick growled. He wasn't about to find himself at another dead end, unable to chase a clue that would lead to the Santana's pendant's eventual discovery. He stuck his finger back into the Russian's heel. "Give me something, asshole. Anything."

The Russian yelped and banged his fist against the floor. "It's somewhere in BonVivant Valley! That's all I know! That's all I know!"

Dick nodded acceptance, then sat on his ass.

The Russian closed his eyes, breath now coming in sudden hitches. Dick had two Russians dead in his apartment. The last thing he needed right now was a third.

Dick rose to his feet and crossed to his medicine cabinet. He tapped out two pills from a bottle of oxycodone and placed them in the Russian's mouth. Where he was going, he needed to avoid feeling the inevitable pain of the trip.

Dick scooped the Russian from the floor and carried him over his shoulder. He entered the hallway, praying to the Almighty that Mrs. Harrison had the common sense not to snoop on him right now. He opened the large drawer of the garbage chute and placed the Russian inside, feet-first.

The Russian slid with little friction, and as the body tumbled down the chute, Dick dialed the emergency services. With any luck, the Russian would find himself waking in the comfort of a nice cozy bed, his wounds tended to, and a deep appreciation for the fact his life had been spared.

Yeah, like that's ever going to happen. The reality was that Dick had set himself up for yet another dickhead in Atlantica who held a grudge. Still, needless death wasn't inside him. Maybe they would hold a grudge, but there was still a sliver of a possibility that they would thank him.

Dick tended to his wounds, cursing at the tear in his jacket and shirt. He spent a few minutes stitching to repair the damage before he downed another measure of Bronze Macaque and headed out the door. On his way to his sedan, he dialed a number and waited for a response.

"Yes?" a woman's voice answered.

"Cleanup in aisle four," Dick responded.

There was a moment's pause. "Again?"

Dick sighed. "An extra ten percent if you don't ask questions."

The line went dead.

As Dick drove away, he glanced up at his apartment, safe in the knowledge that by the time he returned, there would be no sign that anything had happened.

CHAPTER TWENTY-ONE

Dick emerged onto the busy street with a pack of cigarettes and a frown on his face.

His hip hurt. Although the bullet hadn't done any major damage, it was still an inconvenience. He could feel it in the way that one leg overcompensated for the pain as he walked, his body leaning slightly to one side.

He popped a hole in the side of the pack and tapped out a cigarette, then allowed himself a few stolen minutes to wallow in the silky-smooth texture of the smoke creeping down his throat. He knew it was a terrible habit, wasn't even sure he remembered how it had started in the first place, but he had come too far to stop now. While other Atlanticans had their relationships, pets, and family, Dick had cigarettes and alcohol.

It wasn't a pretty family, but he could rely on them whenever he needed comfort.

Dick climbed into his sedan and thumbed through his cell. It was mid-afternoon, which left him some time until he would get the chance to meet Santana. He opened an encrypted message from Chuck that required a voice-activated password Dick had given the man during their first encounter. The file opened to show a video of the disgruntled Chuck speaking into the camera of his cell.

"The results are in," Chuck declared in a tired tone. "According to the AJS databank, you were in the presence of one Sadie Turnberry, and one Erik Burgess."

At least we know for sure that was Erik's real name.

"The hair belonged to Sadie, who is down in the AJS system as a former mercenary. According to the data I could pull—and please, as always, remember that I can only read the information that appears on the screen, I have no clue if it's factually accurate or a decoy—Sadie has been clean for years. She resides at Wellington Park, number one forty-seven. Must be some kind of fancy bitch with a *lot* of dough. If you want more information, she's sixty-three, a Pisces—understandably, given her profile— she's five-foot-seven-inches tall, her parents are Croatian with a little bit of UK bred into her, and her blood type is O rhesus negative."

Chuck removed his glasses and cleaned the lenses with one hand. "I assume that's all you need to do what you do. If you need any further help, please hesitate to ask." A voice called from somewhere above Chuck. He shouted back, "Just a second, please! I've already told you!" He sighed, then absently rubbed his temple. "Duty calls."

The feed shut off.

Dick played the video again and scribbled down the key points on his notepad. If what Chuck said was true, then he could finally be onto something. Sadie Turnberry was real, *and* he had an officially registered address from the AJS databanks.

Still, it could be another red herring.

Dick chewed his lip and debated what the truth could be. He checked his watch and, seeing that he had a few hours to kill, decided to visit Wellington Park.

Dick shut off his phone while he drove, conscious of the Russian's words to him. Dick always had the feeling of being watched, but he had never felt it more acutely than with this investigation.

The names whirled in his head as he drove. DL, Sadie Turnberry—they sounded like a prestigious power couple who ruled one of the many corporations operating in Atlantica. When he arrived at Wellington Park, his suspicions were confirmed.

He had never traveled this far west in Atlantica since he had never had a reason to. The more money you made, the easier it was to cover up your corrupt operations. Most of Dick's cases concentrated in the built-up districts in the heart of Atlantica city, but now he drove down a road where great estates and mansions filled the spaces on either side. The buildings stretched almost fifty meters in width, and Dick could only guess how far in length. He couldn't see past the high white-brick walls and the black and golden gates, woven and twisted with bright flowers and neatly manicured shrubs.

"To have this kind of money..." Dick chuckled and continued his hunt for one forty-seven.

He eventually found the building and drove past far enough to remain out of sight of the inevitable volley of cameras that guarded the property. As he passed, he glimpsed a red-brick path that snaked toward the front of the building and what appeared to be two large stone fountains.

Dick made a U-turn at the end of the street and parked as close as he dared. Knowing how closely Sadie had been watching him when she had led him on a wild goose chase to the luxury apartments, he wondered whether she would be aware of his presence there now.

If she were, she showed no sign.

Dick pulled a pair of binoculars from the glove box and glanced through the lenses, scanning as much as he could see of the property. A large three-story mansion peered out from above the pristine white walls. Its roof was a mash of geometric shapes, with bubbles and corners of cubes carved from glass. To Dick, it looked like something that he would expect from an aviary or some kind of botanical gardens, although at this distance he could neither confirm nor deny the fact.

Covering a large portion of the rest of the building were the tops of exotic trees, and on a couple of occasions, Dick wondered if he had seen the flashing of a brightly-colored bird appear for a moment before disappearing from view.

"Interesting." Dick exited his car and pulled up his collar. He put on a pair of dark sunglasses and fished in his pocket for his scrambler. He found the device without looking, and as he neared the property, he pointed in the direction of the gates and pressed the button.

While he couldn't be certain that the cameras had frozen, their LEDs changed color from green to red. That was a good sign, right?

He strode quickly toward the gate, his intention to walk straight on by without arousing suspicion. He slowed as he passed the gate, and without turning his head, tried to drink in as much as he could see of the property.

His stolen glance confirmed his suspicion. Flanking the main mansion was a series of greenhouses and large, expensive-looking cages. While Dick couldn't see what was inside them, he could chance a guess, having read on the online news channels about the increase in Atlantica's wealthiest ferrying in exotic animals and keeping them as pets. Dick wondered if this were such a situation and what kinds of creatures might be captive inside.

Hopefully, they won't all be trained guard dogs.

Dick walked to the end of the street, then came back down the other side, allowing himself another look through the gates, only this time from farther away. He gleaned no new information, and when he climbed back into his car, his mind had filled with questions.

The clock on the dashboard read a little after 5:00 p.m. Dick thumbed the ignition, spared one last look at the house, and drove back into the city with his stomach rumbling.

Dick ate a healthy portion of porterhouse and eggs, and washed down the impressive plateful with three glasses of whisky, served neat, and a Blue Moon beer.

As he sat alone in the diner, he chipped away at his internal questions while using his cell phone to dig out any information he could on The Warehouse and its operations. At one point he called Jimmy, hoping that the scumbag who had put Dick onto the trail of Jessie Jackson a few days ago might know something that he was missing. Unfortunately, all that he got was a scrambled load of mumbling and the hearty reassurance that if he found out anything, he'd let Dick know.

The diner Dick sat in was three blocks from BonVivant Valley. From where he sat at the glass window, he was in full view of the evening foot traffic, the residents of Atlantica going about their everyday lives, fresh off a day of shopping or crunching the numbers in their corporate towers.

The majority of the civilians' arms were laden with bags filled with their purchases they'd made from the local upper-class stores, with price tags starting somewhere in the quadruple digits.

The whole thing made Dick feel sick.

But not sick enough to put him off a large chunk of apple pie, topped with whipped cream.

When Dick finished, the evening was wearing on. Darkness covered the city, and he made his way across the road toward a bar with flashing neon signs and an illuminated cocktail menu in the window.

Dick had been to places like this before—hipster establishments. He knew that it was unlikely he'd get the drinks he favored.

The place was busy but not full. Dick maneuvered around the crowd and found a spot hidden in the crevice beneath a spiral staircase's smooth wood. He removed his jacket as he watched the clientele and did his best not to feel *so* out of place.

Dick felt thankful that the smoking laws that had overtaken most of the advancing world had yet to be established in Atlantica. For residents who paid a premium to live on the island, the general rule was that you could live your life however you wanted. Sure, some businesses had erred on the side of caution and were offered out as smoke-free zones, but Dick avoided these like the plague. There was something satisfying about sitting in a cloud of haze. It created something of an enigma of the man behind the fog.

Santana finally arrived. She looked good. He had to give her that. Walking into the bar in a pair of combat shorts, hiking boots, and that goddamn whip still fastened to her side. There were a few grubby marks on her arms and legs that suggested she hadn't bothered to make herself civilized before she hit the town with her buddy Terra.

"How was dinner?" Dick rose as Santana caught his eye and came to join him.

She slung her heavy backpack down and took a seat. "Delish, but pricey. I'd heard rumors of the cost of food in this district, but had no idea what I was getting myself into."

Dick raised an eyebrow. "I thought you were a thoroughbred Atlantican."

Santana chuckled. "Even *I* don't know all the secrets. You think a girl like me spends much time in this part of the concrete jungle? I wouldn't last an entire night out here."

"Me neither." Dick pointed to the bar. "Can I get you a drink?"

Santana ordered a grasshopper, not bothering to elaborate when Dick waited for a punchline. After twenty minutes of elbowing patrons out of his way, he reached the front of the bar. A half-dozen gorgeous women and a handful of well-groomed men scurried around, pouring various quantities of brightly-colored liquor into metallic shakers before flinging them around their body in displays that made the crowd "Ooh" and "Aah."

When a young woman with dark hair came to Dick, she leaned across the bar and bent her ear toward him. The music was loud, but Dick made himself heard. He ordered the grasshopper, glad to see that Santana wasn't playing some prank on him, then a few minutes later she presented a neon-green drink and something that she had called a "whisky sour."

Dick didn't have the patience to ask why they served whisky sours, but not straight whisky. He returned to Santana and placed the drink in front of her. "There. I think it's blended with real grasshopper. Might as well be for all the time it took to make the damn thing."

Santana laughed. At least Dick could hear it. Under the stairs, they were far enough away from the speakers that they could talk. "Why are you in such a hurry to drink, John?"

"Call me Dick." Dick took a sip of his whisky sour, winced at its sharpness, then nodded approval. "Not bad."

Santana rolled her eyes. "Give it up. I'm not calling you that. If you want to play into some weird notion that you'd rather be called male genitalia than the name your mother gave you, take it elsewhere. Where I come from, family matters."

"Where I come from, family doesn't exist," Dick quipped. That wasn't necessarily a true statement, but he didn't fancy going down that avenue right now.

Santana must have sensed this effort, because she followed with, "So how goes the investigation? I assume there's still no news on the pendant. I mean, surely that would have been the first thing you'd given me, not this drink." She glanced down at the grasshopper. "Unless this is another weird ploy you put in place to sleep with pretty women?" She narrowed her eyes, but the look wasn't unkind.

"Are you calling yourself a pretty woman?" Dick grinned.

Santana returned a smile. "Your eyes are. Remember, John. This is strictly professional. I know the type of man you are. I've seen it all before. You want to strip back the bedsheets and have a good tumble, find some other bimbo to satisfy your urges. Me and you, it's strictly business."

Dick half-shrugged. In truth, as pretty as Santana was, he would never threaten his professional relationships with the notion of romance or sex, and judging by the look in her eyes, Santana knew that to be true, too. "You can't blame a guy for trying."

Santana sat silently for some time while Dick explained the nuances of his investigation so far. Omitting his helpers' identities, Dick told Santana about his journey, from his interception of Grunch in the alley to the solo raid up the tower of the Russians. He spoke of the wild goose chase that Sadie Turnberry had set him on, and his investigation of Erik Burgess' apartment. When he informed Santana about the Russians waiting in his apartment, her hand moved to her mouth.

"I'm so sorry I got you tied up in all of this." She reached across the table and placed her hand on his. He expected her hands to be soft, but her pads were calloused and tough. *Probably from her adventures in the jungle.*

Dick leaned forward, eyes darting around to ensure that no one else was eavesdropping. "What the hell is the significance behind this pendant, Miss Sokolov?"

Santana shook her head and momentarily turned her eyes down to her lap. "I honestly don't know. It was a gift my mother wanted me to have. That's all I can speak of. The rest of it is all gibberish. The map, the inscriptions, all of it. It's a total mystery to me. I wish I knew more, but I don't."

Over at the bar, a group of twenty-something men gave a

raucous laugh. Dick caught the hungry eye of one staring at the back of Santana's head, clearly debating whether or not to make a move.

"You said your mother passed a while back," Dick stated. "What happened to her?"

"A cave-in," Santana replied. "That's pretty much all I know. My mother was always secretive about her work. I'm sure that even my father didn't know half of what went on in her professional life." A nostalgic smile painted her lips. "She was tough. Vibrant. She was a born leader, and she led the early expeditions across the wilds of this island to discover its secrets. Atlantica has a rich and enigmatic history, as I'm sure you're aware, and if there was one thing that drove my mother to near insanity, it was turning secrets into knowledge."

Santana leaned back and sipped her drink. "The cave-in happened twelve years ago. I was only a girl at the time, navigating my way through the city's education systems while discovering my love for the wilds. My father... Well, he was an archaeologist too, but his work was mostly museum and laboratory research-based. When we first heard the news, it was a tough nugget to take in. My mother was my inspiration, my role model. I wanted only to follow in her footsteps."

"You said your father *was* an archaeologist. Is he..."

Santana let out a soft laugh. "No, he's alive and kicking. A few weeks after my mother's passing, he shipped us off to his Russian homeland. My mother was a thoroughbred Atlantican, but my father felt that a good way to escape the pain and start a new life was to defect and travel miles away from the source. He was right to, in a sense. Russia has some incredible sights to see. Have you ever been?"

Dick shook his head.

"The snow-covered mountains, the night skies, the wildlife." Santana's eyes grew glassy with wonder. "After years of living under this blanket of fog, I never knew how beautiful the night sky could be. Like someone had scattered fireflies across a sheet of swirling purples and blacks."

Dick finished his drink and debated getting another, although he knew that he was only inviting the hungry jackal still staring at Santana to take his chance if he left the table. "Yet you came back."

Santana chuckled. "Yeah. Enough time passed that the wound wasn't so fresh. I realized I missed this place. Russia is great, but the real mystery is here. I can sense it. There's a reason my mother, one of the most inquisitive minds I've ever known, chose to do her research here. I just don't know what it was. Yet."

"Yet?" Dick nudged.

"I've made enough discoveries over the years to know that something happened here, John." Santana's eyes grew wider with excitement. "There are so many places and lost treasures to discover, and it is for these that I returned. I always wanted to work with my mother, but in her absence, I can at least carry on her legacy by picking up where she left off."

"Which was?" Dick asked.

Santana's shoulders softened. "Honestly? I don't know. They never released the cave-in's location. There was no photo evidence, no further information other than the fact it had happened. There was only one survivor, but she passed away a few days after the accident—a delayed reaction to the grief."

Santana fell silent. Dick tried to allow himself a moment to process everything, but his throat was parched. He needed a beverage.

He offered Santana another, and she accepted, asking for another grasshopper. As Dick strode to the bar, the jackal sniffed out his chance and started to break away from the pack. As they brushed shoulders, Dick gripped him by the bicep and pulled their faces closer together. His mouth barely moved as he informed him, "You so much as breathe the same air as her, and you'll have me to deal with, son. You got that?"

The man gave a derisive snort, eyes struggling to focus after the numerous drinks he'd consumed. When he finally saw the seriousness in Dick's eyes, his cocky expression faded. "Fine. Probably a shit lay anyway."

"The best you'd ever get," Santana called between cupped hands.

Dick returned to the table ten minutes later. "You can read lips?"

"I have a lot of skills." Santana took a long draught of her drink.

Dick laughed. "Well, Miss Sokolov. It's rare that anyone presents me with a mystery that keeps me entertained, threatens my life, and extends far beyond the initial brief's magnitude. But you've certainly given me a challenge, so thank you."

He raised his glass. Santana's met his with a gentle clink. "Find that pendant, Mr. Chambers."

"I'm trying." Dick's eyes narrowed. "Believe me, I'm trying."

CHAPTER TWENTY-TWO

After Santana yawned for the third time in as many minutes, Dick brought their meeting to an end.

He liked her. She was a breath of fresh air in this city. She was someone you could tell on the surface was pure of heart and worth her weight in gold. More than that, she had a profound dislike for the city, which sat well with him.

He hailed her a cab and paid the fee for her. He held open the door like a gentleman and waited until the self-drive cab disappeared around the corner.

He wondered where she lived, what her life was truly like. There was more to her than met the eye, and Dick wanted to find out more.

Still, you have a job to do first. Maybe earn the rest of your paycheck before you scramble down rabbit holes in search of a new friend.

Dick chuckled to himself. "Friend." Dick didn't have too many of those. It was difficult to trust anyone in Atlantica when it felt like you had a permanent target on your back.

Dick lit a cigarette, adjusted his collar, then strolled down the street. It was nearing 11:00 p.m., and he had a gambling ring to find.

BonVivant Valley was heaving. Although the shops were closed, the numerous blocks that accommodated Atlantica's finest boutiques marked a thoroughfare from the theater and bar establishments to the various luxury apartment blocks.

Including Miss Turnberry's fake address. Dick scowled and startled a young couple wandering nearby. They ducked their heads and gave him a wide berth.

He wasn't sure where to start his search for The Warehouse. All he had gleaned from the Russian was that the entrance was located somewhere in the Valley. That was a big area to scour, akin to finding the secret doorway somewhere in Times Square. Where the hell did you begin?

Dick strolled around the blocks three times to get familiar with the Valley as he kept his ears open for any nuggets of information that could be useful. He studied the passersby, hunting for anything that might suggest a group of people on their way to one of the city's largest gambling operations.

After his fourth loop, Dick dialed some acquaintances and dug around for information. No matter who he spoke to, the answer was always the same. "No idea, Dick. It's like asking where the lost city of Atlantis is. No one knows."

Dick scratched his head and scanned the streets in frustration. For all he knew, every single damn building had some kind of underground space to host something like this. It wouldn't surprise him if the original architects of Atlantica created a network of underground rooms and chambers where most of the city's shit was conducted.

But how to find something? Anything?

Dick sat on a metal bench in the middle of Vivant Square. A grotesquely ornate three-tier fountain occupied a large portion of the well-groomed common in the center of the Valley's primary block. Water trickled down its edges, and white lights illuminated the ripples. A bronze statue of a man who had done nothing of worth to the city other than donating the capital used to fund the display topped the fountain.

Money talks. That's all there is to it.

Dick watched the people pass. A place like this would be the perfect location for The Warehouse. There were plenty of people up top to lose yourself in, and a thousand places to hide.

Dick narrowed his eyes at a man in a tuxedo with a briefcase in his hand. He wore dark shades and a fedora low over his brow. The man cast a glance around, then waited by the fountain. Five minutes later, he walked away and left the briefcase in the shadows.

Predictably, a woman swung by a few seconds later and picked it up, walking as if nothing strange had happened as she headed in the opposite direction.

Dick gave a disapproving head shake before realizing that his phone was ringing. He fished out his cell. He didn't recognize the number on the screen.

"Hello?"

"You don't give up, do you?" a modulated voice replied.

Dick frowned as his heart rate accelerated. "There's a reason I'm in this profession. What do you want?"

"The question is, what do *you* want?" The voice fell silent.

"Answers." Dick exhaled smoke into the air. "That's what anyone wants, right?"

There was a moment of quiet when Dick believed the person on the line might have disappeared. "You're a gambling man, aren't you, Mr. Chambers?"

"I dabble."

A small chuckle answered. "Follow the address. Bring your A-game."

Dick glanced at the phone as the line cut. A few seconds later, a message popped up on his screen with a location sent from another unknown number.

Yangle's Accessories. Right alley. Third door. "Cha-ching."

"Cha-ching?" Dick repeated. He scanned the storefronts and found the bright lights of Yangle's Accessories on the square's other side. The store sold high-end vintage clothing, and the building displayed a strange array of steampunk-inspired wheels and cogs along the front of its façade.

Dick rose to his feet and soon stood in the alleyway entrance.

The alley was narrow, not wide enough for Dick to walk straight ahead. He leaned against the wall and waited for the perfect time to slip farther inside without arousing suspicion from the passersby. He had to walk sideways to navigate the space, and his chest still rubbed against the wall.

This would be a great way to get trapped and killed, Chambers. Do you know what you're doing? Why do you trust this person?

Dick wasn't sure that he *did* trust the caller. The only thing he knew was that bold moves made progress. He hadn't solved any crimes by sitting on his ass and playing it safe. If the military had taught him anything, it was that you get stuck in the trenches if you want to win wars.

He passed two doors and found his way to the third. He wasn't sure why the doors were there. Perhaps this building had stood alone at one point, but the city's rapid growth had forced the structures to swell and expand and left little room between them all. He only hoped that the doors opened inward. Other-wise, he was screwed.

Dick knocked on the door and waited.

A slit opened near the top of the entrance. Dick couldn't make out anything in the darkness inside.

Now's a great time to have my head blown off.

"Password?" a voice requested.

Dick rubbed his fingers together. "Cha-ching."

The slit closed. The locks clicked. The door opened.

Dick stepped through the threshold into total darkness.

CHAPTER TWENTY-THREE

Dick navigated his way through the darkness, which was easy enough. The walkway was only as wide as the door and led in one direction. Ahead, he could make out the footsteps of the person who had allowed him entry, but otherwise, he had no idea where he was heading.

After a minute of blindly walking, they came upon stairs which descended beneath the city. Dick used the walls for balance and followed the person straight down. After a short while, they reached a level walkway, and the person in front stopped so abruptly that Dick almost bashed straight into them. A female voice spoke softly. "I am to check you for weapons."

Dick gave an approving grunt, and hands patted him from shoulder to toe. When she found his pistol, she removed it from his person, although Dick thanked his lucky stars that she appeared to dismiss the smattering of small objects in his pocket as non-threatening.

Satisfied, the woman declared, with the slightest hint of an accent, "Welcome to The Warehouse, Mr. Chambers."

Bright light erupted as she pushed open a door that Dick hadn't known was there. He shielded his eyes and squinted as they adjusted to the glare, and he tried to regain his focus. It took a lot to surprise him, but this was something special.

It was like a scene from an old Bond movie, with the casino unfolding under the overhead fluorescents' glow. There were craps tables, roulette, blackjack, and a place to play poker. A couple of hundred men and women strode around with martini glasses in their hands, sporting an array of high-end cocktail dresses and tuxedos. While Dick had never visited Caesar's Palace personally, it was like someone had airlifted one of their rooms and buried it below Atlantica.

"What do you think, Mr. Chambers?" The woman eyed Dick expectantly. His eyes turned to her for the first time, and he was breathless. She was stunning and wore a black cocktail dress that hugged her figure, and a feather in her hair. She had long black gloves that came to her elbow and glittered with shimmering sequins.

Dick regained his composure with a clearing of his throat. "Impressive. I suppose the more impressive thing is that you know my name. Tell me, who gave you your intel?"

The woman shrugged, her shoulderless dress exposing her soft flesh. "It is all of our business to know who enters and who plays here. We are a community. We are one. We know each other, and we understand that we are each transparent unto ourselves. It's the only way an operation like this can exist. Total, unequivocal trust."

Dick nodded approval, feeling the poker table's pull where a small crowd of well-groomed men and women watched as the game reached a heated crescendo. The center of the table held chips, watches, pieces of paper, and necklaces, too.

"You want to play?" the woman asked.

Dick smirked. "You say that this place runs on transparency and trust, yet you led me through the dark and haven't told me your name."

The woman gave a soft chuckle while looking abashedly at

the floor. "Of course, you're right. How rude of me. My name is Alison Miller. Pleased to meet you."

Dick took her hand. "Miller?"

"Is that a problem, Mr. Chambers?" Alison had a playful look in her eye.

Dick tried to work out where the hint of the accent was from but thought not to pursue that line of questioning with Alison right now. "No, not at all."

Alison dug a cigarette out of her purse and lit it between her lips. She offered one to Dick, but he refused. Trust had to be earned. While everyone here might trust each other, Dick was still the outsider, and his guard was up.

"Very well," Alison stated. "Come. Follow me. Miss Turnberry is dying to meet you."

Dick kept his composure, although his throat grew dry. Sadie Turnberry was here? The very woman he was seeking was present in this room, and he had walked straight into the lion's lair.

As Dick followed Alison across the gaming floor, he could not have been more out of place. His shoes were shabby. His jacket was crudely repaired from his scrap with the Russians, and he could easily have passed for a garbage man compared to the rest of the clientele. Still, he gleaned no looks from the patrons of this gathering, which he found odd.

He fought to keep his eyes away from checking out Alison as he walked, beyond noting a little extra wiggle in her hips. He wondered whether this was on purpose, then realized that it was when she reached the poker table and gave him a cheeky wink. She leaned down toward a woman in her sixties who sat at the head of the table and whispered in her ear.

"Finally," Sadie Turnberry declared. "You're here."

"In the flesh." Dick spread his arms to present himself.

Sadie gave him a crooked smile and shooed Alison away. Dick wished that she had stayed. Something was comforting about her presence, particularly compared to the rest of the clientele at the table.

Sadie looked at Dick with ocean eyes. Not the steady calm of an azure cast on a summer's day, but rather the dark tones of a storm brewing as black clouds roiled over the seas and tossed the waves in mountainous motions. "Won't you take a seat, Mr. Chambers? I hear you're quite the poker player yourself."

Dick looked for an empty seat but found none. "I'll wait until this game is over."

"Nonsense," Sadie replied. She was well-spoken, with a short crop of silver hair that complemented her eyes. Around her neck was a string of impressive pearls, and there was a tattoo on her neck of a dagger with words coiled around it in a language Dick couldn't read. "Andre. Move."

Her words were harsh and directed at a man who sat beside her. He was easily large enough to crush her between his massive palms. He glared at Dick, nostrils flaring, then silently obeyed, leaving behind a modest stack of poker chips and two facedown cards.

Sadie motioned for Dick to sit beside her. He obeyed, and took a moment to study the situation as he did so. In his experience, head honchos hardly ever enacted any of their dirty work, so it was the other players that Dick inspected.

There were three other players involved in the game. A woman with a mane of brunette hair who hid her eyes behind a pair of dark glasses, a man in his fifties who Dick assumed from his build, scars, and demeanor might once have served in the military, and a man so dashing that he could have been a prince in a fairytale story.

A glance showed Dick no sign of weapons. It was almost impossible to conceal a pistol on someone without leaving a bulge that he had learned to detect over the years. The only way to avoid the telltale lump was to hide the weapon in difficult to reach places like the ankle or armpit.

This simple maneuver was slow and compromised the position of the people trying to hide their gun. It added precious seconds to the time it took to attack and gave victims a chance to defend themselves.

Satisfied for now, Dick took his seat.

Sliding the cards toward him, he raised the corners and peeked at his hand. The king of spades, and the seven of clubs. Not the greatest hand, but not too shabby, either. He craned his neck toward the big guy who took a stand behind him. "You bet all your shit on this? You need to work on your game, pal."

Sadie laughed, a scratchy sound from her throat. "Already trying to play mind games? I like your style." She threw a chip into the center. "Your move."

Dick matched the amount in the center, knowing that he had to be careful here. The big guy knew the hand, and it became obvious that he was feeding signals to Sadie. Dick lost more chips on that one hand than he would have liked, but at least in resetting the board, he reset his chances of claiming some of the mountain that Sadie had accrued.

"So, Mr. Chambers," Sadie mused as she studied her new hand and gave no telltale sign that he could read. "Tell me, is there a reason you've been stalking around my people, trying to discover where I live and who I am? You've been making quite a stir."

Dick glanced at the other faces, trying to read if this was one big ruse or if Sadie was simply a single player in this venue with her agenda.

"I'm paid to perform certain duties," Dick replied as a waiter appeared at his side with a Blue Moon beer. Condensation beaded the glass, and the very presence of it made his mouth water. "There's nothing personal. I follow where the trail leads, expose the truth to my clients and take my paycheck."

"And what trail, pray tell, has led you to prod around my business?" She spoke calmly, not even a hint of annoyance in her words, but Dick knew better. "I have men dead at your hands. That is something that I don't take kindly to."

Dick took a cautious sniff of his Blue Moon, then sipped. Still wary of a poisoning attempt, he swilled the liquid around his mouth, unable to detect any tampering. He swallowed and set the drink down. "With all due respect, I'd like to have a question answered first."

The dashing gentleman raised his eyebrows in surprise and glanced at Sadie as if Dick had committed an act of blasphemy.

Sadie smirked. "I had no doubt you would. Proceed."

"You have me at a disadvantage," Dick continued. "You seem to know a lot more about me than I know about you, and for someone like myself who has worked in investigation and detection for some years, I'm impressed by the lengths you've gone to research me." He raised the Blue Moon. "Fantastic choice." He raised the bottle to his lips and drank half of it.

Sadie gave an approving nod. "I've yet to hear a question."

"What is your interest in me? Why march your troops against a lone detective like me if you have nothing to hide?"

Sadie laughed, eliciting chuckles from the other players across the table. "Oh, I never said I don't have anything to hide." She tossed a chip onto the table, and Dick followed suit. The dealer turned the third card. "You know as well as I do that Atlantica isn't for the average citizen. If you have nothing to hide, you don't belong in this city. It's because of the intricacies of people's personal lives and business that this city thrives. Secrets are power, and power is currency. I have plenty to hide, but then so does everyone in this room. We play our cards close to the chest, and that's where we keep them. Once you know how to play the game of Atlantica, life gets a lot easier."

Dick studied the new card, the jack of hearts. He threw two more chips in the pile. "You talk as though I don't know the city."

Sadie gave him a hard stare. "You're not from around here, are you? You've been in the city less than a decade, and your nose has already dipped into places where it isn't wanted." Her voice took on a keen edge. "I'm not prepared for you to start invading my privacy, Mr. Chambers. I won't have it. I don't wish to warn you twice."

The dealer called for the reveal of hands. The woman with the glasses displayed a pair of jacks. The veteran threw down a pair of tens. Prince Charming lay his cards flat and shook his head, then drained the contents of a gin and tonic.

Dick waited for Sadie to reveal her hand. She shook her head and motioned for Dick to go first. "After you."

Dick placed down his jack and a two, giving him a full house. He turned to Sadie expectantly and found that she was frowning. She placed her cards facedown and muttered a bitter, "Well played."

Dick scooped the chips and various items into his pile, pleased to see that he had reclaimed a good deal of the game back in his favor. The woman in glasses was nearly out, Prince Charming nursed five chips, and the veteran was third in the running with a handful of colored chips to his name.

The bulk of the pot was split almost evenly between Sadie and Dick.

Dick leaned back while the dealer served and drank from his Blue Moon. "You know, Miss Turnberry, you talk about invasion of privacy, yet I still wonder how you managed to lure me to an empty location of your choosing. It was quite impressive."

Dick made a point of mentioning nothing about finding Sadie's real address, wondering if there was a part of her that knew he had found alternate methods to track her down.

"I have my methods." Sadie's lips grew tight as she was dealt her next hand.

Her tell?

Dick waited for her to say more. When she didn't, he prodded, "Where do we take this from here, Miss Turnberry? It appears we're at something of a stalemate. You have secrets, but they're directly tied into my work. It's not within my manifesto to bow out and leave a job unfinished. I'm paid good coin to pursue what others won't."

Sadie sighed and scratched her temple. "I was afraid you were going to say that." Her eyes darted to the other players. "I must insist that we talk in private."

"I'm not sure that's wise," Dick replied.

Sadie smiled. "Oh, come, Mr. Chambers. What's the worst you think a woman of my age could do? Now, let's speak no more of this nonsense until the game is won, and your pockets are turned out."

Dick stared at Sadie levelly, his mind repeating images of the DNA samples he had found in Erik Burgess' apartment. Judging by the scene that unfolded, there was a lot that an older woman could do, and her age was the perfect cloak to throw a normal Atlantican off the scent.

Unfortunately for Sadie, Dick wasn't a typical Atlantican, and she would soon see why.

CHAPTER TWENTY-FOUR

The Warehouse went deeper than Dick could ever have imagined.

After cleaning out the table at poker, Dick claimed his winnings in the form of a digital transaction validated by a clerk who operated a regulating table in the room's corner. Sadie grumbled as they walked over to the table together and looked pained when Dick tapped his phone and the transfer completed.

Dick also won a Rolex, a Versace necklace, and the keys to a brand-new Lamborghini. These three he gave back to their original owners, stating how little he cared for egregious displays of wealth. As long as his bank account was healthy, that's all that he cared about. Why would he want to draw attention to himself with sparkly things and vehicles that roared?

Sadie led Dick to a gold-plated door near the counter. She touched her finger to a plain panel, and the doors opened to reveal an elevator. Sadie ushered Dick inside. He entered without hesitation, knowing how important it was to keep face in situations with people such as her.

The elevator went down another six floors. When it *dinged* at the bottom, Dick followed Sadie into a small corridor that almost made him forget he was underground. He had seen corridors like this in apartment buildings and offices, and it was only the absence of natural light that reminded him he was buried more than six floors under.

Sadie led Dick to a doorway that she touched the pad of her finger against once more to reveal an office. Dick was curious about her security protocol. If he was right in his estimations, the locks weren't activated by her fingerprints but by a small chip embedded beneath her skin.

He had seen this on a few occasions, but never this close, and wondered why Sadie would risk such a move when an enemy could easily cut off her finger and have instant access to her properties.

The office was spacious, with a large walnut table that Sadie sat behind, its surface polished and gleaming. Aside from the table, a computer, and a few potted plants, there was little of note.

"You have your office here?" Dick asked.

Sadie smiled. "Why shouldn't I? This is all my operation, after all."

Dick was taken aback. "You're the ringleader behind The Warehouse?"

"Something you weren't expecting?" Sadie steepled her fingers together. "Yes, everyone needs a side project to keep them busy and network with the powerful. This is my hobby. It brings me a considerable amount of cash and keeps me in the loop of the city's goings-on."

"So all those people up there are spies for you?" Dick asked. "That's how you know so much about me?"

Sadie laughed. "Oh, no. Not at all. I have other means for that. Things that I wouldn't dare to discuss with even my closest advisors." She studied Dick closely, then leaned forward. "How much is this going to cost me?"

Dick raised an eyebrow.

"Whatever Miss Sokolov is offering you, I'll double it." Sadie waited for a response.

Dick adjusted his position in his chair. "I can't be bought."

Sadie prodded, "Triple."

"No," Dick rejected.

Sadie sighed and rubbed her head. "Mr. Chambers, we have two avenues of progress here. Number one, you give me the chance to purchase your silence, and you leave this path well alone, or number two, we find an alternate way to settle this score."

"Like you did with Erik Burgess?" Dick replied.

Sadie flinched, not expecting Dick's retort. While she was great at remaining composed, Dick saw her calm begin to crumble. "I have limited patience, and you are pushing me to the edge of it. People do not deny me, *Dick*." She spoke his name like a swear word. "I am a force to be reckoned with. I built this underground kingdom. I am a purveyor of luxury goods. I own properties and collect wildlife the likes of which Atlantica has never seen. If you deny me, it will be your error, and I will not ask you again."

"Why wildlife?" Dick asked as if Sadie hadn't spoken. "You seem like a rational human being. Why not stick with the power and wealth that comes with profiting from humans? Why gather and abuse animals, too?"

Sadie's lips tightened. "Another animal rights activist, are you?"

Dick shook his head. "Merely a curious bystander." He grinned internally, knowing that he'd pushed a button.

"For what it's worth, my animals are protected and cared for. I have staff caring for them around the clock. The cages and exhibits are well within reasonable limits to keep them satisfied, and I have a team of expert advisors armed with the latest knowledge on the survival and care of every last one of them. Mr.

Chambers, I may seem like a monster to some, but I assure you that my hardness does not extend to my zoo."

Oh? It's a zoo now, is it?

Dick chewed this over, pleased to have found a nerve so quickly with Sadie. Often it would take hours of prodding before you found the weak spot, but Dick had managed it in only a few minutes of being alone with her.

Sadie shook a hand. "But to the business at hand. Ten times what she paid. Final offer."

Dick considered this, momentarily mulling over the impact this would have on his bank account. He pictured Santana sitting across from him in the bar, her bright eyes, and long legs. She was the true innocent in all of this. All she wanted was to discover the truth behind her mother's passing, and here she was, caught up in a homicide and a theft of her possessions.

Dick studied Sadie, boring into her eyes. He wondered what the alternative was here, and how he would escape without receiving a down payment on silence.

"That's very generous of you, Miss Turnberry." Dick rose from the chair and rested a hand on the table. "However, I reject your offer. Now, please show me the way out of here."

Sadie let out a long breath, pained by Dick's conclusion. "Very well, Mr. Chambers." She rose and placed a hand on Dick's. Her voice grew harsh. "You won't like what you discover. Don't say I didn't warn you!"

Sadie moved her hand to her waist and revealed a short, slender dagger. The hilt was gold, and the edge was keen. She shot forward, aiming the knife for Dick's chest. However, he blocked the movement with a sweep of his forearm and pushed her arm away.

Embracing the momentum, he swiveled his wrist and clutched Sadie's, twisting it sharply to force the dagger from her hand. It clattered to the table, next to where her other hand clamped Dick's.

Sensing that she was about to strike again, Dick flipped his hand and secured her other wrist before picking up the dagger. With a quick slash, he hacked down point-first through her index finger and into the table.

Her fingertip separated from her hand. The knife stood on end, buried in the flawless walnut wood. Sadie cried out in pain as blood leaked from the stub.

Dick picked up the severed digit and ran from the room. He pawed it at the panel and the door unlocked. As Sadie screeched behind him, he sprinted down the hallway toward the elevator. He tapped the finger against that panel and climbed inside.

As the doors closed, he caught a final look at Sadie, and his blood ran cold. She was fumbling behind the desk and searching for something. A moment later an alarm rang out around Dick, piercing inside the elevator.

"Oh great," Dick uttered. "Here comes the fun."

The doors closed, and the elevator started its journey to the surface. The alarm howled, and Dick kept his hands on his ears to block it out. When the elevator stopped, and the doors opened, the customers of The Warehouse were in a state of confusion.

A group of patrons hurried toward the exit. The dealers and the serving staff were clearing the place as if to hide the evidence from the Feds, and a handful of burly gentlemen in tuxedos ran toward the elevator, straight at Dick.

Dick tried to act coy until he found the burly man whose seat he had replaced at the poker table. The man glanced at Dick's hand, which cradled the stub of Sadie's finger accompanied by a few streaks of dried blood.

Putting one and one together—painfully slowly—the burly man commanded his men to attack.

Dick placed the stump in his pocket and ran straight at the group, a move they weren't expecting.

They faltered, taking a stance as Dick closed the gap between them. They readied their fists, but at the last minute, Dick faked a right before quickly switching and rolling around their left. It was a maneuver he'd seen in NBA games when players picked and rolled at the edge of the key, and was surprised at its effectiveness now.

He put some distance between them, but it was only slight. The door to the outside was still fifty feet away, and the brutes recovered quickly. Dick glanced over his shoulder and discovered them closing the gap, their tall frames giving them an advantage as their long legs sped toward him.

Dick was halfway there when a hand grabbed his shoulder. It felt like a vice clamping onto him and dragging him back. Dick whirled, met his confronter head-on, and threw a haymaker that caught the brute's chin. The grip released, but now the others closed in around him.

He couldn't let that happen. While Dick was a practiced fighter, he couldn't take down five bears at once.

Dick twisted away from the closing circle and broke through the gap. As he did, he kicked one of the brute's legs, caught the side of the knee, and forced him to buckle. A blow from behind caught Dick on the shoulder and knocked him off balance, but he recovered.

Dick turned to face them, their faces all masks of hate and determination. The Russian whose seat Dick had taken leered with hungry pleasure.

Dick backed up against the craps table. The brutes believed they had him, but Dick jumped backward and stood on the green. His hand found the rattan dice stick—a long wooden stick with a curved edge—and he brandished it before them. "Let me leave, and you won't go through the pain you'll inevitably face otherwise."

The Russian smirked and muttered something Dick couldn't understand. They encircled the table. Dick sighed. "Very well."

Knowing that they wouldn't listen to him, Dick dug a hand

into his pocket and grabbed one of his small metal orbs. He tapped the side, then threw it at the lead Russian who caught it instinctively. Smoke poured from tiny vents on either side before a flash came and the cloud it created engulfed them.

Dick got to work.

He spun the stick around him, hoping that his memory of where all the brutes had been standing was accurate. He jabbed out, avoided hands that grabbed blindly at him, and felt the satisfying vibration running down the wood as the stick found its mark. He caught three of the brutes, not knowing exactly *where* he had hit them, but reassured by their growls and groans of pain.

After a hop back, Dick leaped from the main honcho's clutches. He momentarily saw the fury in his face before the smoke thickened. Dick made his best guess at a gap and took it by jumping from the table and moving toward the door.

The Russian shouted something that might have been, "Get him!" from the tone.

Dick passed a dealer's table and grabbed a stack of playing cards. He tossed them behind him, scattering them all over the floor. A moment later, one of the Russians slipped and fell with a colossal thud.

Almost there, surely?

The cloud of smoke followed Dick, which made his smooth escape a little harder to navigate. Once or twice a game table barred his way, appearing as if someone had magicked them in front of him. He swerved around them and finally found the exit.

He reached for the handle and opened the door. A hand grabbed the back of his head and threw him against the wood.

Sparks bloomed in Dick's vision. He tasted blood on his tongue as the hand gripped his hair.

He reached back and grabbed his attacker's thick wrist with one hand, and used the other to lash the rattan stick behind him.

He caught the attacker in the crotch, which loosened his grip and afforded him a glance at his enemy.

The lead Russian. Of course, it was.

The door was closed, and Dick knew he'd never get it open without removing this final hurdle. He put both hands on the stick and attacked, hitting with both ends. The Russian blocked with his meaty forearms and occasionally threw blows that shoved Dick against the door and sucked the wind from him. The brute was strong, but Dick was nimble.

The Russian charged at him, hoping to press him against the door and take advantage. Dick released the stick and rolled sideways. The man hit the door so hard that it bowed in the center and a crack appeared around the hinges.

After moving behind his opponent, Dick did the only thing he could think of at that moment. He leaped onto the Russian's back and hooked an arm around his throat in a chokehold while using his other hand for leverage to tighten the grip.

The man's arms were so thick with muscle that he couldn't bend them enough to reach behind him. Even with the stick, the most he could manage were a few weak taps. Dick held tight as both men grew red in the face. The Russian gave a guttural choke, his movements slowing as his oxygen-starved body gave up. Dick played his hand with the same cool he played poker and released his grip when the brute fell to the floor.

He hopped off, then crouched. He checked the man's pulse and was pleased to see that he was still alive.

One more enemy running loose in the city, but at least it's not a smudge on my conscience.

He moved once more to the door and managed to squeeze through the minute gap he could make, given that the door was now partially blocked by the Russian's body.

Darkness swallowed him once more. The sounds of the other attackers finally reaching their leader rang from behind. Using his arms to guide him, Dick found the stairs and made his way to the surface. He stumbled a few times, but soon emerged in the narrow alley.

He breathed in the chill night air and closed his eyes. When he opened them again, he strode into the open streets of BonVivant Valley and disappeared into the crowd.

CHAPTER TWENTY-FIVE

Dick stood in the shadows of the alley and stared up at his apartment window.

The lights were off, but that didn't mean anything. He had walked back, afraid of leaving a digital trail by hailing a cab, but as he approached his home, he couldn't help but feel as though something was waiting for him again.

Not getting nervous, are you Dick?

Dick placed a cigarette between his lips but didn't light it. He didn't want the spark to draw attention to his location. Where he stood, he was all but invisible. The few civilians left walking the streets didn't turn their head to the alley.

If Sadie had led three Russians to his apartment before, who was to say she wouldn't do it again? Particularly now that he'd shortened a finger on one of her hands. Sadie was the type of person who held a grudge, and Dick had a bad feeling that he'd awakened the hornet's nest.

He took out his notepad and flicked through the notes, angling the paper to get enough light to read them. There were pages and pages of scribbles from previous cases, as well as a smattering of information he had left from Santana's quest for her pendant. A name jumped out at him, "Dexter Lockhart."

Dick's brow creased in confusion. The Russian in his apartment had mentioned a Dexter Lockhart, then backtracked. He had cried Lockhart's name in a blind panic, yet it was Sadie's blood at the scene of Erik Burgess' murder. Some things Dick couldn't let go, but first, he had to look where the man had said. Sadie worked *with* a Russian, but would that mean that the three Russians who had attacked Dick were hers?

So many questions and so few answers.

Dick debated chancing a return to his apartment. His mouth craved scotch. He wanted to collapse on his bed and sleep off the past few hours of excitement, yet he knew it would not come. He needed to find somewhere safe to lie. Somewhere away from the mess that was building around him.

Dick turned away and passed through the alley.

Dick sat on the stoop outside the colonial-inspired apartment building until daylight seeped into the night sky. He clutched his jacket around him to fight off the chill. Beside him was a brown paper bag with a cheap bottle of scotch he had purchased from the corner convenience store.

Dick took a deep drag of smoke before bringing the bottle to his lips and taking a long swig. He closed his eyes and enjoyed the warmth that spread inside him as a woman in a maroon evening dress strode past and shook her head.

He didn't blame her. He was hardly the picture of the advanced society that Atlantica liked to project to the rest of the world.

At some point, Dick closed his eyes and fell asleep on the stoop. He awoke to the sound of someone clearing their throat, and he tore his face away from the guardrail, feeling the deep imprints the metal left behind on his face.

Terra Kris tilted her head, a pitying look on her face. "Well, this is a fall from grace, isn't it?"

Dick rubbed his eyes and peered up at her. Dawn had lightened the sky to a hazy pink, and the road traffic was building up again. "Not so much a fall, as a toss down from the heavens." Dick cleared his throat and felt its dryness. "Not all angels are born equal."

Terra studied Dick for a few seconds. She walked past him and scanned a card against the apartment door. A buzzer groaned as she opened it and stepped inside. "Are you coming in? Or are you getting into the mind of a criminal homeless man?"

Dick picked up his bag and followed Terra inside.

The kettle whistled as the water reached its boil. Terra poured the scalding liquid into two cups, then added a measure of milk to hers while leaving Dick's black. She gave him the mug and sat on the couch across from him.

Her apartment was nice—standard issue for a woman of her position within the AJS. There were no frills or eccentricities, everything served a purpose, and everything had its place. The only note of extravagance that Dick could find were the displays of flowers in several vases and pots around the room.

Terra gave an appreciative gasp after her first sip. "Are you going to tell me why you were hanging around my apartment steps until I finished my shift? I assume you haven't forgotten my 'no booty-call' rule?"

"What makes you think that's your rule?" Dick replied.

Terra shrugged. "Because I made it." She stared at Dick expectantly.

Dick pawed at his tired eyes. "I'm in a bit of a jam, okay? I can't really go back to my apartment right now. It's not safe for me there."

"So it's safe for you to be here?" There was no blame in Terra's voice, only a genuine question. Dick liked that about her. It took a hell of a lot to scare or intimidate Terra Kris.

"I hope so," Dick answered honestly.

Terra waited for Dick to say more. When he didn't, she nudged. "Look, Dick. I know that your work is veiled in secrecy. I get that, I really do. There's a lot of work on my side that I'd be instantly fired for if I so much as breathed the wrong information to a coworker, let alone a private investigator famed for his…questionable methods. But you need to give me something. I've not seen you this tired in years."

Dick drank from his coffee, then found Terra's gaze. "I'm in the middle of a case. I may be onto something big here. I don't know what, yet, but I know I'm about to crack it wide open."

"Is this to do with the homicide?" Terra asked. "The one you were investigating the other day?"

Dick told her it was, all the while debating whether to mention Santana's involvement in the case. He decided against it, keeping his cards close to his chest.

"And you can't share *any* details?" Terra asked.

Dick gave her a look.

She held up her hands defensively. "It was worth a try." She finished her coffee and returned to her kitchenette to refill her drink. She offered Dick a second, which he politely refused. "What is it you need from me, Dick? If it isn't advice or utility, why were you on my doorstep?"

Dick looked at her levelly. "I need a place to crash. A few hours tops."

"Oh?" Terra's eyebrows raised. "So, you'll have your case closed before tonight, will you? That's impressive."

Dick smirked. "You can read me like a book."

"I may be the only one who can," Terra returned. "Look, I need to catch some Zs before I'm up again for another night shift. If you want to take the couch, then feel free. I have nothing in the way of amenities for guests, so don't expect PJs, fresh towels, and pancakes when you wake."

Dick chuckled. "Fine. I hear you." He eyed Terra's mug. "Coffee before bedtime? How does that work?"

Terra shook the mug with smug satisfaction. "Decaf."

"Oh?" Dick replied. "So I got decaf, too?"

Terra winked. "Guess you'll have to find out. Goodnight, Dick."

Dick made himself comfortable on the couch after kicking off his shoes but leaving pretty much everything else on. His hip ached and gently pulsed, reminding him of the bullet that had grazed his side.

Funny. That didn't once cross my mind at The Warehouse. Amazing what adrenaline and distraction can do.

Dick closed his eyes and prayed that Terra hadn't played some cruel trick in pumping him full of caffeine.

His answer came when sleep did, only a few minutes later.

Dick woke up to the sound of the front door closing.

It startled him awake. He had been so deep in sleep that he hadn't even dreamed, but now he was here in a strange room, wondering for a few moments where the hell "here" was.

He sat up and looked around, then remembered his early-morning visit to Terra's. There had been a part of him that believed she wouldn't let him stay, but underneath her tough exterior, Terra had a kind heart. If only more AJS officers had that quality.

"Terra?" Dick called, although he knew that she was gone. Her bedroom door was ajar, the smell of fresh coffee hung in the air, and she'd left a note on the table.

"Dick, I left some coffee for you. Caffeinated, this time. I want you gone before I'm back. T."

Dick chuckled. "She's quite the compassionate gal, isn't she?"

Dick poured himself some coffee and settled back down on the couch. He rubbed his temples and contemplated his next move. He could only think of one avenue forward, and it wasn't one that he particularly looked forward to.

Sadie Turnberry was the next link in the chain, and as much as she tried to put him off the scent, she only ignited his curiosity. She was hiding something. Whether it was connected to the pendant or not, and Dick fully believed that it was, he needed to discover the truth. There was some game afoot here, and he wanted to get to the bottom of it all, wrap it in a big bow, and present it to Santana. *Here you are, Sokolov. Your pendant, and all the answers you sought. Now give me my cash.*

Not that the cash was his only incentive. Dick yearned for closure, for truth.

For justice.

Dick rose to his feet and wandered around Terra's apartment. He paused by her bedroom door, wondering if he could get away with a quick shower, but thought better of it. If he abused Terra's hospitality, it was unlikely that he'd ever be able to seek succor at her place again, and he needed all the people on his side he could get right now.

Dick poked his head into the bedroom, unsurprised by its untidiness. The bed wasn't made, there was a pile of clothes in the corner, and a chest of drawers held four dirty mugs. The blinds were drawn, casting the room in a hazy glow.

A voice spoke from behind. "I leave you alone for two minutes, and you're already sniffing around the delicates."

Dick whirled around and saw Valentina Winters standing in the middle of the apartment. Against the neutral colors of Terra's place, her red jacket and hat stood in stark contrast, drawing the eye.

"Question," Dick started, "Why do you wear vibrant red if you're supposed to be a mercenary? Doesn't it draw attention?"

"The closer I am to danger, the further away from harm," Valentina replied. "A wise man said that once."

Dick raised an eyebrow. "That's from The Lord of the Rings."

Valentina chuckled. "Yes, Meriadoc Brandybuck is quite the wise hobbit." She sauntered toward Dick, causing his heart rate to accelerate. "What are you doing here, Dick? I hunt across the city for you and find you in another woman's apartment. Should I be concerned? Have you got wandering eye syndrome?"

Dick's eyes darted to the ruby red of her lips before settling on her cleavage. He tore his eyes back up to meet hers.

She smirked. "I suppose that's a yes."

Dick collected himself. "I needed somewhere to stay, and I had no idea where to go. Terra and I, we go back. She's good stock, but there's nothing between us."

"Look at you, getting all flustered." Valentina's perfume was intoxicating and clouded Dick's thoughts. "I only asked since I was concerned about you. I kept an eye on you since your run-in with the Russian family a few days ago. I was concerned, so I visited you again and saw the state your apartment was in. It took me nearly two days to track you down."

"Quiet at the office?" Dick asked.

Valentina shrugged. "A slow patch."

Dick moved past her and sat, then brought the coffee to his lips. "I was attacked. Three Russians were waiting for me at my apartment. I took out two and left one in the hospital—I hope. Turns out this case goes so much deeper than I'd originally thought."

"Don't they always?" Valentina sat beside Dick. She leaned back and spread her arms over the back of the couch and crossed her legs as she did.

Dick shook his head. "Not like this. There's something I'm missing. Some piece of the puzzle. I just don't know what it is yet."

"Who's your next target?" Valentina asked.

Dick gave her a considering look.

"Oh, come on, Dick," Valentina encouraged. "We both work in secrecy, and we both work in private business away from the Feds and prying eyes. You can tell me. You've shared with me before." Her eyes drank in his body. "In more ways than one."

He cleared his throat. "Fine. Here's where I'm at."

Dick explained to Valentina the bare bones of what she needed to know to understand his interaction with Sadie Turnberry. He was pleased with the sour expression that grew on Valentina's face when he mentioned that he had been led to a bogus address since there was a minute part of him that pinned Valentina as a suspect in leading him there.

Everyone is a suspect until proven otherwise.

He told her of his visit to The Warehouse and his face-to-face encounter with Sadie.

"That's why you're here and not at home?" Valentina replied, not a question. "And you say you have her true address?"

"I believe so." Dick gave it to Valentina, who pulled her phone from inside her jacket's depths and tapped the screen. Dick leaned over to look at what she was doing. He didn't recognize the operating system or the phone's firmware. Knowing Valentina, it was likely a custom build of her making.

"Here." She held out the phone to Dick, and he couldn't believe what he saw. The screen was a grid showing the feeds from security cameras. "Tap one to make it bigger."

Dick glanced over the phone at Valentina. "This is…this is her house? But how?"

Valentina gave Dick a look that said, "Do you really think I'm going to share that information?"

Dick scrolled through the camera feeds and zoomed in on the mansion's various rooms. Although it didn't give him a proper idea of the house's layout, he could see much more of what lay inside.

There were dozens of camera feeds, with at least two-thirds

of them showcasing the interiors of the cages and buildings he had witnessed from afar. There were exhibits with alligators, tigers, parrots, and a whole host of other mammals, fish, reptiles, amphibians, and birds. Many of the displays were far from zoo standards since the spaces were almost complete replicas of the natural outdoor habitats. It was more a wildlife park than a zoo.

On top of that were the many layers of shrubs, flowers, and trees that grew around the habitats. There were hedges carved into the shapes of animals and staff wandering around the mansion with firearms clipped to their sides. Dick examined the house's main rooms and found taxidermy animals and skeletons on display, plus several reception rooms downstairs.

The cameras didn't show the upstairs, presumably because Sadie was dumb enough to believe that no one could get past the downstairs security and wildlife displays.

The final image Dick looked at before handing the phone back to Valentina was a series of cages somewhere near the back of the house that housed many angry-looking dogs. These cages were nothing compared to the other exhibits. They were small, bare, and looked as though they hadn't been cleaned in days.

"It's a defense technique some people employ," Valentina explained. "Make the dogs angry, make them resent their cages, and they'll be all the more fierce against intruders."

Dick rubbed a hand over his face, momentarily overwhelmed by the challenge presented to him. He lit a cigarette before letting out a ream of smoke. The instant he saw it in front of him he remembered that he wasn't in his apartment and snuffed it out. He waved a hand to clear the air.

Valentina watched him with an amused expression on her face. "Everything okay?"

"I think I'm going to need some help," Dick replied.

Valentina shook her head. "Don't look at me."

"I wasn't," Dick confirmed. "I have someone else in mind.

Although I'm not sure how willing and able she is to help me right now."

Valentina scoffed. "Another lady? I suppose that's my cue to leave."

Dick grabbed her wrist and pulled her toward him. He kissed her deeply, not caring that her lipstick would smudge on his face. When they came up for air, he looked deep into her eyes. "Thank you."

Valentina kissed him once more. "Don't mention it."

CHAPTER TWENTY-SIX

Before Valentina and Dick parted ways, she checked through his phone for bugs and digital tracing frequencies.

"Nope, clean as a whistle from what I can see," she stated and handed the phone back to him. "Are you sure you're going to be okay, Dick?"

Dick grinned. "Of course. Have you ever known me to get into a scrap I can't get out of?"

They kissed once more, then she left. Dick stood a moment, taken aback by the force of the kiss, then glanced around the apartment. A pistol left on the counter drew his eyes. Although there was no note attached, he wondered if it hadn't been left on purpose.

Dick closed the front door of the apartment block, then stepped out into the street. It was approaching night, and he realized then that he missed the sunshine. Back when he'd lived in the US, daylight—real daylight—had been a staple of his life. Living under Atlantica's haze of fog kept him in a permanent state of wonderment, as though he were living in a dream, the edges of his reality hazed no matter where he went.

There was no point going back to his sedan. He was almost

certain that he'd been tracked and that Sadie would know the car by its registration. *It's all on foot now, buddy. Don't bother hailing a cab, because this system is rigged to work against you.*

Dick took a stroll while thinking through the next stage of his plan. He found himself a few blocks in the other direction of his favorite diners and sat in a red leather booth of a place that called itself "Waffles."

Dick ordered another coffee, and after the waiter brought over his customary toast, he dialed Santana's number and waited for her to answer.

She picked up on the second ring. "Good news?"

"Afraid not. I need your help."

Santana chuckled. He couldn't work out where she was, but he was sure he could make out road traffic in the background. "I thought I paid you to take care of this for me."

Ouch. Right in the pride.

"You're an expert on all things animal, aren't you?" Dick asked.

"I am," Santana replied. "Why do you ask?"

Dick explained what he had seen on the camera feed Valentina had hacked into, and that she had ensured Dick could access even now with a simple touch of a button.

Santana growled. "That makes my goddamn blood boil. Animals aren't our pets and playthings. They're beautiful creatures, designed to run free. What is it with you aristocrats that makes you think it's okay to deny majestic creatures their primal liberties?"

Dick raised his hands defensively. "Don't put me in a box with those freaks. I've never owned a pet in my life."

"Really?" she replied, surprise in her voice.

Dick grunted. "Absolutely. Who needs something extra to clear up after?"

Santana sighed. "Look, I can come and lend a hand, but I can't be gone for hours. I have shit I need to deal with. A girl has to make a living, you know." She paused a moment. "Still, I'd do anything to make sure those animals make it back to the places they came from."

"What is it that you do exactly?"

Santana chuckled. "Well, have you ever played Tomb Raider?"

Dick told her he had. Santana said no more.

They arranged a time and a place to meet, and Dick hung up. He tucked into his toast, leaving nothing behind on the plate but a few crumbs, then drained his coffee. He ordered a second and asked if the diner had any whiskey available.

"I'm sorry, sir. We don't sell alcohol on these premises," the acne-ridden waiter replied.

"That doesn't mean you don't *have* any." Dick tapped a figure into his phone and showed the waiter. "That's your tip if you can do this for me."

The waiter returned a few minutes later, hands shaking as he poured a measure of whiskey into the black coffee. It was a small bottle, but it did the trick. The waiter glanced in disgust as Dick drank from the cup. "That can't taste nice."

Dick shook his head and grimaced. "It takes like shit. But does the job." He tapped his phone against a receiver pad strapped to the waiter's waist, and a small ding rang out. "There. Happy birthday."

"But it's not my..." The waiter stopped. "Oh."

It would have taken Dick a few hours to walk all the way to Wellington Park, but he found an alternate method.

After the first three blocks of walking, Dick came across a bicycle locked to a metal fence. He lit a cigarette and loitered near the bike for a few minutes before deciding that he was safe to pick the lock. It didn't take much. Most of the U-shaped bike locks fitted the same mechanisms inside, so it was merely a case of jimmying the right way to open it.

He discarded the lock and straddled the seat. A moment later, he was speeding along the city's cycleways, heading west in search of Sadie Turnberry's house.

It took all of two minutes for Dick to grow breathless. Although he considered himself a relatively strong man, his cardio needed work—cigarettes and alcohol would do that to a man. However, after pushing through the pain in his side, he found his second wind.

He took the back roads, avoiding anywhere he knew there to be an association with Sadie. It added an extra twenty minutes to his ride, but soon enough, he'd made the several-mile trip and was in Wellington's impressive suburbs.

The street was deadly silent. Dick assumed that the residents here kept to themselves during the witching hours and hoped that would be the case as long as he was here. He made his way to the corner of the long street, hid the bike behind a tall hedge, and made a mental note to return it when this was all over. Satisfied that it was out of sight, he waited in the shadows for Santana to arrive.

Passing the time, Dick raised a cigarette to his lips and took a long drag. The cherry lit brightly, and anyone passing might have seen the rugged PI for a moment in the gloom. Dick let the smoke seep through his pores before exhaling a cloud. He patted his side and checked he still had the pistol. If he wasn't mistaken, it looked like AJS issue. A custom GLOCK 99—created specifically for the AJS.

Bitch gave me a traceable firearm.

He wondered whether Terra had an ace up her sleeve somewhere. His gut told him that wasn't the case, and usually, it was right. However, you could never be too careful in this city.

"Burning the midnight oil?" Santana strolled around the corner wearing the same attire she had worn the previous night.

Dick couldn't help but stare at her long legs. "Eyes up here, Mr. Chambers."

Dick smirked. "Hardly the type of clothing one would expect in the chilly evenings."

Santana tilted her head and placed a hand on her hip. "You should know by now that I'm not your typical Atlantican." She nodded down the street. "Is it down there?"

They both turned to the long row of impressive housing. "Sure is. Are you ready for this?"

"Have you got my back?" Santana replied.

Dick was taken aback by that question. "Of course. Do you doubt it?"

Santana shrugged. "Can't blame a girl for being cautious. I've been burned before."

"Well," Dick continued, "if there's any burning done tonight, it's that establishment and the liberation of all its creatures."

Santana gave him an accusing look.

Dick rolled his eyes. "I won't burn the place with the animals still inside. It's an expression, anyway. I don't plan on using literal fire. There's no way to draw attention faster than sending plumes of smoke into the sky." Dick drew out his phone. "Here."

He showed Santana the video feeds of the animals within their exhibits and noticed how her stare hardened. "This woman is a real piece of work. These aren't simply rare specimens. They're endangered species, too. A Siberian tiger, a Mexican wolf...she has a goddamn snow leopard in there."

"You know your animals," Dick commented.

"I'm paid to." She studied the feed, then gave the phone back to Dick. "What's the plan, then? I imagine we're not only here to liberate the creatures. You want something from Sadie, don't you?"

Dick nodded. "Sadie is my only link to your case. She near enough confessed to me in person that there was a trail to follow. Whatever we're after, it'll be in that house. I'm all but certain."

"We have to get past the security," Santana added.

"Exactly," Dick replied. He glanced down the street. "Exactly."

A quick study of an online map showed Wellington Street and its surrounding neighborhood. Sadie Turnberry's house backed onto the beginnings of the wilds that stretched and spanned over Atlantica's hills, and on toward a central dormant volcano that would have towered over the island had it not been for the blanket of fog.

Santana identified the leafy canopy as their way in. While the back wall of Sadie's mansion stood an easy twenty feet tall, Santana was confident that she could breach it. The trees would give them adequate cover to sneak closer and to perform the reconnaissance they needed to break in and explore.

Dick followed Santana down a side road and through the thin alleys which broke between a megamart and a retailer of high-end vehicles to access the wilds. When they emerged in the trees, Dick felt the cloying damp of the jungle fog.

"Man, it's like the trees are breathing on me," he noted as he wiped a hand over his sweating brow. He removed his jacket and folded it over one arm.

Santana's eyes found the pistol holstered at his side. "AJS issue? Should I be concerned?"

Dick laughed.

"What?" Santana asked.

"Nothing," Dick replied. He wasn't sure why, but he liked that both women were in the dark about the role he played in each of their lives. It would undoubtedly come to a head at some point, but he could keep his secrets until then.

Santana led Dick at least fifty meters into the forest before she turned and skirted around the back of the mansions. Dick didn't know how she could keep her bearings so well, particularly when it was this dark, and there were so many obstacles. Every step revealed more of the same. Trees, bushes, and more trees.

Santana stopped a couple of times and put a finger to her lips. A moment later, she'd crack her whip and send something scurrying off into the undergrowth. He had to admit that her skills were impressive. It was like being led through the jungle by a female version of Tarzan.

Jane?

After almost twenty minutes of maneuvering in the dark, with Dick managing not to trip more than twice, Santana pulled him to a stop by holding up a fist.

Dick was all too familiar with the military command.

He froze. Santana cupped her eyes toward a source of light a short distance away. A dog's bark rent the night.

She motioned Dick over. He stood by her side and peered ahead. He could see the faint shade of the wall through the trees. There were small cutouts in decorative shapes along the barrier, none of them large enough to fit a hand through, but enough to see the garden's floodlights as they filtered through.

The sound of metal hitting metal was followed by more dogs barking. They sounded furious as they went into a frenzy.

"The same dogs from the camera feed?" Santana whispered.

"I guess," Dick replied. He took a few cautious steps closer before Santana grabbed him and pulled him back.

"Careful," she warned. "We're upwind. One strong gust and they'll catch our scent."

Almost as if spurred on by her comment, the dogs fell silent. Through the tiny gaps, Dick thought he could make out a few of their group sniffing the air. One of them moved toward the wall and exploded into barking. The others quickly joined as they scratched and clawed at the barrier.

"Is someone there?" a voice called.

Santana grabbed Dick's wrist and pulled him farther into the wilds. She guided him away from where they stood until the barking and shouts were considerably quieter.

"You think they have their guard up?" Dick asked.

"Hard to say," Santana replied. "Dogs kept in conditions like that will bark at anything. For all they know, there's a squirrel or a mouse by the wall. We can use this as a distraction. Come on, let's find another place to get nosy."

They came to another section with similar decorative patterns cast into its façade. They snuck closer with Santana taking the lead and reassuring Dick that there were no dogs here.

When they made it to the wall, they crouched and peered through the holes. They could almost make out a large courtyard, the edges rimmed with exotic-looking trees and plants. Where they stood was deep in a cluster of trees, but a handful of guards were visible beyond that. They wore black uniforms without insignia, and each held a rifle.

"She's well protected," Santana commented. "Dogs, exotic creatures, and paid guards? Who does this woman think she is?"

"A woman with something to hide," Dick replied. He craned his neck to the top of the wall. "How do we enter without detection?"

"I thought that was your specialty?" Santana smirked.

"My specialty is domestic covert ops and disabling technology," Dick commented. "This is way over my head." He looked at the wall again. "Literally."

Santana chuckled. Dick spotted the guards resuming their usual places, seemingly pacified that nothing was on the other side of the wall from where the dogs were barking.

"Wimp." Santana winked. "We climb. Come on."

Dick lit a cigarette and put a hand in his pocket. "I'll wait here. Let me know if your way works."

Santana shook her head and scaled the wall. When she neared the top, she peeked over, trying to determine if the cover was sufficient to drop to the other side. From his position on the ground, Dick had a fantastic view. He stared at her ass for a while, almost forgetting the job at hand. It wasn't until Santana hissed in his direction that he turned to face her. "Focus."

Dick was about to reply, but in one swift movement, Santana swung her leg over and disappeared on the other side.

Dick sighed, extinguished his cigarette, then started climbing.

CHAPTER TWENTY-SEVEN

Dick's climb wasn't nearly as graceful.

When he reached the top, he fumbled with his leg and almost managed to lower himself without hurting himself. His landing was heavier than he anticipated, and they both froze for a nerve-wracking moment, expecting the guards to turn their way and close in on their location.

After a few silent minutes, they breathed sighs of relief and retreated deeper into the exotic plants.

Dick recoiled at the touch of a strange leaf. It was a deep red and the size of a saucepan. The edges were twisted upward and serrated. "There's nothing here that's going to sting me, is there?"

Santana shrugged. "No idea. You'll probably want to worry more about the things that could eat you. Or the stuff that stinks. Did you know that there's a flower that literally smells like a rotten corpse?"

Dick tried to imagine it. He didn't like the result.

Santana ushered him through the artificially placed under-growth until they found its edge away from the guards. They came across a red brick path that snaked its way from the outdoor courtyard with the dogs toward the closest greenhouselike building. There was a twenty-foot gap out in the open they'd have to cross if they wanted to find their way inside.

"Are you ready?" Santana asked.

Dick nodded.

Santana waited until all the guards were facing the other direction, then tore off from cover. Dick followed swiftly after, and somehow, they made it through the slatted plastic curtain that covered the entryway.

Not knowing if there were more guards inside, they dashed to the edge of the building and found cover behind three large boulders placed neatly together.

Dick wiped his brow. "I thought it couldn't get any hotter than the jungle. I'm sweating buckets."

Santana seemed unaffected by this change. "You need to get out more, city boy. Living with other humans is messing up your natural responses to outdoor conditions." Her eyes narrowed as she scanned around the space. "I don't remember seeing this room on the cameras. I wonder what she's keeping in here."

Dick checked his phone and thumbed through the feeds. Santana was right. This room wasn't on them.

"Maybe it's a new addition, and they haven't installed CCTV yet," Dick suggested. He couldn't see anything of note around them, only the faint silver edges of rocks, trees, and a water feature trickling through the exhibit's center as the floodlights outside leaked through the glass.

A squeak came from beside Dick. He turned and jumped a little at the creature sitting beside them. Its eyes were orbs on its tiny face, and its hands clutched a berry. It examined them both with a curious look.

Dick slowly eased away. "What is that thing?" Its eyes freaked him out. They glowed a strange gold in the dark.

"Aww," Santana cooed as she leaned closer, a grin on her face. "It's a tarsier."

"What the hell is a tarsier?"

"One of the only extant entirely carnivorous primates. Isn't he adorable?" Santana reached slowly toward the creature.

"Carnivorous?" Dick questioned. "As in, it eats meat?"

Santana nodded, her eyes fixed on the tarsier's glowing orbs. "Mostly insects, so you can simmer down. There's no threat here."

Her fingertips touched the tarsier's fur. It bristled slightly and recoiled, but changed its mind and clambered up her arm when she eased toward it once more. It soon found a nesting place on her shoulder.

Dick examined the plastic strips they had walked through. "Is it safe having them in an enclosure where they could escape if they wanted to?"

Santana considered this. "Depends how trained they are. If they prefer living where they're fed regularly and have all their friends and family, then why wouldn't they stay? Still, it does seem a bit odd."

They skirted the room, keeping their voices low as they spotted more tarsiers. Well, Santana spotted them and pointed them out to Dick. They were assembling around the pair, curious about their new companions.

When they reached a door on the left wall, they found it ajar.

"Maybe that's where they came from?" he suggested.

Santana chewed her lip. "Maybe." She reached up and helped the tarsier off her shoulder. "Sorry, cutie-pie. It's not safe for you where we're going."

A flashlight shone on the other side of the door. Dick and Santana tucked themselves against the wall and held their breath. A guard strode down a dark corridor, casting the light in all directions as she completed her circuit.

When she was gone, Dick poked his head through the doorway. This room was long and acted as a walkthrough from the house to the courtyard, with several other exits heading in different directions. Where the room they were in now was almost entirely made of glass, this one had a low ceiling and was dark. The only light source was the ultraviolet lights of the glass displays set into the length of the wall where Dick could make out the shape of several bugs, insects, and other invertebrates.

He spotted a camera in the corner of the room and clicked his device in its direction. Santana studied him with interest. "What's that?"

"None of your business," he replied as he took her hand. He dragged her into the room, where they quickly sprinted half the corridor's length before a light appeared around the corner. They ducked into a crevice and hid in the darkness.

Someone whistled. The door opened, then closed. The footsteps drew closer.

Dick pressed back into the crevice and found that what he thought was a wall was a doorway. It opened silently on its hinges, and he and Santana passed through. They eased the door closed behind them.

Dick wiped the sweat from his brow, thankful they were in a cooler room. He pressed his head against the door and took a deep breath.

"Thank God for small miracles," he muttered. When he turned, the sentiment faded as he found Santana with her knees bent, arms outstretched, and eyes fixed on the amber-ringed pupils of a Siberian tiger.

Dick's breath caught. "Santana—"

Santana hushed him, eyes unmoving from the predatory beast as it lowered onto its haunches and examined its new guests. The exhibit wasn't huge, giving the tiger only enough room to walk in circles. There was an artificial river running through, and a selection of foliage to make it feel more like home. The entire section of one wall was glass, although it was pitch dark on the other side.

Dick scrambled the camera's circuits while Santana slowly moved her hand to her satchel. Each movement felt like it lasted a lifetime as the tiger bared its fangs at the pair while advancing with tiny steps.

"Easy, now…" Santana cooed. "Easy…"

She popped the clasp on her satchel, and the tiger growled. Santana flipped open the top and pulled out a hunk of nondescript meat in a plastic bag.

What animal Santana had gotten the meat from, Dick couldn't guess. Drops of blood trailed onto the floor as she held it in front of her.

It caught the tiger's attention. She waved it back and forth hypnotically.

Santana whispered to Dick. "When I give the signal, run."

Dick was about to ask where, until he saw the door on the other side of the exhibit, almost lost against the backdrop of greenery. Santana rose to her full height, then tossed the meat past the tiger.

It roared as it leaped to catch the meat, missing by inches. It whirled and tore straight into its food, tearing the chunk to shreds in seconds. It wasn't a meal for the tiger. It was barely a snack. By the time Dick and Santana had made it to the doorway, the tiger smacked its lips and wanted more.

Santana tried the door. It was locked. Dick looked for a keyhole but couldn't find anything. There was only a digital panel on the side and an LED light.

Santana pressed back against the wall. "Come on, infiltrator. Do something."

Dick scrambled through his jacket pockets, moving aside the devices he had acquired from Ringo through the years. His fingers found something soft, and he took it out to see he was holding Sadie's fingertip.

"Now, John!" Santana urged while digging to find another piece of meat, which she tossed over the tiger's head. This time, it didn't take the bait.

Dick pressed the fingertip to the panel and couldn't believe that the light turned green and a lock clicked open. He tugged the door open and pulled Santana through as the tiger leaped at them, its bodyweight shutting the door closed behind them both.

They landed on the floor, Santana on top of Dick. They remained there for a moment, breathing heavily. Dick looked down at Santana. "If this is *your* way of bedding a strong, handsome man, I don't approve."

They both laughed. Santana climbed off Dick and offered him a hand up. Dick checked for cameras and quickly triggered his device.

"We may have given away our position," Dick informed Santana.

Santana's face hardened. "Then we'd better move."

They both paused when they noticed the security guard who had entered through a nearby door. One hand was on her waist, hovering over a gun holster.

Dick sighed. "That was fun while it lasted."

The guard flinched, but before she could grab anything or make a move, Santana flicked out her bullwhip. The lash coiled around the guard's neck. Then a strong tug jerked the woman forward, where she landed on her hands and narrowly avoided hitting her face on the floor.

Dick took the initiative, moved forward, and kicked the woman in the face. She was out cold in less than a second.

"We make a great team," Santana commented.

Dick raised his eyebrows. "Enough advances. Come on, get your head in the game. We have a mansion to explore."

Santana scoffed, but a smile grew on her face.

CHAPTER TWENTY-EIGHT

They dragged the guard into a nearby utility closet and bound her hands and mouth in tape.

It happened in stages. Santana remained on the lookout for other guards and kept her ear pressed against the door, informing Dick when another guard was performing their rounds.

By the time he'd satisfactorily bound the guard, Santana deduced that the rounds happened in five-minute circuits. "It's like clockwork. Precisely to the minute. Who the hell are these clowns?"

"People we should avoid," Dick replied. He asked Santana to keep watch and let him know when the next free break would be. Two minutes later, they sneaked back into the corridor.

They tiptoed around the place and found a set of stairs after walking through a few doorways. They could make out the iridescent blues of fish tanks and more vivariums scattered around the house down the corridors.

This woman loves her animals. Hopefully, she doesn't have a protocol to set them all off on intruders at once.

They paused at the top of the stairs, attention caught by

another flashlight. Dick and Santana tucked around the corner while Dick checked his feed from the digital cameras. He was pleased to see that the cameras he'd frozen were still out of action, although the one near the tiger enclosure—showed their blurry, dark shapes. Luckily it was dark enough that the forms were questionable, but it wouldn't be long before whatever guards were watching the monitors would be drawn in with suspicion.

Another flashlight joined the first. Dick peeked through a glass window in the door, then retracted instantly. "A pair of them. There may be no video feed up here, but there's still no lack of guard."

Santana moved past Dick and had a look for herself. "Any bright ideas, Mr. Chambers?"

Dick considered this. "Wait for them to move on. Sneak up and take them from behind."

"You romantic," Santana quipped.

Dick raised an eyebrow. "You got a better idea?"

Santana grinned. "I thought you'd never ask." She pulled out two sharp objects from her satchel and a reed pipe. "Let's make the guards go sleep bye-bye."

She crawled along the floor and eased the door open enough that she could poke her head through. The top of the stairwell was dark, but emergency lighting kept the corridors dimly lit. Santana placed one of the objects inside the reed pipe and moved it to her lips.

Dick's eyes widened. "Are you kidding me?" he hissed. "No one could make that shot. That's your idea?"

Santana raised a finger to silence him. She inhaled deeply, then blew sharply. The reed made a slight musical note as the projectile launched.

She rapidly placed the next projectile and repeated the action. The target was more difficult this time since the first guard had been hit in the neck and swatted as though a wasp hovered nearby. Still, she found her mark, and soon both of them were flailing.

She rose with a graceful confidence and stepped through the door. Dick watched from behind the glass as both guards saw Santana and stared at her in disbelief. Both men checked out her long bare legs as their bodies gave up on them.

"Neurotoxic paralysis," Santana informed them. "Atlantica has a plethora of impressive and unique creatures. But none more impressive than the Sokolov bullfrog." She turned her head back to Dick. "I named it after my mother. Not sure if anyone else has discovered one before, but I'll take the credit until I'm proven otherwise." She strode toward the guards who had fallen on the floor and now lay still. "A powerful sleeping agent that shuts down all motor functions and clouds the memory of those it enters. Please don't ask me how I discovered that."

Dick nodded, impressed. "I won't."

They worked together to move the guards out of the open. The corridor had many rooms spawning off each side, and they found a guest bedroom to place them in. To add extra humor, Dick set the pair up to make it appear as though they were spooning, one guard with a slight grin on his sleeping face.

"They make a cute couple, don't you think?" Santana offered.

Dick smirked. "Maybe we're matchmakers? They'll wake up and realize they had feelings for each other all along. There's a movie in there somewhere."

"Eurgh." Santana stuck her tongue out in disgust. "What is it with the modernized world and movies?"

Dick laughed. "I should have known that Miss Primal hated the digital revolution."

"I love the digital revolution," Santana retorted. "I just hate TVs and films. Why would anyone spend hours staring blankly at a box in the room when they could be outside experiencing the world? Sure, you can catch up on National Geographic, but there's nothing like experiencing it all and being out in the open, exposed to the elements. The smells, the textures, the sights, the adrenaline rush when a leopard thinks it's got the drop on you and you outsmart it. That's what life is really about."

Dick smirked.

"What?" Santana asked. "What's so funny?"

Dick shrugged. "Nothing, really. Remind me to find you when the apocalypse hits and the power lines go down. We're going to need people like you to remind the pampered A-holes of Atlantica how to live."

They headed back out into the corridors and cautiously worked their way through the various rooms. The upstairs looped around in a large square, with the majority shooting off to the left as they walked in a clockwise motion. There were considerably fewer doorways on the right, each locked by a series of digital panels and locks.

After checking the tenth door on the left and finding yet another guest bedroom, Dick examined the door on the right. "What's the guess that the queen has taken the center of the house?"

"That'd be a big old bedroom," Santana whispered.

Dick pressed his ear to the door. "Let's hope Miss Turnberry isn't at home."

Santana raised an eyebrow. "It is the middle of the night. What are the chances she's out in the city right now?"

Dick grinned. "High. Rats and other scum come out when the lights are low, and shadows cover the world, do they not?"

He pulled out the stump of a finger and held it in the air.

"Ew." Santana recoiled in disgust. "Where did you get that?"

Dick winked. "I have my methods."

He tapped the finger to the panel, and an LED light flicked green. Not a moment later, footsteps sounded in the stairwell, followed by muttering voices.

Dick and Santana opened the door and slipped inside.

The room was enormous, lit entirely by the looming glass

ceiling that allowed a full view of the night sky above. The full moon cast a silvery glow across the area, displaying as much light as possible through the haze of fog.

There was a four-poster bed centered on one of the walls, and a smattering of bureaus and closets around the room. Compared to the rest of the house, this room was stripped bare, its only function seemingly to allow Sadie Turnberry the pleasure of a full night's rest.

Dick stalked into the room and aimed straight for the bed with its bunched-up duvet. In the darkness, it appeared as though someone was snoozing. He tiptoed across and craned his head, but couldn't see what was beneath the cover.

Santana pointed questioningly. Dick shrugged.

He peeled back the duvet enough to get a glimpse at the moving shape. Leopard-skin pajamas greeted him, furry and with a faint hint of an earthy scent. Dick wondered how Sadie could sleep in something as warm-looking as that, but who was he to question her methods?

Dick took the initiative and pressed the advantage as he leaped onto the bed and bundled the duvet around Sadie. He bunched the corners up and closed them around her, surprised by how tiny she felt in his hands.

Sadie kicked and flailed and…

Growled?

An animal noise erupted from the duvet, loud enough to cause Dick to flinch. He tried to hold the duvet, but now something was shredding its way out. Santana encouraged Dick to toss the duvet back since the noise risked exposing them in Sadie's room if a guard were to pass now.

Dick took several leaps backward and stared at the duvet where the material fluttered and wriggled around. A tail appeared, then a paw, then the face of some kind of cat—larger than Dick had seen kept as a domestic pet. It bared its fangs and hissed in their direction.

"What the fuck is that thing?" Dick asked.

Santana stepped in front of him and held one hand out to ward off the creature. "An ocelot. Have you never studied biology?"

Dick bit back his retort. Of course, he had studied biology. Who hadn't? What the school teachers didn't tell you was every variation of goddamn big cat and what to do if you pissed one off.

The ocelot leaped off the bed and stalked toward Santana, eyes catching the faint glimmer of moonlight. Santana cooed at the creature and softly spoke to it. "Easy, kitty. We're not a threat to you. Calm down, breathe…"

Dick rolled his eyes while his hand reached for his pistol. "We're not teaching the damn thing yoga, just restrain it."

Santana spoke through gritted teeth. "Shut up and let me work, won't you?" She addressed the ocelot, which was now only a few feet away and looked ready to pounce. "Calm down, kitty. We're not your enemy."

Santana slowly reached into her bag and removed a bottle of something that looked like sanitizer. She quickly squeezed some into the palm of her hand, then rubbed until the gel had sunken into her skin. She held her hand out again—

As the creature leaped at her.

"Santana!" Dick exclaimed as the ocelot brought its paws up to Santana's chest. She folded backward with the creature pinning her to the floor. Santana remained silent and wore a confident expression. The ocelot growled and bared its teeth at her face. Dick imagined those teeth slicing straight through her skin and making mulch of her head, but instead, the growl turned into a rolling purr as the ocelot's rough tongue licked Santana's cheek.

Santana let out a relieved laugh and stroked the creature's head. One hand found its chin and the ocelot purred as it closed its eyes and surrendered to the petting.

Dick didn't realize he still pointed the gun at the ocelot.

"What have you got that out for?" Santana reprimanded. "You could've raised the alarm for the whole damn building."

Dick gave her an incredulous look. "What the hell just happened?"

Santana tossed the bottle to Dick as she sat up and cuddled the ocelot in her lap. Dick read the label. "Big cat pheromones?"

"You got it." Santana smirked. "A girl is always prepared. Specifically, that formula is for ocelots, but can also work on lynxes and margays. Don't ask me how I know."

Dick opened the cap and sniffed the bottle. He poured some on his hands and rubbed them together. The ocelot's ears raised and it sauntered over to Dick, allowing him to stroke its soft fur. "Why the hell didn't you use this on the tiger?"

Santana pushed herself to her feet, rubbing off the fur which had shed onto her top. "Did you not hear me? It works on ocelots, lynxes, and margays."

Dick looked at her blankly.

"You should brush up on your big cat knowledge." Santana placed her hands on her hips.

Dick glanced down at the creature. The ocelot was about the size of a Rottweiler. "How can you call this a big cat? Those are lions, tigers… Erm… Other cats."

Santana called the ocelot back over and stroked her ruff. "Your knowledge knows no bounds." She hooked a thumb in the pink collar and read the golden heart name tag. "Her name's Sabrina."

Dick brushed himself down and scanned the room again. "I don't care. In case you'd forgotten, we have a job to do."

Santana chuckled, then muttered, "A thank you would do the trick."

Dick strode over to a dressing table that had caught his eye. The unit was at least three meters wide, with an array of mirrors of different sizes and angles. There were boxes with tiny drawers for all kinds of jewelry, and a padded chair that fit underneath.

Dick looked at the collection in awe. "There must be thousands of dollars' worth of jewelry here." There were diamonds the size of game dice, necklaces of beaded pearls, silver chains, and rings upon rings resting on the stumps of ornaments in the shape of hands.

Dick rooted through the drawers, a strange feeling in his chest that something was close. While Santana cuddled the ocelot, Dick investigated, going through each drawer. He found rings and pendants, but nothing that looked vaguely familiar. At the end of the unit was a lamp, carved into the shape of a Hawaiian woman dancing. Dick turned on the light, a little too rough when handling the button hidden in the shade's neck.

The lamp jogged. Beneath it, Dick glimpsed a hint of silver. He lifted the light and found a key.

Dick examined the key, then looked for a lock.

There was none in sight.

"What have you got there?" Santana arrived behind Dick, Sabrina nestled in her arms like an infant. The ocelot's eyes were closed as it tucked into her neck.

Dick ignored the question, his curiosity ignited. He moved to the floor and examined the sides of the unit. He looked in the drawers for a hidden entrance of some kind and came up empty. When he was beneath the unit's center nook, where the seat would usually rest, Dick found the keyhole above him. "Bingo."

He placed the key in the lock, then turned it once, twice, three times.

A mechanism ratcheted inside. With each turn, a hidden compartment slid out like the tongue of a hungry beast. Dick couldn't see what was inside from his position on the floor, but looking up at Santana and Sabrina, he knew they'd found something significant.

Santana's face fell. Her mouth opened. She stared dumbly at the contents of the drawer. "Dick..."

Dick didn't bother giving lip service to the fact that Santana had used his colloquial name, but instead crawled out and stood by her side.

The compartment was the size of an old vinyl case with a red velvet-lined interior.

Santana's pendant sat in the center of the drawer.

She let out a disbelieving exhalation and reached for it.

Dick held her wrist. "What if it's alarmed?"

Santana snatched up the pendant. "I don't care." She turned it over in her hand, unable to believe they'd found it. She undid the clasp and investigated the inside, finding the folded pieces of paper that Dick had only seen in photos. "This is it. John, it's really it."

"What happened to Dick?" He smirked, but Santana paid no attention. She kissed the gold, the movement eliciting a disapproving nod from her ocelot pal, then held the pendant to the only piece of her chest she could reach. Dick was surprised to see tears falling from her eyes. "Thank you so much. Thank you."

Dick rubbed his neck. "Don't mention it." He twisted the key in the opposite direction, placed it back where he found it, then moved over to the other drawers and spaces around the room.

"What are you doing?" Santana pocketed the pendant. "Let's get out of here."

Dick continued to search, ignoring Santana's question.

Santana frowned and cast a longing look at the door. "John. Listen to me. We have what we came for, so let's get out of here. I can only pay you the remainder if we're still alive."

Dick shook his head. "You could pay me now if you wanted to, so that's not an issue." He determinedly moved around the room and checked under the bed, looking for something that Santana didn't understand.

Finally, Santana caught him by the shoulder and turned him

around. She let the ocelot jump onto the bed where she curled up and slept. "John!" She stared into his eyes. "Let's get going."

"I can't. Yes, we have the pendant. That's great. But there's something more here, I can feel it."

"Like what?" Santana hissed. "What are you hiding from me?"

Dick drew a deep breath. "Dexter Lockhart."

Santana looked at him blankly.

Dick continued. "Those Russians that attacked me, they said that Dexter Lockhart sent them, but I've found no trace or sign of the man so far."

"So you think that Sadie is hiding a Russian mob leader?" Santana asked, accusation in her eyes.

"I think there has to be a connection," Dick replied. "I encountered more Russians standing as her bodyguards when I was…" He didn't want to tell Santana he'd discovered the fabled Warehouse's location, so he swerved the topic. "When I was on my search. Don't you think it's coincidental that she would have Russian guards, the people who attacked me were Russian, and the Guardian was a Russian family head who used his entire Russian family to try and bring me down when I was on the trail of that goddamn pendant?"

Santana blinked. She looked as if she were going to say something, then bit it back. "Fine. I can see that you're going to be as stubborn as ever." She smiled. "Let's get digging."

They hunted together for a few minutes before Dick found a lockbox beneath the bed. He pulled out the wooden box with a combination code and gently shook it. Something metallic clanged around inside.

"You got any bright ideas for opening that?" Santana sat beside Dick on the floor.

Dick shook his head. "Combination locks are my Achilles heel. Shy of smashing the damn thing, I have no idea."

Santana exhaled. "Maybe Sabrina knows the code. She lives

here. Maybe she's watched her mistress enter the code." She laughed. "Sabrina, got any bright ideas?"

She looked for the ocelot on the bed, but it was empty. She scanned the darkness and found Sabrina scratching the bedroom door. Santana clicked her tongue. "Sabrina? What are you doing?"

Dick looked up as a beep indicated the door opening. They ducked behind the bed as Sadie stepped into the room. She cooed over the ocelot. "Hi baby, did you miss mommy? I know. Mommy's been gone for some time. But don't worry, I'm back now, ready to give my baby some of her food. Yes, I am." She fell silent and drew an audible breath.

Dick leaped out from behind the bed and pointed the pistol at Sadie. Santana jumped to his side and held her bullwhip ready.

For a long moment, they were silent. Dick's eyes darted to the bandages around the woman's finger. She growled, then looked doubtfully at the ocelot, as if wondering why her prized pet hadn't attacked.

"Well," she offered at last. "I guess that explains why my security seems so lax upstairs."

Dick took a step toward her, gun trained at her face. "Don't do anything stupid, and you'll be fine."

Sadie cast her eyes to the floor and sighed. "It's too late, Mr. Chambers." She turned and smashed a button on the wall that Dick hadn't seen before. A shrill alarm bleated out around them. "Do your worst."

CHAPTER TWENTY-NINE

Sadie dove to the floor as Dick took his opening shot. The bullet caught the doorjamb and wood splintered in all directions.

Santana cracked her whip and caught Sadie as she tried to push herself to her feet. She tugged backward, forcing Sadie to trip and smash her head against the floor.

Sadie groaned and moved her hands to her bleeding forehead. "Security! Get them!"

Although they couldn't hear any guards approaching yet, another sound greeted their ears and caused Dick's blood to turn cold—dogs barking.

"We've got to move, quick," Santana exclaimed. She grabbed Dick's wrist and pulled him toward the door. He didn't need encouragement. He found his feet and swiftly followed her.

Not knowing the layout of the manor was their biggest weakness. They looked left toward the stairs where flashlights bounced against the walls.

"This way!" Santana urged.

Dick followed. Both of them took a right at the end of the corridor and found another set of stairs. The barking grew louder with every passing second, and Dick knew it wouldn't be long until the hounds were on them.

If only they knew the damn way out of here.

They burst through the doors of another stairwell and once again met with flashlights below. No one had gotten a good look at them yet, so cutting their losses, Dick grabbed Santana's hand and pulled her upstairs toward the third floor.

Dick had no idea what they'd find up there, knowing that there were animals below and bedrooms on the second floor. What could this place possibly need on the third floor? Pool tables? A swimming pool? A cinema?

They burst through the doors, spurred on by the shouts and barking from below. They needed to put as much distance between them and their pursuers as possible if they didn't want to feel the dogs' fangs chomp into their skin.

The upstairs was an aviary, a large, open ring that looped around the house where hundreds of birds nestled on perches. They bristled and flapped their wings as Dick and Santana ran through, avoiding trees and bushes that—impossibly—had been planted into the house's structure.

Santana took the lead, which allowed Dick to take her cues for when to jump and avoid hazardous roots. Dick would later look back on this moment and marvel at the sheer architectural impossibilities of what he saw, and the amount of money that had to be sunk into the building to make something like this structurally sound, but for now, his focus was to run.

The doors slammed somewhere behind them. They reached the far wall and met with calls and shouts from the doors at the other end of the house.

They were surrounded.

Santana stopped and wildly looked around.

"Got an exit strategy?" Dick asked.

Santana grimaced. "Shouldn't it be you leading here? You dragged me into this mess."

"I needed a guide," Dick replied. "Go. Guide."

The barks grew in volume. Something streamed toward them. In a flash, Santana cracked her whip into the undergrowth. Something yelped and fell back. That didn't deter the others.

Santana cracked the whip toward the upper branches of a nearby tree and scaled up into the thick denseness of its boughs. She left the whip hanging, spurring Dick on to climb up and join her.

He did, although not nearly as gracefully as Santana.

They reached the heart of the leafy canopy and looked down. From here, they could see the shapes of guards closing in on either side. The dogs were at the base of the tree, scrambling, barking, and jumping, signaling for the guards where the intruders were.

"Shit," Santana grumbled. "Where do we go from here?"

Dick turned upward to where the glass ceiling he'd viewed from afar covered the room. The top of the tree couldn't have been more than ten feet from where they sat. He spotted a latch for a large portion of the glass to lever open like a window, supported by concrete shelving.

Dick pointed. "There."

Santana's face hardened. "Are you kidding me? That's suicide. One wrong move and the entire thing will shatter and collapse before we get a chance to escape."

"That's exactly what I'm hoping for," Dick replied.

A bullet flew past them and embedded itself in the tree trunk. The guards were swarming them, and somewhere in the distance, Dick heard Sadie calling commands.

"Here goes nothing." Dick took his pistol and shot the glass. The panel exploded into a thousand silver fragments that rained down on the guards who covered their heads with their arms. The dogs ran out of harm's way, scattering into the underbrush as Dick's shot started the domino effect.

Glass panel after glass panel cracked under the additional

strain and showered down into the exhibit. Santana mumbled something about, "the animals," before Dick roared at her to flick her whip.

She coiled the whip around the tip of a small chimney now visible through the glass. Santana leaped, using the whip for stability and support. She scrambled to the roof and offered a hand. Dick stood, his footing uncertain as he balanced on the branch. He jumped, but his weight snapped the branch and jerked his leap. He flailed his arms and managed to catch the whip in one hand, and Santana's outreached hand with the other.

Together they climbed and pulled until Dick was secure on the roof. He was aware of blood trickling down his arms from the glass edges that remained, but that was a problem for later.

"Let's go," Dick growled and ran down the roof's sharp angle as he plotted his next move.

There was a thirty-foot drop to the ground from where they stood. Dick peered over the edge, found the windowsills below, and considered scaling down, but he wasn't the best climber. By the time they made it down, the dogs would be on them again.

This was evidenced by Sadie's urgent screams.

"This way," Santana instructed, then took off along the roof's edge without waiting for Dick.

She turned her head in all directions, looking for something that Dick was oblivious to. When she reached the far corner of the house, she muttered, "Bingo."

Dick scoffed. "You have to be kidding me."

Santana shrugged and coiled her whip over a power line that stretched from the corner of the roof and down toward the wall that lined the back of the house. It cut short a little way off from the now empty dog cages.

"Santana, don't!" Dick warned.

It was too late. She grabbed either side of her whip and jumped. The whip caught on the line, which grew taught as she rapidly slid down the wire. Dick watched with mounting horror as she showed no sign of slowing, every second growing closer to the concrete wall.

When Santana was ten feet from the ground, she released her grip and let herself fall. She landed on her feet, then collapsed into a perfectly executed roll that dispersed her momentum to minimize the damage.

She looked back up at Dick. "Your turn."

Dick looked forlornly at his pistol. He hooked the V shape of the weapon over the wire while thinking how bad an idea this was. He took the leap, closed his eyes, and prayed to the god he didn't believe in.

The first few meters were fine as he rode down the line. When he was halfway across, the wire bent with his weight, and the telltale sign of crumbling roof tiles came from behind.

Dick jerked as the cable snapped. He was still fifteen feet above the ground and moving fast. Santana's eyes widened, and she moved out of his trajectory. Dick fell.

He landed indelicately on the balls of his feet before trying to mimic Santana's roll. His military training kicked in, and he remembered the basics, only instead of arriving back on his feet, he finished the maneuver flat on his back.

Dick struggled to get his breath back. His legs felt bruised all over.

Santana loomed over him. "Need a hand?"

"Give me a second. I'm not as nimble as I once was." He patted his stomach. Although there wasn't much gut there, Santana still laughed.

A dog barked and sprinted around the corner, paws scrambling for purchase as it changed direction and beelined for them.

Santana grabbed his arm. "No time left. Get your ass up."

He got to his feet and followed Santana as she found a large crate and climbed atop it. She hopped up onto the wall and swung her leg over before plopping gracefully down on the other side.

Dick was about to grab the wall when something tugged his leg. He grunted as the dog yanked his pants and the material shredded in its teeth. Dick kicked the dog but couldn't get enough momentum to remove it.

"Are you coming?" Santana's eyes appeared through the holes in the wall. When she spotted the dog, she muttered, "Oh, shit."

More dogs arrived, catching up with their comrade as they also skittered and scrabbled to remain upright on the stone path.

Dick fought the dog. "Don't you have any more of those pheromone things you can use?"

"Not on a domestic dog. I'm armed for exotic wildlife, not Chihuahuas."

Dick grunted in pain and finally managed to grab the dog and release it from his leg. It jumped back, then came in for another attack. Dick used the moment of relief to hop off the box and find a place where he could grab some cover as guards arrived and started shooting in his direction.

Dick studied his surroundings, looking for anything that might offer some cover. He found what he was looking for and dug in his pocket for the distraction he needed. A bullet whizzed by his ear, encouraging his urgency.

"Here goes nothing." Dick thumbed the gas device and hurled it toward the guards. It exploded into smoke that covered the courtyard and allowed him to make for the hiding spot. He careened toward the dog cage and shut himself inside. It wasn't elegant, but at least he was out of the way of the hound's jaws while he debated his next move.

"What's your plan, bozo?" Santana muttered as she appeared at the wall behind him while the guards fought to see in the smog.

"How about you give me a hand?" Dick growled, then turned to the wall to find that Santana wasn't there.

Something landed on top of the cage. He looked up and saw

Santana creeping along its roof, her whip in one hand and something small in the other.

She placed the object between her lips and blew. The dogs quieted. It was disconcerting—the din lost its vigor as the dogs shut up, and all that remained were shouts and bullets.

The dog nearest to Dick stared up at Santana, eyes trained on the whistle in her mouth. Dick didn't hear any noise, but he was familiar with dog whistles and the frequencies that humans couldn't hear. She blew again, and the dogs sat on their hindquarters. She hopped down, whip poised, ready to enforce obedience in any dog that chose to disobey.

A man loomed out of the fog. His eyes widened as he found Santana and Dick. He looked as if he was about to call out and raise the alarm, but Santana silenced him with a flick of the whip. It coiled around his throat. She tugged him toward them, and Dick, who had eased out of the cage, socked him in the face with his fist.

The guard went down.

Somewhere in the fog, Sadie called, "What the fuck do I pay you for if you're not going to stop intruders? Kill them. They're on my property, dammit! Kill them both!"

The guards charged into the fog but found Santana and Dick far too late. Dick engaged with many of them, using his fist to knock those nearest to him out. On a few occasions, he whipped out his pistol and shot those who were about to send bullets into his flesh, and soon enough, their number thinned.

Santana focused on the dogs and tossed them a few treats from her bag. Occasionally, she lashed her whip at a guard getting too close to her, and by the time the smoke had cleared, the courtyard was full of the dead and unconscious.

Only one woman remained.

As the smoke subsided, she approached them both with a .22 caliber rifle pointed at Dick. He held his gun on Sadie as they faced off across the courtyard.

"You're impressive, Mr. Chambers. I'll give you that." Sadie looked disheveled with her gray hair twisted into knots and odd angles. "I can't deny the talents of a man with your abilities. I'll give you one last opportunity. Then you can taste the steel of these bullets."

"What makes you think I won't shoot you first?" Dick asked, lips tight.

Sadie grinned. "Because you're a man of honor. You wouldn't attack a poor old lady in cold blood, would you? That's not in your nature."

Dick gave a derisive snort. "My nature is to survive."

"And mine is to thrive," Sadie retorted before turning sharply to Santana, who had looked ready to crack her whip. "Make another move, bitch, and it'll be both of you who dives into the dirt tonight."

Santana held the whistle in her lips and glanced in Dick's direction. Dick fixed his attention on Sadie.

"Join me, Chambers," Sadie repeated. "Final offer."

Santana blew the whistle. The dog's ears pricked up.

Dick saw movement behind Sadie and fought to keep his eyes focused. "Rot in hell," he crooned.

Sadie sighed and lowered her head. "Very well…"

Before she could pull the trigger, a growl crept out of the brush behind her. A moment later, Sabrina sped into the courtyard and lunged at her mistress. Her paws landed on Sadie's shoulder and knocked the woman backward. She landed on the stone with a loud *thud* and cracked her head. A slow trail of blood leaked from the wound.

Sabrina took the whistle from her mouth. She winked at Dick. "It's not only dogs who respond to inhuman frequencies."

Dick lowered his pistol. "Good to know. Let's get the fuck out of here."

Santana scaled the wall once more and disappeared into the wilds at the back of the mansion. Dick followed swiftly after, pausing only at the top of the wall to get a final look at Sadie. She was moving...barely. Her arms slowly reached around to the back of her head as Sabrina licked her face.

Dick lowered himself, aware of the pains shooting through both of his legs from his earlier fall. Santana waved him on, flying to the edge of his limited vision in the darkness. He drew a restorative breath, then followed her into the gloom.

CHAPTER THIRTY

Santana opened the door of her apartment building and helped Dick inside.

The way back had been tough. They ran through the wilderness, keeping out of sight of the edge of the city on the off chance that Sadie had another ace up her sleeve. They leaped over roots and slalomed around the trees until they came to the open car park of a megamart.

The car park was almost empty. A couple of shady figures loitered in the dark reaches, clearly up to no good as money and substances exchanged hands. One car had tinted black windows and rocked on its axles as the people inside got down to the dance that grown-ups do, spurred on by the thrill of getting caught in the open.

Santana offered to hail Dick a cab, but he wouldn't take the risk. Instead, they walked together toward the main road, making sure to remain out of the streetlights' reach as much as possible. At one point, a fleet of AJS cars roared by in the direction they had come, but Dick wasn't afraid. All of the actions that had taken place that night had happened on Sadie's property. As much as they could look down their noses at Dick if they discovered he was involved, they couldn't convict him.

When they were a mile or so away, Santana instructed Dick to hide in the bushes. She extended her thumb, and within a few seconds a bearded man with a beer gut and a mouth full of gold teeth pulled over, feasting on her with his eyes. Dick emerged from the bushes. Although clearly disappointed that he wouldn't be solo with the pretty lady, the driver offered to take them both back into the city proper.

They climbed the stairs until they reached the uppermost floor of the apartment building. Santana asked Dick to wait outside as she eased her head through her front door and examined inside for anything suspicious. She crept in, looking more like a cat burglar than a resident, and for the next few minutes, he simply waited.

When he began to think she was giving him a non-subtle hint to fuck off, the door opened wide. Santana ushered him through, and Dick's eyes were drawn to the string of traps and wires that littered her apartment space.

"Paranoid much?" Dick commented.

Santana raised an eyebrow. "In case you've forgotten, someone broke into my apartment and stole my mama's pendant before murdering the man who gave it to me. I think this is justified."

Dick studied the room and noted the walls lined with dusty books and cracked tomes. There were odd artifacts scattered around the shelves and open spaces, treasures from Santana's previous adventures. Printed maps hung on the wall in glass frames. Dick couldn't help but think this place looked more like a research facility than an apartment. There was no couch for guests to sit, only a single chair in front of a table that might once have held a television.

"What makes you think they won't come back?" Dick asked. "We've stolen the pendant from Sadie. She knows where you live if she was able to orchestrate getting the damn thing in the first place." He grew restless. "We should go. We shouldn't be here."

Santana smirked. "If they come here, they won't find us."

Dick looked at her questioningly.

"Come on," Santana instructed. "Follow me. I want to show you something."

She led Dick to the farthest window and raised it wide open. "Wait here." Then she went back to the front door and activated her complicated network of alarms and traps. Dick had underestimated her. While he recognized many of them as wailing alarms and alerts, Santana revealed several hidden triggers that he couldn't work out what they did. He wondered if any of them would induce bodily harm. Knowing Santana's experiences out in the forests, he imagined they would.

Santana wiped her brow as she rejoined Dick. She motioned to the window. "After you."

Dick poked his head out and looked down the steep drop to the curb. "No thank you."

Santana laughed. "Fine." She leaned out of the window and swung a leg around. With a flick of her wrist, she cracked the whip. Dick leaned out and saw that it had coiled around a section of guardrail on the apartment's roof. Santana held tightly to the whip and used it to pull her up as she scaled the building's side, showing little care for the sixty-foot drop below before she disappeared onto the roof. "Are you coming?" she called back. "Bring that whip with you, please."

Dick's lip turned up. Never one to shy from a challenge, he grabbed the whip's handle and levered himself out into the open. "The last time someone asked me to bring a whip was very different to this one," he quipped to himself, then swung a little as a gust of wind caught him. He focused on climbing and eased himself over the lip of the roof to join Santana.

The top was pebble-dashed with a single emergency doorway on top. Dick threw the whip to Santana and nodded at the door. "Couldn't we have gone the easy way?"

"Where's the fun in that?" Santana smirked. "Besides, that door has been out of commission ever since I arrived here. The super doesn't bother with it. Says there's no point. The only things that ever come up here are birds and clouds."

Dick gave Santana a quizzical look. "You're telling me it's a coincidence that the moment you moved into this apartment, the door broke and the super leaves this space unattended?"

Santana smiled, a beautiful addition to her face. "You tell me, detective."

Santana made her way to the roof's edge and sat on the stone lip. Her legs swung freely below her, and she leaned back on her hands. The sky was tinged with pink, the Atlantican sunrise doing its best to fight off the pervading fog and cast a little color onto the city. Streams of gold gleamed between the droplets of moisture and covered everything in a mystical glow.

Dick joined her, more cautious as he sat. They were silent a long while, staring into the strange glow and listening to the city waking up around them. A bird flew overhead, some type of eagle, Dick guessed, although he knew that Santana could name it in English, Russian, and Latin.

"So, we got the pendant," Dick offered at last, not looking at Santana. "All of this for a tiny piece of gold jewelry. Do you feel better for it?"

Santana shook her head and smiled. "No. Do you?"

Dick considered this. "I will when the money clears."

"Do you honestly believe that?" Santana asked.

Dick mimicked Santana's head shake as the humor drained

from his face. "No. We've unlocked something, but I still don't know what it is. Sadie wouldn't have gone through all that trouble if there wasn't something significant behind that pendant. There's more out there, but I'm not sure what it is or where to start looking."

"I'm not paying you to investigate further," Santana clarified. "Just want you to know that."

Dick laughed. "Miss Sokolov, you'd have to pay me not to."

Dick fished in his pocket for his cigarettes, unsurprised to find the box crushed and in a state of disrepair. He clawed out the broken stump of one of the remaining cigarettes, examined its crooked stem, then put it back in the box. "Something else I'll have to fix on the way home."

"You're going home?" Santana asked, concern on her face. "What if they're waiting for you?"

Dick didn't reply, instead choosing to stare out into the glowing fog.

Santana stroked a thumb over the pendant as a nostalgic smile crept up her face. She flicked open the clasp and examined the contents while rubbing the metal as if it was something precious that could fade at any minute. A single tear fell on her cheek before she closed the locket and placed it in her pocket.

"What's next for you?" she asked to distract herself from her thoughts.

Dick's eyes narrowed. "The same as always. Take the next case, and try to clean up the trail of the mess I've uncovered. Injustice doesn't rest, so why should I?"

Santana nodded appreciatively. After another long stretch of silence, Dick glanced down over the building's lip to where another fleet of AJS cars raced along. "That's my cue to leave." He looked expectantly at Santana. "Are you going to help me down?"

To Dick's surprise, Santana shuffled along the edge and rested her head on his shoulder. She placed a hand on his thigh and drew a long breath. "Thank you, John. I can't express how happy I am to have this back. It's all I have left of her."

Dick sat in discomfort, unsure of what to do. He looked down at Santana's head, then rested his against hers. "Don't mention it." A pause. "And my friends call me Dick."

Santana laughed.

CHAPTER THIRTY-ONE

Dick stopped at the corner store for a fresh pack of cigarettes before heading back to his apartment.

He remained out of plain sight, navigating the alleys he had grown to know so well and avoiding the morning rush's foot traffic. He was tired. All he wanted to do was sleep in his bed and wake up feeling refreshed.

But something told him that wasn't going to happen all that easily.

Along the way, Dick found the spot where he had stolen the bike locked to the railing. A young lad was holding his head, looking up and down the street forlornly. Dick ran across the road and handed the kid a business card.

"Who are you?" the boy asked.

"A detective." Dick chose not to elaborate further. "Your bike was stolen, kid. You'll have to move on. Hopefully, that will help."

The kid turned the card over to reveal a set of instructions to complete a bank transfer worth three times what the bike was worth.

"Wow, thanks," the kid murmured. When he looked up from the card, Dick was halfway down the street.

He turned into the alley, and after another twenty minutes or so, he stared up at his apartment from the same spot where he had been the previous night before submitting to his fears and catching some Zs at Terra's. From what he could deduce from where he stood, everything was normal. No one was watching his apartment, no one was inside, and everything was fine.

Which was exactly what Sadie would want him to think.

His only solace right now was the fact that Sadie would no doubt have had to go to the hospital for examination. Dick hoped that she hadn't put out any orders on him in that time and that he could grab a few essentials before figuring out his next move. Deciding to cut his losses, he turned up his collar, dug his hands in his pocket—keeping one hand firmly clasped on his pistol—and went inside.

Making it to his floor, Dick was pleased to find that Mrs. Harrison wasn't standing in her usual position in her doorway. He placed his key in the lock and drew a long breath, ready for whatever waited inside.

Dick shoved the door open and hid out of the way, memories of his previous experience with the Russians filling his head. When no gunshots came, Dick cautiously entered his apartment and scanned the rooms for any sign of a hidden intruder or tampering.

After ten minutes of searching, Dick was finally satisfied, although he still didn't feel comfortable. He moved to his bedroom and grabbed a large duffle before stuffing handfuls of clothes inside. He took an array of shampoos and soaps and toothbrushing paraphernalia from his bathroom and threw them in, too. He also loaded a couple more of his pistols, a box of devices and trinkets, and for good measure, his one remaining bottle of premium bourbon.

Dick cast a final glance around his apartment and headed for the door. When he got there, he stopped in his tracks as he noticed the written note taped to the wood.

He tore it from its moorings and read, "Mr. Chambers. You can run, but you can't hide. I play to win."

Dick screwed up the paper and tossed it into the nearby trashcan. A smirk crawled up his cheek. "So do I, bitch. So do I."

First, THANK YOU so much for picking up this book and reading all the way through to my author notes here at the end.

The genesis of *Atlantica* goes back to Cabo San Lucas in early 2019. I was sitting at a small table at the Pacifica Hotel on an outside walkway, looking out at the waters where the Pacific meets the Sea of Cortez.

And I was thinking about Gotham City. You know, the one Batman™ inhabits?

What did I like about it, what called to me, and finally, what did I NOT like about it.

I liked the dark, gritty areas and the fact that it is a huge city and it has high-class areas and rat-infested trash-filled alleyways. In short, it's *real*, and it's a place I want to know more about.

Except, I only know about Gotham from the animated adventures, and there are a few things I don't like about that city. It lacks the excitement of the future. I want more technology (which I love) and spectacle (which I would love to see on the big screen.)

In short, I wanted to create a city that was a character in and of itself.

Now, I'm also fascinated by the rumors and the stories about Atlantis. Advanced technology and capabilities thousands of years into the future, yet we can't find this place. Or if we find the location, it might be buried under clay where none of the secrets can be unearthed.

But what if it isn't? What if Atlantis was an island shrouded in mist and mystery that successfully stayed hidden until satellites came into being, looked down at our planet, and noted a location that was always hidden in mist.

And then we found records of battles way back in World War II?

All countries want it, but no country can own it. It must be a neutral location with its own laws.

And someone decided the laws benefitted the powerful to lure them there?

The brightest and darkest of humanity would be drawn like moths to a flame, often to burn up in the same fashion. For some, they say Mother Earth doesn't care if you live or die. For others, they say Atlantica actively tries to kill you.

Of course, that's just a saying.

Thus we have the beginning of the story, one that could unearth humanity's biggest opportunities or create the apocalypse to crack open the world.

What will humanity do? Well, on Atlantica, one never really knows what will happen.

But it will be explosive. I guarantee it.

Ad Aeternitatem,

Michael Anderle

*PS – Note the similarity between the names of the location I was staying—the Pacifica Hotel—and the city (and island) of Atlantica?

There is a reason for that.

If you ever want to stay where the island of Atlantica was named, just go to the Pacifica Hotel and Resort in Cabo San Lucas, Mexico. I plan on going back just as soon as it is deemed safe.